Books by Joy Reed

Seraphina Fox Mysteries

*The Ghost in the Machine*
*Poison in Jest*
*All Hallows' Eve*
*Night Music*
*The Hanged Man*

Published by Unconsidered Trifle Publications

## <u>Historical Romances</u>

*An Inconvenient Engagement*
*Twelfth Night*
*The Seduction of Lady Carroll*
*Midsummer Moon*
*Lord Wyland Takes a Wife*
*The Duke and Miss Denny*
*A Home for the Holidays*
*Lord Caldwell and the Cat*
*Miss Chambers Takes Charge*
*The Baron and the Bluestocking*
*Lord Desmond's Destiny*
*Lord Yates and the Yankee*
*Mr. Jeffries and the Jilt*
*Catherine's Wish*
*Emily's Wish*
*Anne's Wish*

## Published by Zebra Books

# Poison
# in Jest

# Poison
# in Jest

Being the Second Volume of the

## Memoirs

of

## Madame Seraphina Fox,

### Spiritualist,

### Describing Her Worldly and Otherworldly

### Experiences

## Edited by Joy Reed, M.A., B.Sci.

ISBN: 0692803076
ISBN 13: 9780692803073

*Dedicated*
*to Dr. John L. S. Daley,*
*esteemed advisor and*
*military historian extraordinaire*

## CHAPTER 1

**"I**s there a disembodied spirit in the room?"

The faintest of breezes swept through the darkened room. The candle in the hanging lantern flickered, and the lantern itself swayed on its hook with a creaking sound. Both clients raised their eyes to look at it, then returned their gaze to the box on the table in front of us. It was a wooden box about two feet in length and half as wide, its edges bound and studded in brass like a steamer trunk. On the top surface was a large dial with the alphabet inscribed around its circumference.

"Is there a disembodied spirit in the room?"

The words elicited another breeze, this one carrying a hint of vanilla-scented tobacco. "Ah," whispered Mrs. Waring.

Her daughter did not speak, but made a little sound halfway between a sob and a sigh. She was a beautiful girl, tall and handsome in a style seen more often in fashion plates than in life. The face beneath the high-piled brunette hair was gravely absorbed in contemplating the box in front of us.

"Is there a disembodied spirit in the room?"

I made my voice purposely dramatic as I asked the question for the third and final time. And in answer, a bell-like chime sounded within the box.

Mrs. Waring let out her breath in a sigh, and a tremulous smile appeared on her lips. She, too, was a handsome woman, despite being well along in her middle years. Studying her beneath my lashes, I thought she must once have been quite as good-looking as her daughter, though marriage, motherhood, and a still-recent widowhood had all left their marks. "Howard," she said. "I would know the smell of your pipe anywhere."

"Papa," agreed Miss Waring in a husky voice.

The bell chimed again, in assent.

And we were off and running. Another day; another séance at the Temple of Spiritualism; and another evening's work for me, the hard-working woman who runs it.

As a Spiritualist, my rôle is to summon my clients' Dear Departed Ones, and to serve as the Medium through which they may speak with their grieving friends and family. Different Mediums do this differently, as perhaps you may know, Dear Reader. Some speak through a Spirit Guide, or communicate through such simplistic devices as rapping or table-turning.

That may have sufficed in the past (and may still suffice for the simple-minded). But in this age of Steam Power and Scientific Innovation, we Spiritualists cannot be behindhand. Change is inevitable in the human condition. The wise human embraces change rather than resisting it—although there is a trick in knowing which changes are enduring, and which are merely passing fads. When one's livelihood depends upon pleasing the public, there is also a trick in knowing one's audience and calculating the innovations that will best suit their tastes and temperament.

I flatter myself that I have mastered both these tricks, along with quite a few others.

My name is Seraphina Fox.

If you are familiar with me from my previous work,[1] you will know my name is not really Seraphina Fox. You may even have some

---

1  *The Ghost in the Machine*

inkling of what my real name might be. But Seraphina Fox is the name I use professionally, and the only name I propose to give in this, my second memoir. As with my previous one, the same bargain applies: if I do not reveal my real name, rest assured there will be very few other points on which I am not willing to treat you, the Reader, with the most perfect frankness.

Passing lightly, then, over ground I have covered before, I will say that I took the name Seraphina Fox ten years ago, when I first came to London. At that time, I was anxious to reinvent myself and to leave my past behind with my old name.

In accordance with my policy of perfect frankness, let me say also that it was a past intermittently scandalous and occasionally even criminal. I would stress, however, that my crimes have all been venial ones, such as might fall to the lot of any person unfortunate enough to need money badly and intelligent enough to see how easily it may be obtained from the foolish and trusting. For "foolish" and "trusting" you may substitute here Mr. P. T. Barnum's forthright term,[2] but I am a woman of refinement—or at least passing nowadays for a woman of refinement. That being the case, "foolish" and "trusting" will suffice.

In leaving my past behind, I was also anxious to leave behind some of the risks associated with my profession. There was a time when a Medium could darken the séance room, drape herself in phosphorescent muslin, and wander among her clients in reasonable expectation that they would take her as a genuine ghostly Phenomenon. I can say with authority, however, that that time has ended. It ended for me when a young newspaper reporter brought me down in a rugby tackle, while one of his brethren relit the lamps to reveal me lying on the floor in an ignominious heap of muslin.

---

2  "There's a sucker born every minute." Like many people, Madame Fox is mistaken in attributing this adage to P.T. Barnum, but it is certainly in keeping with his philosophy. *–Ed.*

As a result of this and similar incidents, I don't do full-figure materializations anymore. The risk is simply too great, even if one is careful (as I am since that incident) to select the members of my audience with the utmost care. Scoffers and skeptics have no place at the séance table, and for obvious reasons neither do the Press. Nor, for equally obvious reasons, do the indigent. My clients pay handsomely for my services, but I take care that they receive their money's worth. From the moment they enter my Temple of Spiritualism in Wimpole Street, they are surrounded by an atmosphere of the Otherworldly. And those whose means and motives pass my scrutiny may then enter into its *sanctum sanctorum*, the Spirit Parlour, there to consult the Electrical Spiritograph, my patented device for communicating with the Other Side.

The Warings, mother and daughter, were among those privileged few. I had been sitting for them for the better part of a year now. They were by this time perfectly conversant with the Electrical Spiritograph and the power by which it operates—or rather, they were conversant with the power by which it *ostensibly* operates: *i.e.*, Spirit Energy.

I could read you here quite a learned disquisition on Spirit Energy, Dear Reader. I could explain how energy pervades all nature, and is itself indestructible, so that when a person dies, their energy is not lost, but only transmuted into a spiritual form which is nonetheless accessible to a sensitive Medium equipped with an equally sensitive device resembling (say) an Electrical Spiritograph.[3]

But since we agreed early on that only complete frankness should prevail between us, I will simply state that my device is battery-powered, not Spirit-powered. I use my feet to discreetly operate its main switches, but can manipulate an alternate set of switches

---

3  In positing that energy is not destroyed but only transmuted to another form after death, Madame Fox ingeniously draws upon the conclusions of her scientific contemporaries regarding the Law of Conservation of Energy and the First Law of Thermodynamics.–*Ed.*

with my hands, in a pinch. And after the spectacular malfunction that prompted my last memoir, I have provided it with an overriding master switch to shut it down completely, should a malfunction occur again. I am happy to report, however, that I have never needed to use the master switch thus far. In all subsequent séances, the bell has rung only when I press my left slipper to the appropriate set of contacts, and the alphabet wheel turns only when I press the right.[4]

Both switches were operating perfectly tonight. As I responded to the remarks made by Mrs. Waring and her daughter, my only concern was lest my batteries should be depleted before our conversation was done. Not only had Mrs. Waring a great deal to say to her deceased spouse (which of course made no demands on me and my machine), she also had numerous matters on which she sought advice from him. And since Miss Waring had her own view of things, and was prone to dispute with her mother and appeal to her father for judgment between them, I had to stay on my toes—literally as well as figuratively—to keep up with the conversation.

"Howard," said Mrs. Waring, addressing the Spiritograph, "I am glad to have your opinion concerning the railway shares. I feel, like you, that selling them is the only thing to be done. But oh, Howard, there is another matter on which I must consult you—a most delicate matter indeed. And it concerns our daughter."

"Mama," said Miss Waring warningly.

Mrs. Waring swept on, disregarding her daughter's objection. "Indeed, I am at my wits' end, Howard. You little knew, when you

---

4  The Spiritograph is bolted to the table on which it sets. This table has four apparently solid legs and a central pedestal base, studded at intervals with brass studs. Madame Fox wears Turkish slippers with a surface of pure silver metal inset beneath their upturned toes. By pressing the toe of a slipper against a particular pair of the metal studs on the pedestal base, the circuit is completed. Metal rods running up through the table legs carry the power to the box—and the end result is that the bell rings (in the case of the left slipper) or the wheel turns (in the case of the right). –Ed.

made your testamentary arrangements, that you would tie my hands in such a *disastrous* manner and leave us open to scandal and ruin."

"Mama!"

"You must know that Julia has contracted the most imprudent engagement," Mrs. Waring swept on remorselessly. "This Captain Ingram—if indeed he *is* a captain, which I doubt—"

"Mama!" said Miss Waring. "You are unjust! I have seen his army photograph. He served with *distinction* under Lord Chelmsford in Africa."

"Distinction," repeated Mrs. Waring with a sniff. "For my part, I don't see much distinction in going to war against a lot of poor souls armed only with spears. *My* sympathies are with the Africans."[5]

"You know nothing about it, Mama," returned Miss Waring. "Francis has told me all about it, and it was quite the most harrowing business. He only escaped at Eshowe by the *merest* chance. Indeed, it was a miracle that he did escape with only a wounded leg. And he limps to this very day because of it. I believe you would rather he had been slaughtered like so many of his fellow soldiers!" Roused to anger by her mother's disparagement, she was an impressive sight, her dark eyes flashing, her bosom heaving, and her voice throbbing with emotion. "I could not believe, Mama, that you would have been so *unfeeling*."

For the moment, I found my services unnecessary, as recriminations flew back and forth across the séance table. I took my feet off the pedestal, leaned back in my chair, and composed myself to watch as if I were at a tennis match.

---

5 Although the spear, or *assegai*, may be regarded as the Zulu's traditional weapon, Mrs. Waring is mistaken in supposing it to be their only one during the Anglo-Zulu War. Firearms had reached Zululand decades earlier, and additional ones were obtained from British casualties on the battlefield. Her opinion that the British were mistaken in entering into the conflict in the first place has, however, since become the prevalent one.—*Ed.*

Between you and me, Dear Reader, the Warings were not quite of the first society. Mrs. Waring had been only a country clergyman's daughter, and her spouse a banker who could boast no more impressive antecedent than a single eighteenth-century City alderman. But if Mr. Waring's birth had been unimpressive, the fortune he had left behind on his death most certainly was not. Mrs. Waring was a well-off widow even by the inflated standard of the day. And her daughter, on whom the bulk of the Waring fortune had been settled, would bring to her marriage a dowry worthy of a princess. With this advantage added to her physical charms, she might have been calculated to make a very great match indeed, even despite the disadvantages of her birth.

It appeared now, however, that she was contemplating marriage with a humbler sort of man. This was the first I had heard of it, which left me rather at a disadvantage. Fortunately, mother and daughter were so busy wrangling that I was not obliged to make any immediate response. I was able to listen and pick up as much as I could as we went along.

"I cannot like the match," said Mrs. Waring tearfully. "And I am sure your father would not like it, either. Whatever Captain Ingram may be, his scraping your acquaintance in that underhanded way does not speak well of his character. And neither does the hole-in-corner way he has been meeting you, without my knowledge or consent."

"That was as much my doing as his, Mama! You make a deal of fuss about nothing. Nobody gives a fig about a girl meeting a man in public nowadays. And as for scraping my acquaintance, it was the merest chance that put us together at the theatre."

"I don't believe it," returned Mrs. Waring. "I know a fortune hunter when I see one. And so, too, would you, my dear, if only you had a little more knowledge of the world."

Since Miss Waring prided herself on being a sophisticated modern, she was not about to take these words lying down. "What utter rot!" she retorted. "Francis did not even know I was an heiress until I told him. And when I did tell him, let me tell you that he was quite put out. For he is very old-fashioned in his thinking, Mama. He believes a man should support his wife, and not the other way around." In a pointed voice, she added, "I would think that would please you, seeing that you are so full of old-fashioned ideas yourself!"

Mrs. Waring shook her head despairingly. "My poor Julia," was all she said.

Miss Waring, seeing this as weakness, sought to press home her advantage. "Indeed, Mama, I think you would like Francis very well if you would only give him a chance," she said. "He is so kind and considerate and *careful* of me. Not like the boys my own age, who never think of anybody but themselves. If you look at it that way, his being a trifle older than me is a real advantage."

"A *trifle* older than you! My dear, I am sure he is closer to my age than yours."

They went back and forth in this style a while longer before remembering where they were, at which point they both appealed to the late Howard Waring. "Howard, I have no doubt you see things much more clearly where you are," said Mrs. Waring, addressing the Spiritograph. "Tell your daughter she ought not to marry this Captain Ingram."

"Papa, you must know how foolish Mama's fears are," said Miss Waring, addressing the machine in her turn. "Please tell her she is mistaken about Francis."

You might think, Dear Reader, that as the Moving Spirit behind the Spiritograph, I would be hard put to mediate on this issue, seeing that I had never even heard Captain Ingram's name until a few minutes ago. Fortunately, long experience at the séance table has given me a few lines to fall back upon at times like these.

"The wheel is moving!" said Miss Waring triumphantly. "Let's see what Papa has to say."

"N-O-T C-L-E-A-R," said Mrs. Waring, following the movement of the wheel intently. "You mean you cannot see clearly at present, Howard?"

The bell rang in assent, and then the wheel began to move again.

"W-A-I-T A-N-D B-E P-A-T-I-E-N-T,'" spelled Miss Waring. "Wait? Oh, but Papa, why? Why must we wait?"

Both women watched breathlessly as the wheel continued to turn. "H-I-D-D-E-N K-N-O-W-L-E-D-G-E," said Mrs. Waring. "Some knowledge that is hidden? Yes, I daresay. If we knew all there was to know about Captain Ingram, I doubt he would show his face in society, let alone dare to court my daughter."

Her daughter let this pass, being intent on following the wheel's movements. "'In time, what is hidden will be made clear.' There, you see, Mama? The whole matter will be made clear in time."

"Let us hope so," said Mrs. Waring absently. "Look, it's moving again!"

Having bought time with the old hidden-knowledge-will-appear ploy, I now devoted myself to pouring oil on troubled waters. "In the meantime, dear ones, love one another," was the wheel's next pious injunction.

"'Love one another,'" echoed Mrs. Waring. She and Miss Waring exchanged rather shame-faced glances.

"Until we all meet again in the Summerland, nothing should divide the two souls I love most," continued the wheel.

Both Warings looked distinctly melted by this address. "Oh, Howard," said Mrs. Waring softly.

"Farewell, my dears. Until next time." Having spelled these words, the wheel stopped short, indicating the sitting was over—and none too soon, considering how near my batteries were to being depleted.

I got up to light the lamps, noting with benevolent pleasure that the Warings, after looking at each other bashfully for a moment, had flung themselves into each other's arms. "Oh, Mama," sobbed Miss Waring.

"There, there, my love," said Mrs. Waring, patting her daughter on the back as if she were a little girl rather than a statuesque young lady. "You know I only want what is best for you. We must simply wait and be patient, as your father says. Very good advice, I am sure. There is no need for either of us to be hasty."

I thought it was good advice, too, and smiled complacently to myself as I followed them out of the Spirit Parlour. My right-hand woman Susan was waiting in the corridor outside with their cloaks.

"The servants are bringing your carriage around now, ma'am," she told Mrs. Waring. "It shouldn't be a minute."

Rather to my surprise, however, when the carriage appeared, Mrs. Waring indicated that her daughter should enter it alone. "You go on home, dear," she told Miss Waring, "then send the carriage back for me. I must just have a word alone with Madame Fox first."

I could not help being a bit dismayed by this speech, Dear Reader, for I was tired, hungry, and ready to let down my back hair (so to speak). But business is business, and it is no part of my business to discourage a good client.

In any case, I assumed she merely wished to arrange for her next sitting with Howard. So I led her back inside the Temple, ushered her into the Sitting Room, and prepared to hear what she had to say.

## CHAPTER 2

My Sitting Room is not as awe-inspiring as my Spirit Parlour. *That* room is frankly meant to impress, with all the solemnity of black velvet hangings that shut out light from the street and suggest dark rites, mystery, and magic. During séances, the Spirit Parlour is lit only by the brass Moroccan lantern that hangs over the table and between-times by alabaster lamps that look straight out of an Egyptian tomb. Statues of gods and goddesses stand along the walls: solemn and stately, or frankly grotesque, their brass and marble limbs gleaming against the black hangings. And of course, the centerpiece of the room is the séance table with the Spiritograph.

My Sitting Room has some exotic touches, too: purple brocade hangings, paintings of mystical subjects, Indian brasses, and the like. But it also has upholstered chairs and a comfortable sofa and little tables standing ready to hold one's cup of tea—or one's glass of brandy-and-soda, as the case may be. It was to the sofa that I directed Mrs. Waring, taking the chair opposite her.

"Do you care for any refreshment?" I inquired, as a good hostess should. "Shall I order some tea?"

"Thank you, no, Madame Fox," said Mrs. Waring. "I don't mean to keep you long. I know it is growing late, and you must be weary after our sitting." She smiled apologetically. "But I did want to talk to you privately about—" she took a deep breath, as though drawing courage for an unpleasant ordeal, "about this matter of Julia's engagement."

I perceived we were not yet done with the subject of Captain Ingram. "Ah," I said in a noncommittal voice.

"Indeed, I cannot deplore it too strongly," continued Mrs. Waring, with a tragic expression. "This Captain Ingram—nobody seems to know where he sprang from, or who his people are. Oh, I daresay he may have a record for bravery in the army, but what is that, after all? Many a man is physically brave, and yet a rogue. And poor Julia is so innocent—so trusting!"

She paused for breath, allowing me to venture a remark. "I had not heard that your daughter was engaged," I said. I kept my voice matter-of-fact, but in truth, Dear Reader, I was pretty peeved about it. I employ agents who are supposed to keep me abreast of major developments in the lives of my clients. I do not like to have surprises sprung upon me at the séance table.

"The engagement is . . . not a formal matter as yet," said Mrs. Waring, speaking as though the words pained her. "We have not told anyone, or announced it in the newspapers. I persuaded Julia that it was improper to do so while we are still in mourning for her father. But between you and me, Madame Fox, it never will be announced if I have anything to say about it!"

"I gathered you disapproved of the match," I said carefully. Some clients believe that the Medium is unconscious of everything that goes on during a séance, Dear Reader. I used to foster such a belief myself in the old days, but now that I am a Scientific Medium, with an Electrical Spiritograph, I see no need to keep up that particular fiction—unless, of course, the client prefers it.

"Yes, I do disapprove the match," said Mrs. Waring. "But unfortunately, Julia is only a few months away from being of age. And if she perseveres in this madness, there is nothing to stop her from marrying Captain Ingram, even if I withhold my consent."

"And does she gain full access to the money left in trust for her, once she is twenty-one?" I asked, wishing to make the matter clear.

"Yes, she does. If only it were not so! For I am sure that Captain Ingram only wants to marry her for her money."

"But your daughter is a beautiful girl," I pointed out. "He might easily have fallen in love with her." I spoke no more than the truth here, Dear Reader. Many a mother fancies her daughter beautiful, but Mrs. Waring had more solid grounds for doing so than is often the case.

"Yes, she is beautiful, but beauty only goes so far with men," said Mrs. Waring, speaking with what was obviously the voice of experience. "They might admire a beautiful girl, but most of them would prefer to marry a rich one, assuming they had to choose between the two. Especially men of Captain Ingram's type."

Not knowing Captain Ingram, I was in no position to dispute this statement, Dear Reader. In any case, my own experience agreed completely with hers. "That is very unfortunate," I said, and meant it. "Still, Miss Waring has always struck me as a sensible girl as well as a beautiful one. She may yet think better of marrying this captain and break the whole business off."

"Ah, but I am afraid she will not do so in time," said Mrs. Waring. Her dark eyes, so like her daughter's, were troubled as she looked at me. "If it were a full year until she turned twenty-one, I might have cause to hope, for few men can go a year without revealing something of their true character. But two months! He can easily keep up the pretence for that long. And poor Julia is smitten, quite smitten. I fear she will not realize her mistake until she has married him and it is too late to do anything about it."

"Ah," I said.

I said it sympathetically, for I supposed sympathy was what she wanted. Certainly I could not imagine what else she might want from me. My error was set straight with Mrs. Waring's next speech, however. "I was so relieved tonight to hear Howard counsel her to wait and have patience," she said. "If only he might continue to do so!"

Once again I said, "Ah," but this time in enlightenment. I could understand now why she had wanted to talk to me privately.

"I am sure it cannot hurt to keep consulting your late husband via the Spiritograph, ma'am," I said carefully. "It may be that he sees the matter more clearly than we do."

"I am sure he does, Madame Fox. If only he were still with us, to advise us in person! It was a tragedy that he should die when he did, at a time when his daughter and I needed him so much."

She continued to ramble on in this manner, assuring me of how certainly the late Howard Waring would have disapproved of his daughter's husband-to-be, how convenient it would be if the Spiritograph were to convey these sentiments at our next sitting, and how grateful she would be to anyone who might succeed in severing the engagement.

I am a long-time student of Human Nature, Dear Reader, and none of this took me strictly by surprise. Yet I still could not help marveling. Mrs. Waring was as sincere a believer in Spiritualism as you might find anywhere. She even sought Spiritual guidance in her financial investments—proof indeed of her sincerity, for though many people give lip-service to their faith, only the truly devoted back it with cold hard cash.

I might add that she was not mistaken in her faith on this point. I have several clients who are men of affairs in the City, and what with one thing and another, I have been in a position to pick up some very useful information about stocks and bonds and market fluctuations which I have then used for both my own and my other clients' benefit. Indeed, being in a position to advise those same men of affairs, I have myself personally influenced the Stock Exchange—which is a thing not every Spiritualist can boast of!

That being the case, let me repeat: I knew Mrs. Waring to be a sincere believer in Spiritualism. Yet here she was, offering me a bribe quite explicitly to influence the outcome of our next sitting. "I would pay a thousand pounds to see Julia free of this engagement," she said, gazing at me earnestly. "If you could do anything to help in the matter, Madame Fox—anything at all—I would be so very grateful. At the very least, if we can keep Julia from taking any irreversible step for just a few more months, the matter may resolve itself."

I told her I would do all I could, and she thanked me profusely. Her carriage having by this time returned, she took leave of me with a final plea to help her avert the dreadful fate that was hanging over her daughter's head.

Susan, as housekeeper, had helped her with her cloak and opened the door to her. She was thus privy to this final plea—and to what had preceded it, as it developed.

"Another thousand-pound reward," said Susan, eyeing me rather satirically. "Let's hope you don't have to risk your life this time around."

"I shouldn't think so," I said. "It doesn't sound that kind of affair at all." I frowned, rubbing my forehead with the back of a lace-mittened hand. "Still, why the devil have I heard nothing before now of Miss Waring's being engaged? Who's our agent there—the butler?"

"Yes, the butler," affirmed Susan. "Haven't heard a word from him."

"Drat the man. I wonder what ails him, not to pass along such a piece of news as that."

"Maybe he didn't know about it," said Susan. "If she's been meeting this captain on the sly, he might not have heard."

"Damn it, *someone* ought to have heard," I said crossly. "I pay enough to keep abreast of affairs in that house."

Susan suggested that the coachman and footmen might have heard something. "If Miss Waring's been taking the carriage to meet her captain, it stands to reason they would."

"Good idea," I said. "Tell Jenny to come up to the Sitting Room in half an hour, and we'll confer."

It took me all of half an hour to remove my Spiritualistic garb, Dear Reader. First, I divested myself of the lace mittens and all ten of the rings. Next I stripped off the veiled headdress and somber jet-trimmed dress with its trailing skirt and plunging neckline. I took down my hair, removing the numerous switches and braids and rats of false hair that enhanced my own reddish-brownish-blondish locks. If you think of a fox's pelt, you will have a very fair idea of the colour, though I am obliged to say it is somewhat tinctured nowadays with an increasing amount of grey.

Lastly, I scrubbed off the paint and powder that whitened my skin and shadowed my eyes. Once reduced to my natural state, I wrapped myself in my dressing gown and went down to the Sitting Room.

Jenny was waiting for me there along with Susan. Susan, a middle-aged woman with a wholly deceptive air of respectability, has been with me for ten years now, ever since I first came to London. Jenny, however, is a more recent addition. I took her into my service only a few months ago, shortly after the affair described in my previous memoir. Jenny is a strapping young woman, as tall and strong as most men, with dark hair and a ruddy complexion. Like Susan, she is far more intelligent than her appearance and manner of speaking might suggest. Since joining our ménage, she has taken over much of the housekeeping work, leaving Susan free to assist me with the Spiritualism business. Thus, it might be more accurate to call Jenny my housekeeper rather than Susan. But whatever title you give them, both women are invaluable to me. I couldn't operate the Temple of Spiritualism without them.

After we had all helped ourselves to tea and biscuits, I began the meeting, as I usually do, by reviewing the evening's sitting. "Excellent work with the pipe tobacco," I told Susan. "It was Mr. Waring's mixture, all right. The Warings recognized it instantly."

"Yes, but I'll have to spend all tomorrow airing out the Spirit Parlour *and* the room next door," said Susan, wrinkling her nose. "Tobacco smoke gets into everything."

"Never mind that: it was worth it. You might pick up some more of the same mixture from the tobacconist next time you have a chance."

You will understand from this, Dear Reader, that I do not content myself with fabricating only *words* from the Other Side. I also fabricate scents to help evoke the Late Loved One in the minds of his or her survivors. Smell is, after all, the most evocative of the senses, and Susan and I have used everything from floral perfume to saddle leather—or (as in this case) the specific pipe tobacco used by the Late Loved One. There is a ventilator on one wall of my Spirit Parlour, concealed behind a Japanese screen. This ventilator communicates with the adjacent room, where Susan is stationed during séances to waft appropriate scents, as well as assisting in other ways.

"I thought the business went off *reasonably* well," I said, thinking the matter over as I sipped my tea. "Especially given how surprised I was to hear of Miss Waring's engagement. It still irks me that the

Warings' butler mentioned no word of it in his last report." Looking at Jenny, I asked, "Did the coachman or footmen say anything about it while they were in the kitchen?"

"Aye, that they did," said Jenny. "Once they'd drunk a couple of pints, they became very free-spoken about it." She smiled mischievously.

I smiled back at her. When I took Jenny into my employ, I had hoped for nothing more than to help her out of a difficult situation as well as easing some of the housekeeping burden on Susan. But in fact, Jenny has proved a valuable addition. While Susan and I tend to the clients in the Spirit Parlour, Jenny remains in the kitchen to entertain any servants my clients might have brought along. She is instructed to dispense beer and whiskey with a lavish hand, in order to make those servants talk as freely as possible. I may say that the information she gains in this way more than defrays both the cost of the liquor and the cost of her salary.

"Thank heaven for servants' gossip," I said devoutly. "Tell me all they said, as nearly as you can remember it."

Jenny frowned in recollection. Susan and I had been labouring to improve her reading and writing abilities, which had been almost nonexistent when she first came to us. She was improving bit by bit, but still relied mostly on her memory. "The coachman don't think much of Miss Waring's fellow," she said. "He says he ought to be called Captain Sharp, not Captain Ingram."

"'Captain Sharp' being a term for a confidence man?" I asked. Because I am American by birth rather than British, some of their slang is still unfamiliar to me.

Jenny confirmed that this was correct. "And Will, the footman, said it was a shame to see a pretty young girl wanting to tie herself to a man old enough to be her father."

I nodded, but privately thought this of less value than the coachman's comment. Though youth may call to youth, as the saying goes, still it is not uncommon to see a young woman enamoured of a man who is her elder by a decade or so—and *vice versa*, of course. Now and then I myself am obliged to fend off advances from young men, even at my own (comparatively) advanced age.

"That's something to go on, at any rate," I said aloud. "Anything else?"

"Aye, both Will and John Coachman was talking about how Miss Waring's been meeting the captain in the park and at the theatre and so on, all without her mother knowing anything about it. 'Deed, and they weren't sure she knows about it now."

"She does," I said, looking expressively at Susan. "It was a matter of considerable discussion at the séance table."

Susan laughed. "Yes, you had to think on your feet pretty quick there, didn't you? Not but what you didn't manage it well enough," she added generously. "'Hidden knowledge will be revealed.' I was hard put not to laugh."

"Yes, it's an old dodge, but a good one," I said. "And it has the advantage of being usually true. In almost any situation, there's something one doesn't know that would make a difference. I only wish," I added ruefully, "that I knew something more about this Captain Ingram."

"You mean to try for the thousand pounds Mrs. Waring is offering, then?" said Susan.

"Most certainly I do. We must start looking into the matter right away. If this Captain Ingram really is a Captain Sharp, we ought to be able to find it out."

Susan agreed that we ought. "But you know it would have to be something pretty bad to make Miss Waring break with him," she warned me. "If she really loves him, that is."

I had to admit this was true, Dear Reader. I had seen enough of Miss Waring to know she had a stubborn will coupled with a warmly affectionate nature. In short, she was just the sort of young woman who would cling to a complete rotter, defying her mother, her friends, and all of society, simply because she had pledged her love to him.

"We must hope we can find something really incriminating," I said. "Another woman, perhaps. I wouldn't think her the sort to overlook *that*."

"Not if he was seeing the other woman at the same time he was seeing her," agreed Susan. "But if it happened before he started courting her, don't you think she'd forgive it? He'd only have to tell her she was the only woman he ever *really* loved, and that all the others before her meant nothing."

I was forced to admit that this, too, seemed likely. "Perhaps we could hire another woman to seduce him away from her?" I suggested half-heartedly.

"If he really is a Captain Sharp, he'd be a fool not to know it was a trap," opined Susan. "Seeing that her mother wants the engagement broken at any price."

Jenny threw in her support behind this opinion. "You can bet he's awake on that score," she said, nodding. "He's only got to behave himself till he marries the girl, and then he can take as many mistresses as he wants."

"Then perhaps we could hire another man to seduce *her* away from *him*?"

"Then you'd be out of the frying pan and into the fire," said Susan bluntly. "She'd be in love with another rascal, and her mother wouldn't like that a bit better than her loving this one. What you need is a suitor who's a real gentleman: honest and respectable. And you couldn't bribe a man like that."

I scowled and stirred sugar into my tea, temporarily deprived of ideas. "You think it's hopeless, then?"

"Not at all," said Susan briskly. "You never know till you try. We might find something incriminating enough that we could persuade the captain to break the engagement himself." She waggled her eyebrows significantly.

"Blackmail, you mean?" I shook my head. "I won't go that far."

It may surprise you to hear that I draw the line at blackmail, Dear Reader. After all, I regularly make use of people's private information for personal gain. But to my mind, there is a vast difference between using private information at the séance table, for what you might call entertainment purposes, and threatening to make that information public for purposes of extortion. Not everyone can see that difference, but it is clear enough to me.

And since I am sworn to complete honesty, Dear Reader, let me say that besides this high-minded objection to blackmail, I also have a practical one. If I were to take to blackmail, I would soon run up against that Milverton creature, who holds a virtual stranglehold on the blackmailing business in this town. I cannot but think he will come to a bad end someday.[6] In the meantime, I much prefer to keep to my own proper business and let him keep to his.

"I won't go as far as blackmail," I repeated. "But I would be willing to try almost anything else. Let us put our heads together and try to plan a strategy. We are all women, after all, and have some experience of the world. What is the best way to make a woman stop loving a man?"

"Time," said Susan shortly. "Or another suitor. And you haven't got either."

---

6  It would appear that Madame Fox is alluding here to the Milverton whose exploits are described in Dr. John H. Watson's story, "The Adventure of Charles Augustus Milverton." If so, her comments would seem to evince a measure of true psychic ability. –*Ed.*

I thought this unduly fatalistic and said so. "I'll keep counseling Miss Waring via the Spiritograph to wait. The longer I can make her wait, the more likely it is that the captain will do something to disgust her, if he's the man her mother thinks he is. *And* the more likely she is to meet another man she might prefer to him." This, after all, would be the best way of ending Miss Waring's unfortunate entanglement. As dear Miss Austen says, a second attachment is the surest, most natural, and most happy cure in these situations. There is nothing to beat the expulsive power of a new affection.

Having expressed this sentiment aloud, I told Susan and Jenny that we would nevertheless pursue the matter in the usual way, in hopes of turning up something useful. "It's worth a little expenditure if it gains me a thousand pounds," I said. "I'll ask Felicity to investigate this Captain Ingram. If there's a dark secret in his past, she'd be the one to find it out."

Susan and Jenny both nodded. They knew Felicity as one of my agents—unquestionably my very best agent. She is a woman capable of insinuating herself into almost any household and uncovering whatever might be hidden there. "'Hidden knowledge,'" I quoted, smiling. "That's Felicity's specialty. And her motto might as well be 'In time, what is hidden will be made clear.'"

"If it comes to that, you might do well to consult Inspector Harper, too," suggested Susan. "Maybe the police know something against this Captain Ingram. It couldn't hurt to ask. This is another case where the two of you ought to be on the same side."

I agreed, Dear Reader, though with reservations. Detective Inspector Thomas Harper and I had worked together on the Langley affair, and though I had chafed against the partnership in the beginning, I could not complain about the way it had turned out. It would not be too much to say that we were friends now, though neither of us trusted the other beyond a certain point. He was, after all, a policeman whose business was pursuing criminals, while I was a fraudulent Medium—*i.e.*, a criminal myself, though admittedly of a minor and relatively excusable sort. That being the case, we had to tread carefully in our relations. He made a habit of calling on me about once a week to discuss cases that were particularly puzzling, in the hopes that my unique perspective—as a woman and a criminal—might be of help in solving them.

"I suppose I might consult the Inspector about this Captain Ingram," I said thoughtfully. "I can't see any harm in it."

We all agreed there didn't seem to be any harm in consulting the Inspector. "Perhaps you ought to consult the army lists, too," suggested Susan. "I heard Mrs. Waring say she didn't believe Captain Ingram was really a captain. Do you think there's anything in that?"

"Miss Waring said she'd seen his army photograph," I said, thinking back over the conversation. "And that he had been commended for bravery." I smiled. "If that's true, we must hope the Duke of Wellington's words apply. He once said something about there being nothing so stupid as a gallant officer. I'll take a stupid man, however gallant, as an opponent anytime over a clever one."

Both Jenny and Susan rolled their eyes at this. "I knew we'd be hearing from the Duke of Wellington before long," said Susan. "And that reminds me, ma'am. There's a note come from Miss Emily Randall, and I expect it's to do with that very thing." She went off to fetch the note, and I leaned back in my chair, happy to turn my thoughts from Captain Ingram to more comfortable and familiar matters.

## CHAPTER 3

S usan and Jenny had good reason to be tired of hearing about the Duke of Wellington. He had become inextricably mixed with my affairs nine years ago, when I first made the acquaintance of Miss Emily Randall.

At the time, Miss Emily was still living with her sister, Lady Morton, who was a widow and the elder of the two sisters. Both were devotees of Spiritualism, which was how I had made their acquaintance. Being elderly ladies, they had numerous Late Loved Ones—parents, an older brother, and in Lady Morton's case a spouse and a son who had passed to the Other Side. You might therefore suppose it was some or all of these whom they wished to contact via the Spiritograph.

But you would be wrong, Dear Reader. Miss Emily and Lady Morton were only interested in speaking to one person on the Other Side. And that person was His Grace, Arthur Wellesley, the first Duke of Wellington.

This is not so curious as may appear at first glance. The British do not exhibit such fervent devotion to the Iron Duke as the French to Napoleon Bonaparte, but this, I believe, is owing to the differing temperaments of the two peoples as well as to the differing characters of their national heroes. Bonaparte, whom we all know to have gotten the worst of that final encounter at Waterloo, devoted his remaining years in exile to consolidating his reputation and making excuses for his loss. The Duke of Wellington, on the other hand, not only exhibited the greatest indifference to the reputation he had gained on the battlefield, but did much to damage that reputation through his subsequent political career.

Still, the years since his death have gone far to rehabilitate his character in the eyes of his countrymen. And to some of his countrymen, who had actually lived through those dark days when Bonaparte threatened Britain's shores and nothing seemed to stand in the way of French rapine and plunder save the exertions of the Iron Duke, he was a hero to end all heroes and a name to conjure with.

So it was with Miss Emily and her sister. They had been thirteen and fourteen at the time of Waterloo: young enough to have been threatened with the Monster Bonaparte while in the nursery,[7] old enough to see his vanquisher as a romantic hero. If you are acquainted with the childhood works of the Brontës, Dear Reader, you will see this same exaggerated hero worship in referring to the Duke. It was quite common among their generation. Nowadays, of course, it is more the fashion for young girls to admire singers or actors, but the principle is the same, and so is the devotion. In Miss Emily and her sister, the devotion had never faded.

Thus, for the past nine years, I had been regularly summoning the Duke of Wellington to the séance table. As a result, I had become familiar with his character, his style of speech, and his opinions on a variety of subjects. Not, indeed, through any actual intercourse with his Spirit, but through my usual resources: the letters, diaries, newspapers, and other written materials I used to acquaint myself with him and his background.

---

7 Madame Fox does not here exaggerate the use of Bonaparte's name as a nursery ogre. Children of Miss Emily's generation might well be soothed to sleep with the assurance that Bonaparte would tear them limb from limb and eat them if they misbehaved.–*Ed.*

In some ways, it was easier than my usual researches, Dear Reader. One can obtain whole volumes of the Duke's correspondence at any bookseller's, while much more can be found in libraries and private archives. In other ways, it was harder: not only was the Duke himself a prolific writer, but he had been a popular subject for historians and biographers, who had shown their usual tiresome tendency to disagree violently on a number of points. I had become familiar with those points and had my own opinions about them, and indeed felt I could now write my own biography arguing for my own particular point of view. If the Spiritualism business ever fails me, I might think about doing so. But at present, it was enough that I could speak with a reasonable degree of authenticity when I sat for Miss Emily.

It was only Miss Emily for whom I sat nowadays. Her sister, Lady Morton, had died just over a year ago. The sisters had lived together in their family home until the time of the elder's death; now Miss Emily lived there alone with her hired companion, Hilda Schmidt. Although it was an old-fashioned home, it was nonetheless a splendid one. Originally it had been called Randall House, but the sisters' devotion to the Iron Duke had caused them to change its name to Waterloo House. And every year on the eighteenth of June, on the anniversary of the great battle, they were accustomed to hold there an annual Waterloo Dinner. I was invited as a matter of course, for my rôle was a most important one, Dear Reader. I was expected to bring the Guest of Honour.

It was early June now, just about time for the invitation to arrive. When Susan presently returned, bearing a heavy cream-coloured envelope sealed in patriotic red and blue wax, I had no doubt of its contents.

"You're right, Susan: it's an invitation to Miss Emily's Waterloo Dinner," I said, glancing over the enclosure. "Of course I must go.

Poor dear, it wouldn't do to disappoint her. At her age, it's not likely she will be able to host many more such parties."

"No séance here on June eighteenth, then," said Susan, making a note in our appointment book. "Of course you'll sit for the company at her house after dinner."

I agreed that I would. "I suppose Miss Emily's nieces will be there," I said, pulling a face. "I always feel I don't give my best performance with them looking on. They're obviously skeptics about Spiritualism, though they don't say so openly out of deference to Miss Emily's feelings. But Miss Morton is always making nasty little remarks about vulgar, encroaching people, and Lady Frost is worse. Her husband, Lord Frost, is pleasant enough, however."

Jenny was looking impressed. "I didn't realize you went into society with lords and ladies, ma'am," she said.

"Now and again," I said. "I don't do it very often."

In fact, this was about the only occasion I did do it, Dear Reader. I am a businesswoman, and most of my business is transacted in the evenings. Thus, I have little time for dinner parties, concerts, balls, and the other diversions with which the leisured class while away their hours. My somewhat equivocal social position would make them a strain in any case. Believers in Spiritualism are wont to regard me with awe; non-believers are apt to regard me with scorn. Neither is a comfortable attitude when one is hoping merely to enjoy an evening's entertainment.

As a result, I decline most of the social invitations that come my way. But I make an exception for Miss Emily. I would do so even if there were no professional fee involved. She is a dear creature, and I believe she has a genuine affection for me—as I do for her, in fact. Just as the Iron Duke has become inextricably linked with my affairs over the years, so too has she.

"I shall need a new dress," I said aloud.

"You just had that black silk with the panniers from the dress-maker's," reminded Susan.

I waved this objection away. "This is a gala occasion. I shall get a new one."

"Black like all the others, I suppose," said Jenny. Her voice was disapproving.

I explained that I preferred black when appearing in a profes-sional capacity. "It conveys mystery and authority at the same time," I said. "*And* it's also practical and doesn't soil easily."

"But it's so dull!"

"You are thinking of *mourning* black," I said. "Mourning black is certainly dull. The dresses I wear are not dull at all. Quite the con-trary, in fact." I have a weakness for jet trim, lace, beads, and so forth that sometimes leads me into excess, Dear Reader. As Monsieur Flaubert says, however, exuberance can be a fair substitute for taste.

Susan good-humouredly fetched a fashion paper, and we all bent over the illustrations. It emerged that Jenny, too, had thoughts of enlarging her wardrobe.

"I like that hat," she said, pointing to one of the illustrations. "Perhaps I'll see if the milliner round the corner's got one like it. Sam wants to take me to the park Sunday, and I don't have anything fit for warm weather."

Susan and I exchanged glances over her head. Jenny, who had once confided her fear that no good man would ever want to mar-ry her, had succeeded in attracting several devoted followers in the short time she had been with us. Sam was the foremost of these fol-lowers. He was a tall young man with sandy hair and a Herculean build who drove his own milk van. He appeared to be a fine, up-standing young man in every way, and I would have liked him very well if he had not bade fair to take Jenny away from me. As it was, I concealed my reservations about their relationship. One must not be selfish, after all, and if she chose marriage to him over working for me, I would have to accept it.

"I think that hat would suit you very well, Jenny," I said, and discreetly changed the subject.

As a result of that evening's events, I was kept busy during the next few days. My first order of business was to call upon Felicity and ask her to undertake the investigation of Captain Ingram.

There are many ways to communicate with Felicity, Dear Reader—through the agony columns of the newspapers, via the penny post, or through one of several receiving offices, to name just a few. But the easiest is to simply drop by her own particular den, The Calico Cat. This is a tea-shop of humble mien, dark and low-ceilinged, where she can often be found around the hour of five o'clock indulging in her favourite cream tea. She was there today, as I had hoped, seated in the corner nearest the fire. Not coincidentally, this place offers a good view of anyone entering the shop. Also not coincidentally, it was located as far as possible from other tables and any possible listening ears.

I may have mentioned before that Felicity's appearance varies wildly from day to day, depending upon the business she has in hand. Today, she was dressed with nun-like austerity in a grey linen sack dress with neat white collar and cuffs. All of her hair and most of her face were concealed by a dark close bonnet. She hailed me cheerfully and beckoned me to sit down in the chair opposite her.

"My dear Seraphina!"

"My dear Felicity," I returned, as I seated myself. She ordered the attendant to bring another round of tea, scones, and clotted cream, then waited until the girl had departed before addressing me again.

"How are you, dear?" she inquired. "You're looking well."

"And so are you, though I'm not sure that bonnet becomes you," I said. She laughed and shook her head.

"No, to be sure it don't, but that's neither here nor there. You know how it is, dear. Sometimes we're obliged to hide our light under a bushel."

I agreed, and after we had exchanged a few more remarks in this vein, we got down to business. "I was hoping you might be free to help me, Felicity. I need to learn as much as possible about a Captain Francis Ingram. He's a middle-aged man—ex-army—fought in the Zulu war and received some sort of commendation for it. He's recently become engaged to Miss Julia Waring."

Felicity rolled a knowing eye at me. "Parents don't approve?"

"That's it," I said. "The girl's mother objects to the match, but without any real grounds as far as I can tell. Mind you, he does seem to be something of a man of mystery."

Felicity made a few notes in a memorandum book. "Can't say I've heard of him, dear, but I can certainly look into it. Is that all?"

"That will do to start. I want everything you can learn about him, both good and ill."

"And how much is it worth to you?"

"*Carte blanche*—within reason," I said. "If there's any extraordinary expense, you might consult me first. But for the ordinary sort of business, proceed as you think best."

Felicity signified her satisfaction with these instructions, and as soon as we finished our tea we parted on amicable terms. My next stop was a dressmaker's in Regent Street, where I meant to order my dress for the Waterloo Dinner.

There are many dressmakers in London, Dear Reader, some of them splendid establishments patronized by wealthy women of fashion. Not being a wealthy woman of fashion, I am obliged to settle for a humbler sort of place. I like a pretty dress as well as the next woman, but I like a bargain, too, and Mrs. O'Meagher's was a very good compromise between price and fashion.

I was waited on by the dressmaker herself. Although her name is Irish, she is an elderly Englishwoman of extreme refinement. We get along well nonetheless. On this occasion, we consulted fashion plates, discussed modes in dinner dresses (square necklines are very much worn nowadays, it appears), and looked at samples of fabric.

Motivated by Jenny's words, I was inspired to choose something a little more colourful than my usual unrelieved black: a summer-weight taffeta that was black indeed, but reflected a tinge of iridescent green in the light. "And for the head, may I suggest a dear little toque of the same fabric, pleated with bands of jet beads, and trimmed with a cluster of coq feathers," said Mrs. O'Meagher, displaying some blackish-green feathers that matched the taffeta to a nicety.

The price she named for dress and toque was rather high, but not too high for my one social outing of the year. I ordered the dress, set a date for the first fitting, and proceeded back to the Temple of Spiritualism well pleased with my day's business.

The next day, Sunday, was the day Jenny was going to the park with Sam. It was also the day Inspector Harper usually came to call. With mixed feelings, I watched Jenny, attired in her new hat, sally out the door with her beau. They made an impressive couple, both being a good head taller and foot broader than the ordinary people in the street. If they ended up marrying, one might imagine them progenitors of a race of super-men and -women. Rather morosely, I shut the door and returned to the Sitting Room. It wasn't long before the doorbell rang, and Susan came to announce the arrival of Inspector Harper.

I stood to greet him as he entered the room. He saluted me with his usual courtesy, then took a seat on the sofa while I resumed my chair. In deference to the nearly summer weather we were enjoying, his long-limbed frame was clad in lightweight tweed, and the hat he surrendered to Susan might more properly be termed a cap. "I hope all is well with you," he said, bringing the tips of his fingers together beneath his chin and surveying me with his keen grey eyes. "Nothing gone wrong, I hope?"

"Not at all," I said, rather surprised by this inquiry. "Why do you ask?"

"There's a little line between your brows when you're worrying about something," he explained.

This was too much like mind-reading for my taste, Dear Reader. Of course I myself habitually scan faces for such telltale signs, but to have it done to me was disconcerting. I promptly smoothed my brow. "Oh, I wouldn't say I was worrying," I said. "It's only that Jenny's out with her young man." Despite myself, I could not keep a forlorn note from my voice as I added, "I am afraid he means to marry her."

The Inspector smiled. "I can see how that would be vexing. But at the same time, you must rejoice to see her with prospects of being so well settled in life."

He knew something about Jenny and her past, so he knew how her hopes had long centred on a home and family of her own. "Of course," I said. I meant what I said, Dear Reader: I did want her well settled in life. It was only that I felt she already had a settled home with Susan and me.

To change the subject, I asked him how business was progressing at Scotland Yard. He told me all about a forgery case they had just wrapped up in Paddington, which had several amusing features. He also thanked me again for the recent help I had provided him in connection with a burglary at a well-known jeweler's.

That had been a singularly successful collaboration, Dear Reader. The burglary had in fact been what is called an inside job. The jeweler himself had concealed the goods, reported it as burglary, and counted on profiting twice, once from the insurance money and once from the later disposal of the jewelry.

As it happened, however, the place had been under surveillance by real burglars, who had been planning their own burglary for the following night. They were so incensed at being defrauded of what they considered their lawful property that they reported the matter to Felicity (who may well have been involved in the matter from the beginning, though I wasn't impolite enough to ask). In any event, Felicity told me what had happened and—knowing my connection with Inspector Harper—suggested I pass the information along to him.

"These amateurs," she had told me with a shake of her head. "To think of the old fool spoiling the game that way! I can't hold with *that* sort of thing."

I did pass the information to Inspector Harper, who was able to bring the jeweler to book for his crime. It was a case where everyone was happy with the outcome, with the possible exception of the jeweler. As what may be termed the middleman (or woman), I had done especially well out of the matter, gaining not only the goodwill of Felicity and her compatriots but of Scotland Yard.

All that had been several weeks ago, but it was clear I was still in Inspector Harper's good books. That being the case, I felt I might ask a favour without appearing forward.

"Have you ever heard of a Captain Francis Ingram?" I asked.

He rolled his eyes upward, as though searching a Rogues' Gallery in his memory. "The name's not familiar to me," he admitted after a minute or two. "Should it be?"

"Not necessarily," I said. "I only heard of him myself a few days ago."

"Is he a criminal?"

"Not to my knowledge," I said.

That apparently sounded too much like evasion, for the Inspector frowned and told me that if I had even a suspicion of criminal activity on the part of the captain or anyone else, he would appreciate knowing about it.

"Yes, of course," I said. "But in fact I know nothing against this Captain Ingram, except that he is engaged to marry a very rich and beautiful young lady, and that her mother doesn't favour the match."

"I see," said the Inspector, his brow clearing. In a jocular tone, he added, "There's no law against marrying rich and beautiful young ladies—assuming the young lady's of age and willing to marry you. And assuming also that you haven't another wife in the background somewhere. Even if her mother doesn't approve, it isn't against the law!"

"Well, she is certainly willing, and she will be of age in only a month or two. I don't know about there being another wife in the background."

I daresay I sounded rather wistful, for I could not help thinking how wonderful it would be if Captain Ingram proved to already have a wife. Even if Miss Waring went ahead and married him, her fortune would be safe, for the Law does not recognize bigamous marriages.

Inspector Harper seemed amused by my wistfulness. "Do you want me to make some inquiries about the fellow?" he asked.

"I would appreciate it if you would," I said, and gave him the little I knew about the captain. He promised to look into the matter and let me know the outcome at our next meeting.

"Now there's something I want to ask *you*," he said. "Miss Emily Randall is one of your clients, isn't she?"

"Yes, she is," I said, trying to hide my astonishment. Miss Emily had naturally been in my thoughts lately, but I could not imagine why she would be in his. It seemed a strange coincidence to have her name brought forward in this way. I felt the unease I always feel when coincidences are a little too pat—or perhaps it was merely hearing Miss Emily's name on the lips of a Scotland Yard detective. She had always seemed to occupy a rarefied world, quite insulated from criminal affairs. Unless you counted my own criminal affairs, of course. I hoped he was not referring to those, as I waited with trepidation to hear what he would say next.

"I thought she was a client of yours," he said, nodding. "And you know her pretty well?"

"Yes, pretty well," I affirmed cautiously. "I have been sitting regularly for her for nine years."

"Then I wonder if you'd take a look at this and tell me if you can shed any light on it." He handed me a much-creased piece of paper.

I smoothed it out on my knee and saw that it was a letter of sorts. Instead of being written, however, the words were made of letters cut from a newspaper and pasted across the paper in a straggling line:

MISS EMILY RANDALL IS BEING POISONED

"Good heavens," I said blankly.

"Do you know anything about this?" asked the Inspector, regarding me more closely than felt entirely comfortable.

"Not a thing. Good heavens. Surely it can't be true?"

"That's what I'm trying to find out," he said. "We get a fair number of anonymous letters, of course. Most of them are just spite, or the work of lunatics. But now and then, there's one that repays our attention."

I could hardly speak, for the thought of Miss Emily being poisoned was disturbing in more ways than one. "This is dreadful," I said. "If it's true, that is." I paused, thinking. "She did cancel our last sitting, saying she wasn't feeling well. That was a month ago, but I didn't think anything about it. I knew Waterloo Day was coming up, and we always have a standing engagement for that."

"Waterloo Day?" repeated the Inspector, raising his brows. "What on earth has that to do with it?"

I had to explain about Miss Emily's Wellington monomania. He listened with incredulity and mounting amusement. "Well, I suppose it's a harmless enough eccentricity," he said. "Makes me sorry I'm not invited to this dinner, upon my word. I'd give a good deal to be there and see you summon up the Duke of Wellington."

I told him that his being there would put me off. "Policemen have a dampening effect on Spirit Energy," I said sternly. "Everyone knows that."

He acknowledged this with a smile. "I wouldn't doubt it. But you don't know anything that would suggest Miss Emily is being poisoned?"

I shook my head. "I can't imagine anyone poisoning her. She's the most harmless creature. And she's an old lady, whom you wouldn't expect to live very long in any case. Her sister was only a year older than she was, and she died about a year ago." I paused. "Just *over* a year ago. Now I wonder . . . ."

"What do you wonder?" asked the Inspector sharply.

"I wonder if there's a motive there. Miss Emily inherited the house—well, not inherited it, precisely. I believe it was deeded to both sisters, or at any rate they both had a life interest in it. When her sister died, it became hers alone."

"Who gets it when *she* dies?" asked the Inspector.

I was not surprised by this question, Dear Reader. *Cui bono*—who profits? —is the first inquiry a sensible person makes when there is a crime to investigate.

"I don't really know," I said. "But I don't believe it's in Miss Emily's power to dispose of the house, or indeed of anything besides her own personal possessions. I think on her death, everything would pass automatically to her nearest relative."

"Is there an entailment?"

"I don't think so. For one thing, there's no male heir. I'd guess originally the property would have been settled on her nephew Arthur—her older sister's son. But he died years ago, which would have broken any entail there might have been. So probably the house would go to her niece instead—her eldest niece—or to both nieces jointly, perhaps."

As I spoke, the Inspector had drawn out his notebook and was scribbling away. I eyed him with misgiving. "I don't wish to be mixed up in another murder case," I told him.

"It's not murder—yet," he returned. "With luck, we can prevent it from going that far."

"We?" I asked pointedly. "I would say that is *your* job."

He smiled as he put the notebook away. "I'm going to do all I can, of course. I'll drop by Miss Emily's house tomorrow and ask a few questions. Probably it's nothing—a disgruntled servant, or just someone playing a stupid joke." He got to his feet. "But if you hear anything in the meantime, I'd appreciate it if you'd let me know."

I promised to do so. He promised in turn to look into the matter of Captain Francis Ingram. Having collected his hat from Susan, he departed, leaving me with much food for thought.

## CHAPTER 4

I lost no time acquainting Susan with the news Inspector Harper had given me. She was as incredulous as I had been.

"Poisoned? Miss Emily? I don't believe it."

"I'm not sure I do, either," I said. "It might be only a joke, of course."

"Not a very funny joke," said Susan disapprovingly.

"Yes, I'm of the same opinion. The whole business makes me very uneasy."

"I don't wonder," said Susan. "You're planning to eat dinner with her, after all!"

It was certainly not a reassuring thought. Still, I comforted myself with the idea that Inspector Harper was looking into the matter. If there really were a poisoner at Waterloo House, he would doubtless discover it long before Waterloo Day and do something about it.

In the meantime, I had Miss Waring's affairs to occupy me. Felicity had undertaken the investigation of Captain Ingram, but had run into some unexpected trouble.

"I've seen your captain, and I'm bound to say he's a taking sort of man," she told me. "It's easy to see why the gel's wild for him. A bit down at heels, but still a handsome fellow, and very pleasant-spoken and mannerly."

I nodded, reaching for my teacup. We had met at the Calico Cat to compare notes. I was being honoured with the personal attention of the tea-shop's eponymous cat, which was lying in my lap purring and incidentally getting particoloured hairs all over my black batiste dress. "I wouldn't have expected him to be other than charming. That's a fortune hunter's stock-in-trade, after all. How old do you think he is?"

Felicity shrugged. "Might be anything from an old thirty to a young fifty. I'd say closer to fifty, if I had to guess. Mind you, that don't seem likely if he was fighting in the African war."

"Have you found anything to tell if he did fight in it?"

"Well, he's got a bit of a limp, dear. It *might* be a war injury," said Felicity cautiously.

"But you haven't been able to verify it?"

"Ah, there's the rub, my dear. I daresay I could verify it easy enough, if I could only get into his room. But his landlady flew up into the boughs at the very idea. I tried to talk her round, but she wasn't having it at any price. It's easy to see he's got her properly wrapped around his finger. And yet I've got it on the word of one of the maids that he's a couple of months behind in his rent. That shows you what kind of a man he is, right there."

I agreed that it did seem pretty telling. "What shall we do, then? It handicaps us terribly if we can't get into his room."

"As to that, I think I've found a way to manage the business. The maid I was telling you about says her mistress is a regular one for churchgoing. On Sundays, she's away all morning and most of the afternoon."

I grasped the idea immediately. "So you think you can get in on a Sunday morning?"

Felicity shook her head. "I might if the captain was a churchgoer, too, but he's not. Nor he isn't an early riser, either. Seems he's apt to stay abed late on other days, too, not just Sunday. But the maid says he's usually out of his room by noon. She says if we go to the house at noon on Sunday, she'll let us in and stand guard while we do our looking."

"*We?*" I repeated.

It was strange, the way people kept trying to draw me into their investigations. First Inspector Harper had suggested the two of us might investigate the allegations in the anonymous letter. Now Felicity was suggesting we share in unlawfully entering the captain's room. Normally, I prefer to remain at a remove in these kinds of affairs. But I could see Felicity's point: it sounded as if an hour or two in the captain's room was the most we could hope for, and two of us could cover the ground much more quickly, especially since I would have a better idea than she of what might ultimately prove useful. The risk seemed minimal, too, with the maid standing guard.

"Very well," I said. "I will meet you at the captain's rooming house this coming Sunday."

⁂

Unfortunately, this conversation took place on Tuesday, meaning I had five days to wait before I could hope to gain any more definite information about Captain Ingram. And Mrs. Waring was not going to let me wait that long. She was besieging me daily, begging for another sitting. Obviously she expected me to take immediate action to save her daughter. She kept hinting about that thousand-pound reward, too: not saying explicitly that she would pay to have her late husband's Spirit warn her daughter away from the captain, but the inference was plain. It was, in fact, one of those desperate situations that call for desperate measures, as I told Susan and Jenny that evening.

"I've put her off till Friday, but I haven't anything more to go on this time than last. Still, I'm going to have to do something. So

I think that in addition to having the Spiritograph counsel delay, I shall reinforce it with a stronger and more personal message."

"What does *that* mean?" said Susan suspiciously.

"It means a materialization," I said.

Susan frowned. "I thought you didn't do materializations anymore," she said. "You've told me over and over that after what happened with that newspaper reporter, back when you were younger, you wouldn't ever take the chance again." Jenny nodded her concurrence. She, too, had heard about that most humiliating episode.

"I did say that," I acknowledged. "And I meant what I said. I won't do any more materializations *myself*. But that doesn't mean I couldn't *produce* one. One that was altogether distinct from me, you understand, and in no danger of being mistaken for me."

Jenny merely looked uncomprehending, but Susan was regarding me with deep distrust. "You're not expecting *me* to dress up in phosphorescent muslin, I hope," she said.

"Oh, no," I assured her. "It's not a full figure materialization I mean. But I shall definitely need your help, and possibly Jenny's, too. Let us go into the Spirit Parlour, and you both can help me decide how best to manage the business."

There were several problems we had to overcome. The biggest was that in order to produce the materialization I had in mind, Susan would have to be in the Spirit Parlour along with me rather than assisting from the room next door. "I could hide behind the screen, I suppose," she said, surveying the room. We had hidden someone behind the Japanese screen once before, Dear Reader, and it had worked reasonably well,[8] but I was uneasy about using it as a hiding place on this occasion. If one of the Warings took it into

---

8 Apart from the destruction of the screen itself, and a few other trifling damages. The screen referred to here would appear to be a replacement, or possibly the original proved repairable. See *The Ghost in the Machine*. –Ed.

her head to look behind it, either before or after the séance, the cat would be out of the bag.

The same objection applied to hiding Susan behind the curtains in the window bay. "In my experience, the more spectacular the materialization, the more likely people are to come poking around afterwards looking for some clue as to how it was done," I said. "There's no help for it. I'll have to have the workmen in again. We need not just a ventilator, but an actual passage between the two rooms. You must be able to go in and out without any chance of being seen."

I was able to employ the same workmen who had installed the ventilator years ago. They worked well and swiftly and were also admirably discreet, showing a complete lack of interest in what might have been considered a rather curious alteration. Under my direction, they cut a hole in the wall between the two rooms big enough for Susan to crawl through. On the Spirit Parlour side, it was covered by a wooden door that blended beautifully into the wainscoting. You would never have guessed it was there, the more so because it was directly beneath the ventilator and thus concealed by the Japanese screen. It cost me something pretty considerable, but I tried to look upon it as an investment. If it helped me earn a thousand pounds, it would be worth it.

By Friday evening all was ready. As I received the Warings and led them into the Spirit Parlour, I could not help feeling a little nervous. I had not produced a materialization in over a decade, and here I was attempting one with an inexperienced partner. To be sure, Susan was the most intelligent and capable of assistants, but there were many things that could go wrong. I tried to put them out of my mind and focus on my own rôle.

We began our séance as usual, seated around the Spiritograph with the candle flickering in the lantern above us. Mrs. Waring, on my left, was tight-lipped and had a furrow between her brows.

On my right, Miss Waring sat stiffly upright, her lovely face set in something remarkably like a scowl. It was easy to see they had been quarreling again. Once more, I set about pouring my own particular brand of oil on the troubled waters.

"Is there a disembodied spirit in the room?"

There was, of course. Both women relaxed slightly as the sé-ance proceeded along the usual lines. We had the scent of Howard's pipe tobacco, an exchange of greetings via the Spiritograph, and the standard assurance that Howard was well and happy in Summerland on the Other Side. From this point on, however, the proceedings became more contentious.

"Howard, you must know how unhappy I am about this engage-ment of Julia's. Haven't you any advice for your daughter?" inquired Mrs. Waring, in what I felt to be a lamentably heavy-handed manner.

Miss Waring obviously thought it heavy-handed, too. "Papa knows better than you do, Mama, how foolish your objections are," she retorted. "I won't listen to a word against Francis."

The wheel suggested again that there was Hidden Knowledge yet to emerge.

"That's all very well, Howard, but what does that mean? *What* hidden knowledge?"

The wheel hesitated, then spelled, "Wait."

"Wait for what, Papa?" inquired Miss Waring impatiently. "And for how long?"

"Wait," spelled the wheel again, and then, "Must speak." After another pause, it produced the word "Danger."

"*Danger?*" said Miss Waring incredulously.

"Danger?" repeated Mrs. Waring.

"Must speak," spelled the wheel again. "Wait."

The Warings exchanged puzzled glances, then looked to me for guidance. "The Spirit is trying to manifest itself," I told them, in my most authoritative voice. "It wishes to speak to you directly. We must concentrate and try to help it."

"Extinguish candle," suggested the wheel.

"Complete darkness will help the Spirit Energy to concentrate," I explained glibly. Getting up, I blew out the candle and then reseated myself. "Now let us join hands again and concentrate. Whatever happens, do not break the circle. *Do not break the circle*," I repeated. "It might be . . . dangerous."

Without the candle, the darkness in the Spirit Parlour was complete. I sat there holding hands with the Warings, unable to see them or anything else. The next few minutes would be the tricky part, as Susan entered the room and set about her work under cover of darkness. In order to drown out any noise she might make, I kept up a steady stream of words in a supplicating voice: "O Spirit of Howard Waring, we are here . . . here and waiting for you. Speak to us, O Spirit . . . we wait to hear your words."

All at once light blazed forth, illuminating the room like a flash of lightning. Both Warings cried out in shock. I could see their faces turned toward me, pale in the cold, blue-white light. But it was not me they were looking at. They were staring behind me, at the source of the light. I did not look at it myself. Instead, I gripped their hands warningly and repeated, "Do not break the circle."

"O God," said Mrs. Waring faintly. "Howard?"

My own eyes were cast down, as though in concentration, but from under my lashes I watched their faces. Both women wore identical expressions of open-mouthed wonder. Only their eyes moved as they watched the light ascend, casting its rays over us like a tiny blue-white sun.

"My dear ones," came a voice—a whispery voice, sounding oddly tinny and distant. "My dear ones."

"Howard?" quavered Mrs. Waring.

"It is I," replied the voice. "My dear ones, I come to warn you. There is danger."

"Danger?" It was Miss Waring who spoke this time. "Papa, what danger?"

"Julia," breathed the voice. "Danger threatens you. You must be on your guard."

"Yes, Papa," whispered Miss Waring.

"Trust no one, Julia."

"Howard," cried Mrs. Waring, sounding affronted. "She can trust *me*, surely."

There was a pause, and then the voice, sounding slightly disconcerted, replied, "Trust no one except your mother, Julia."

I frowned at this deviation from the script, but it seemed to pass reasonably well. "Yes, Papa," agreed Miss Waring docilely. "I will be on my guard."

In a more assured tone, the voice continued, "The energy is waning. I must go. Take care . . . my dear ones . . . until we meet again."

The light was visibly dwindling as these words were spoken. I could see it now only as a tiny spark reflected in the Warings' eyes. In a another moment, it winked out altogether, and the room was in darkness once more.

"Do not break the circle," I said again. "Let us shut our eyes and concentrate once more. Concentrate now on releasing the Spirit Energy . . . relaxing . . . releasing . . . letting the energy of the Spirit flow back to the Other Side."

I kept this up for a few more minutes, until I was sure Susan had had time to gather up her equipment and withdraw through the door in the wainscoting. A slight thump marred the silence of her departure, but I was reasonably sure the Warings did not notice it. When I got up to relight the candle, they both appeared as awestruck as they had during our dialogue with the Spirit Light.

"That was . . . astonishing," said Mrs. Waring in a faint voice.

"Yes," agreed Miss Waring. She was looking very subdued, as well she might. I hoped I had given her something to think about.

Both Warings were too stunned to say much as they got up to go. It was the highest form of compliment. I was careful to do nothing that might spoil the mood, but merely pressed their hands and looked soulfully into their eyes as we parted on the doorstep.

As soon as Susan had shut the door behind them, I threw my arms around her and embraced her exuberantly. "Susan, you were brilliant! Very well done, upon my word!"

"Thank you," said Susan, looking shyly pleased. "I thought it went off pretty well."

"Not pretty well, but excellently well. If they hadn't been believers before, they would be now." I laughed aloud at the recollection. "Oh, it was masterly! I don't know when I've been so pleased. Miss Waring will think twice about her engagement to her man of mystery, if I'm any judge. We must have a little party to celebrate."

The three of us did have a party, once I had changed out of my working clothes. I insisted on opening a bottle of champagne to celebrate the night's achievement. I told Susan that the champagne in her case might also serve as a restorative, for she had had a strenuous evening.

The manifestation had been achieved in this way, Dear Reader. As soon as the lights were out in the Spirit Parlour, Susan had to open the door in the wainscoting and crawl through. In the darkness, she had then to feel her way along the wall to the window bay and slip behind the curtains.

Once inside the window bay, there was a little light from the street—not much, but enough to assist her in the single most critical part of her task. Before the séance started, we had placed a stoppered bottle of phosphorescent oil on the floor just behind the centre parting of the curtains. Susan had to remove the stopper from the bottle, then retrace her steps behind the curtains and along the wall, until she was once more behind the Japanese screen.

As soon as the stopper was out of the bottle, the oil within began to react with the air, producing a blue-white light. The bottle was round, and tied around its neck was a strong black thread. This thread ran upward to a small hook set discreetly in the ceiling of the Spirit Parlour in *front* of the curtains. From there the thread ran to a second hook just above the Japanese screen. The end of it hung down behind the screen. Pulling on this thread made the bottle rise up from the floor and swing forward through the curtains, bringing it into sudden, spectacular view of the séance table.

As Susan continued to pull, she could make the bottle climb higher and higher—or lower it, of course, if she so desired. This was the moving Spirit Light that had so amazed the Warings.

The Spirit Voice had been produced with a speaking trumpet—a long metal horn that Susan had brought with her into the parlour and placed ready behind the screen. Such trumpets were often used during séances years ago. Seated around a table with her clients, a clever Medium could whisper into peoples' ears from across the table, or direct her voice so it seemed to come from the floor or ceiling. Susan had directed hers toward the light. The distant, metallic quality of the voice, together with the light, were enough to produce a wonderful otherworldly effect.

Even after Susan had spoken her piece, her work was not yet done. She had to put down the trumpet where she could find it in the dark and carefully let out the thread suspending the bottle of oil until it rested on the floor once more. It was then her job to remove all the evidence by going again behind the curtains, collecting and re-stoppering the bottle, and pulling the thread down from the ceiling. With these items in hand, she had then to make her way back behind the screen and retreat through the door in the wainscoting— not forgetting to take the speaking trumpet with her. As you can see, Dear Reader, it was a complex operation. Yet it had all gone off splendidly, as I told Susan, raising my champagne glass in a toast.

"I wish I could have seen it," said Jenny, looking wistful. She had attended our rehearsals beforehand and helped me critique the performance, but of course it was not the same as being there on opening night and seeing the audience's reaction. By way of consolation, I offered her a glass of champagne. She accepted it gingerly, confessing that she had never tasted it before.

"Tickles your nose, don't it? I must say, though," she said, taking another cautious sip, "I believe I prefer beer."

I gave her permission to bring up a pitcher of beer from the kitchen, while Susan and I continued to drink champagne. "If you'd told me years ago I'd be earning my living in such a way, I'd have said you were potty," said Susan, shaking her head. "A woman of my years, scrabbling about on my hands and knees pretending to be a spirit."

"Woman of your years be damned," I said, flourishing my glass. "You're in the prime of life, my girl. Just as I am."

"That's as may be," retorted Susan, but her usual acerbity was slightly mellowed by champagne. I thought it a suitable moment for a spot of constructive criticism.

"Regarding the warning you gave Miss Waring," I said, "I don't say your way wasn't more *impressive*—but I thought we agreed you were to say, 'Julia, take care whom you trust' rather than 'Trust no one, Julia?'"

Susan looked embarrassed. "I can see now that was a mistake," she said. "But you remember I said beforehand that 'take care *whom* you trust' sounded like a schoolmarm talking?"

"Yes, I remember your saying that."

"Most folks'd say 'take care *who* you trust,'" continued Susan, her tone argumentative. "And from everything I hear of Howard Waring, he was a plain-spoken man without a lot of education—not someone who'd be likely to follow all the finer points of grammar."

"True," I said in a conciliatory voice.

"So I just thought I'd simplify matters a bit. But I can see now it was a mistake. It made it sound as though she shouldn't even trust her own mother."

"Or me," I pointed out.

It was clear Susan had not thought of this. She looked so stricken that I assured her she had recovered nicely from what was, after all, only a minor error. "All's well that ends well," I said, topping off her glass of champagne.

"If it went anything like the rehearsals, I've no doubt you knocked 'em back on their heels properly," said Jenny. In a shy voice, she added, "It fair knocked me back, the first time I saw it. I never heard of oil that lights up before."

"We used to use it a lot in the business," I said. "Sometimes we'd have eight or ten bottles of the stuff blazing away at the same time, all around the room. Sometimes, too, we'd put a length of gauze over the bottles, to give them the effect of Phantom Forms."

Susan gave it as her opinion that this would be gilding the lily. "To my mind, nothing could look better than your plain round bottle. It was something to see it rise up like that—like a star, against those black curtains."

"Like the embodiment of Spirit Energy," I agreed happily "But it doesn't always go so smoothly, believe me."

I told them about the time I got careless opening a bottle of phosphorescent oil and splashed it all over my arms. "And of course it lit up as soon as it came into contact with the air, so everyone at the séance table could see me and my glowing arms. I couldn't slip quietly out of the room to wash it off, either, but had to sit down at the table and brazen it out."

"What did you say?" asked Jenny, her eyes round.

"I told the clients that not only had we succeeded in summoning Spirits to the room, they had given me—" I lowered my voice dramatically, "*Spirit Arms*."

Susan laughed. "Spirit Arms," she said. "Did they believe you?"

"I fear not," I said regretfully. "But at least they weren't rude enough to say so." Dividing the last of the champagne between my glass and hers, I added, "At any rate, it taught me to take care in opening those damned bottles. And to do it behind cover where possible—and to have an assistant do it if it can be managed. So, as the Duke of Wellington once said, 'I learnt what not to do, and that is always something.'"

As usual when I quoted the Duke, Susan and Jenny rolled their eyes. "I can see you're all ready for Waterloo Day," said Susan. "We hear from the Duke of Wellington every time you open your mouth."

"He had a lot to say about insubordinate staff members," I said meaningly, as I drank off the rest of my champagne.

It was after midnight when our party broke up. I told Susan and Jenny they might sleep as late as they liked the next day, and that Susan might take the whole day off. People don't appreciate how much work it is to be a Moving Spirit.

## CHAPTER 5

The next day was Saturday. Since Susan had the day off, Jenny assisted at my séance that evening. It was her first time doing so, but it was an ideal first outing, as I was sitting for Lady Haverhill, one of my regular clients—and also, incidentally, my least demanding client.

Lady Haverhill is an autocratic old lady who pays me generously to summon up the Spirit of her deceased husband once a week. Being a confirmed egotist, she is not interested in asking him about his own existence in the Spirit World, but rather in telling him about hers in the Earthly one. I gather she rather bullied the poor man during his lifetime, and she certainly bullies him now that he has passed to the Other Side. It's rare he gets a word in edgewise. This naturally makes for a very easy, undemanding evening's work for his Medium.

Jenny and I had no trouble managing it between us. Indeed, she expressed disappointment afterwards that Lord Haverhill hadn't spoken through a Spirit Light. I had to explain to her that that sort of thing was risky, and the whole reason I invented the Spiritograph was to minimize the risks associated with my profession. As long as Lady Haverhill was satisfied by the Spiritograph, I wasn't going to suggest using anything else.

Of course, I was a fine one to talk about avoiding risks. I was, after all, intending to meet Felicity the very next day to unlawfully search Captain Ingram's room. It was hardly behaviour suited to the Sabbath. Nonetheless, on Sunday morning I departed the Temple of Spiritualism as though dressed for church, reasoning that this would make me less conspicuous on the street at that time of day. If I had possessed a prayer book, I would have carried it.

As it was, I was wearing a high-necked brown chintz dress with a loose jacket—an ensemble designed to conceal any slightest vestige of feminine charm. With it, I wore a straw bonnet ten years out of date with a spotted veil thrown over my face. This may surprise you, Dear Reader, knowing my predilection for stylish black attire. But the very fact that I always wear black professionally, as well as enhancing my eyes and complexion and adding those other touches that give me such a distinctive look, means that when I eschew those touches, I appear a thoroughly ordinary-looking woman and very nearly unrecognizable.

I reached the captain's lodging house without attracting any undue attention. Felicity was waiting for me there. She, too, had dressed to be inconspicuous in a cotton print dress with a cap and apron. This made her look exactly like a serving woman—which was, of course, an excellent disguise, if the captain happened to catch us during our illicit search. I was sorry I hadn't thought to do the same. Felicity, however, assured me it was no matter.

"Esther will warn us in plenty of time, if she sees either the captain or Mrs. Marker returning. Mrs. Marker is the landlady—and half gone on the captain, by all Esther tells me."

I was introduced to Esther, a dour-looking maidservant also clad in cap and apron, who permitted us into the house and showed us to the captain's room. The house was a regular rabbit warren, with half-flights of stairs and long winding passages and odd little landings stuck here and there a few steps above the hallway level. The door to the captain's room opened from one of these landings.

While Esther was unlocking the door, I went a few paces down the hall to see the lay of the land. There were several other doors, but all of them were locked. At the end of the hall, however, the corridor turned a right angle and became a flight of stairs leading upward. I marked it down mentally as an exit in case of emergency.

As I stepped across the threshold of the captain's room, I was uneasily aware that I had just broken the law. I was glad Inspector Harper couldn't see me. Felicity was already on her knees in front of a shabby chest of drawers, rifling through the contents of the bottom drawer with professional efficiency.

I knew our time was limited, but rather than immediately following her example, I first went around the room just looking. The bed was unmade, a sordid tangle of linens left for the maid to straighten or not as she pleased. An empty whiskey bottle—a cheap brand— stood on the table beside the bed, along with a water carafe and a tumbler containing the dregs of a drink.

There were a few clothes hanging on hooks behind a curtain. I noted one of the suits bore the name of a Savile Row tailor, though it was grown somewhat shiny about the knees and shabby around the cuffs. Clearly the captain had some pretensions to style, even if he had fallen on hard times.

There was nothing in any of the suit pockets. I examined the lining, too, for this is one of the classic places of concealment for those handy with a needle, but I could not detect anything in the way of concealed papers or valuables.

On the wall were a couple of luridly-coloured lithographs of religious subjects. I judged them to be to be the landlady's property rather than the captain's, but there was also a framed photograph showing a row of stern uniformed men against a desert-looking background. The inclusion of a couple of dark-skinned men in a more picturesque dress suggested it had been taken in Africa.

"This must be his army photograph," I said aloud. "Miss Waring spoke of seeing it. I wonder when that could have been? Surely she didn't come here to his room?"

"Ah, you never know what young ladies will get up to nowadays," said Felicity, inspecting a box of collars and cuffs. "A bit shabby, poor dear," she commented, holding up a frayed and yellowed collar for my inspection. "Money not too plentiful, by the look of it."

"Either that, or simply squandered on drink and debauchery," I said, with a nod at the whiskey bottle. "Can you tell me if the captain's in this picture?"

Felicity got up and came over to squint at the photograph. "I'd say that's him right there," she said, pointing to a man in officer's uniform who stood at one side of the group, a little apart from the others. "Looks like him, anyway."

I scrutinized the figure. The scale was so small it was hard to see much detail, but Captain Ingram appeared to be taller than average, with a fine athletic figure and dark hair. What I could see of his face seemed attractive, but since he affected the extravagant mustachios to which military men are so partial, it was difficult to be sure.

"Ah, *here's* something," said Felicity with satisfaction. "Come take a look at this, my dear."

She had found the captain's collection of pornography. We went through it together, but agreed it was all completely standard and unimaginative. There were, unfortunately, none of the more exotic variations that might hint at a possible way to detach him from Miss Waring. Of course, even ordinary pornography ought to shock a gently-bred young lady, but unless we brought her here and showed it to her, there wasn't any way of proving he had it. And even then, she might not believe it was his. It wasn't as if he personally appeared in any of the photographs. She might simply accuse us of placing it there ourselves, and there was no way we could prove otherwise, as Felicity sapiently noted. "Let's keep searching, dear. You might have a look at his desk, there."

I went over to the desk—really just a scratched and battered table with a shallow drawer set in the side. There were several bundles of papers in the drawer tied up with tape. I reached for the nearest, then drew back my hand and bent down to inspect it more closely. A single almost invisible hair was resting across the top of the bundle.

"Aha," I said. "The captain has taken precautions to see if anyone disturbs his papers."

This seemed to indicate I might have stumbled onto something interesting. Having made careful note of how the hair was placed, I set it aside and looked through the first bundle. I found nothing incriminating, but much that was suggestive. They were letters from a lady named Louisa Tate, affectionately inquiring after her dear Francis and hoping he might soon return to gladden her eyes. As you may know, Dear Reader, no respectable woman corresponds with a man in this style unless she is related to him or engaged to marry him. Unfortunately for my purposes, they were dated almost a year ago. Miss Waring would not see them as proof of her lover's perfidy, unless there was something more that did not appear in the letters. I made a note of Miss Tate's name and direction just in case, replaced the letters and the hair, and went on to the next bundle.

These were from Miss Waring herself. I was dismayed to see that not only had she written to the captain, she had given him a lock of her hair. There it was, long and dark and lustrous, tied up with a romantic red ribbon. "Silly girl," I said aloud.

My dismay increased as I skimmed through the letters. There could be no doubt that Miss Waring was completely smitten with the captain. Reading her gushing, high-souled sentiments in that squalid room was a curious illustration of Human Nature.

The last packet appeared to be merely bills, all unpaid. I put everything back, making sure it was just as the captain had left it, and shut the drawer.

"Here's something, dear," said Felicity suddenly, from the other side of the room.

She had found a paper granting a captain's commission to Francis K. Ingram, along with a few other official-looking documents. There were also newspaper clippings spanning the years of the last decade, describing the military actions of the captain's regiment. He was mentioned by name in several of them. I am not an expert in such matters, Dear Reader, but it all looked dismayingly authentic.

"Damn," I said. "I had hoped the army career might be a fabrication. Finding out he wasn't really a war hero might have been enough to put Miss Waring off the match, if nothing else offered."

As Felicity opened her mouth to reply, the maid Esther appeared in the doorway. "Hist!" she said urgently. "The captain's just walked through the front door. I need to lock the room afore he gets here, or he's like to suspect something."

Felicity and I flew about, making sure all was in order. The maid hurried us along, saying over and over that the captain would be here at any minute. Indeed, I could hear a heavy tread coming up the stairs as we hastily exited the room. Felicity boldly set off down the hall along with Esther. She did not fear to meet the captain, since she was dressed in servants' garb and might be taken as having business there. Dressed as I was, however, I thought it might appear a little odd if he saw us together. So I withdrew to the other end of the hall, where the staircase turned upwards, went up a few steps, and waited.

I could hear footsteps approaching now. There was just the slightest hesitation in the tread, hinting at a limp. I thought I wouldn't have noticed it if I hadn't been expecting it. I heard him inserting the key in his door, and a rattle as he unlocked it. Then there was a pause.

I was taken with a sudden desire to see him, Dear Reader. After all, it might be my only chance. The photograph had been too small to give any detail. Pulling my veil over my face, I came down the stairs and around the corner, passing the half landing where the captain stood with his key still in his hand. He glanced at me briefly and without interest, then swung open the door, went inside, and shut the door behind him.

I continued down the corridor, as in a dream.

Never in my wildest dreams, indeed, had I expected to see that face here and now. It had changed a bit in twenty-odd years, and so had the rest of him, but nonetheless he was familiar to me, though not under the name of Captain Francis Ingram. Twenty-odd years ago, he had been calling himself Professor Erasmus Brooke.

And I, Dear Reader—I had been calling him my husband.

## CHAPTER 6

In novels of a romantic kind, when the heroine finds herself in a situation of peril, her blood is often described as running cold. You, like me, Dear Reader, may have taken this merely as a writer's cliché. But to my surprise, I found the expression perfectly apt in the aftermath of my meeting with Captain Ingram (so-called). I felt suddenly chilled, exactly as if my veins were full of ice water.

The shock extended to my mental faculties. If I spoke to Felicity before I left the captain's rooming house, I don't remember it. I don't even remember walking home. I only became fully conscious again when I walked into the Temple, to be met by Susan with the words, "Jenny's out with her young man again."

I blinked, trying to bring my mind back from wherever it had been wandering. "Ah," I said. "Jenny. With Sam. Yes."

Susan eyed me oddly. "Are you all right?" she asked.

"I don't think so," I said, quite truthfully.

Susan's expression became one of concern. "Don't tell me you got caught in the captain's room?" she demanded. "I told you that you ought to have left all that to Felicity!"

I shook my head. "We didn't get caught. And it's just as well I went there. At least, I think it was." I put a hand to my brow. "The fact is, I have had a shock. And I must think what to do."

Susan, looking more concerned than ever, suggested I lie down on the Sitting Room sofa and let her bring me some tea. "Or brandy," she added. "If you've had a shock, that might be more to the purpose."

Brandy sounded very good to me at that moment, and I was about to accept, when it occurred to me that I could not afford the indulgence of alcohol just then. I needed all my wits about me in what was likely to prove a most complex and delicate matter. "Tea," I said with decision. "Please bring me tea, and then see that I'm not disturbed."

As I sat on the sofa, drinking my tea, I pondered the strange twist of fate that had brought back into my life the man known as John Colley—alias Professor Erasmus Brooke, alias Captain Francis Ingram, and doubtless half-a-dozen other aliases as well.

As mentioned earlier, Dear Reader, some twenty years ago I had called him my husband. We had, at that time, been passing ourselves off as a married couple. And we were indeed as coupled as it is possible to be without the formal blessing of Church and State. Yet we came together first in the way of business, and business always came first and foremost with both of us. I will not deny, however, that John (his real name, I believe) had attractions that made me very ready to fall in with the arrangement.

He was, at that era, as handsome a man as you might ever hope to meet. Not only was he tall, and magnificently formed, and possessed of a smile that was all flashing white teeth and laughing dark eyes, his attractions were completely natural. Without being indelicate, Dear Reader, I may say that he looked quite as magnificent in a state of nature, first thing in the morning, as he did dressed and brushed and polished into a more publicly presentable form.

And indeed, I often felt more envious than admiring of this excess of natural beauty. I am not an ill-looking woman, but I have never been beautiful. Even at that era, when I possessed all the advantages of youth, I required at least an hour, and everything that cosmetics and corsetry and the higher flights of hairdressing could do, to make me a fit companion for such an Adonis.

You may be wondering what business brought us together. It was a variant of the Spiritualism business—a two-person act, which John proposed to take on the road as a traveling show. At the time, the fashion was for full-figure materializations, which involved bulky cabinets and a lot of other cumbersome paraphernalia. I had just lost my father, who had served as my manager ever since I entered the business. As my mother had died years earlier, when I was only a child, I was at this point a woman alone. That made it very challenging to earn a living as a Medium.

It was an earlier time, in which a woman was really handicapped if she had no husband or father to manage her business affairs. This was especially the case in such a business as mine. There are a lot of gentlemen out there who imagine any woman who is a Spiritualist must also be a practitioner of Free Love. Sometimes they take a lot of persuading to be convinced otherwise.

John was very useful in this regard, of course. He also took charge of renting halls and theatres in the towns we visited, advertising our performances, and shipping our equipment from town to town. He was Professor Erasmus Brooke, Man of Science; I was his wife Mrs. Brooke, Spiritualistic Medium, able to produce the most convincing three-dimensional Spirit figures "under scientifically controlled conditions." As Felicity might say, it sounded a good wheeze.

And indeed, it proved quite profitable—so profitable that on the final stop of our tour, John had apparently been tempted to partake of the profits beyond his legitimate fifty-per-cent share. I had returned from an evening spent with a circle of Spiritualistic admirers to find he had absconded with everything—profits, paraphernalia, and even my own clothing and personal items.

It was the single lowest point of my life.

I have no wish to dwell on that period, Dear Reader, so let us pass over it as quickly as possible. In the fullness of time, I pulled myself together, started over, and made good. Of course, I could not help thinking about John now and then, and wondering if I would ever meet him again, and imagining how much pleasure I would take in such a meeting, provided I happened to have in my hands a knife or gun or horsewhip or some other weapon. I don't believe I am an unduly vindictive woman, but you will agree I had cause for resentment.

Still, my resentment had faded with the passage of a couple of decades. During that time, I had recouped all the losses I had suffered and then some. And there is truth in the adage that living well is the best revenge. I was living very well indeed these days. Memories of John and his treachery hardly crossed my mind from one month to the next. If I thought of him at all, it was only to suppose that he must by now have come to the bad end he so thoroughly deserved.

Obviously I had been mistaken, however. Here he was back again, like the proverbial bad penny, and I had to decide what I was going to do about him.

The irony of the situation was not lost on me. I had been feeling sorry for poor Miss Waring, caught in the toils of a blackguard, but I had been feeling a little superior, too. Now I knew us to be fellow labourers under the same delusion. In only one thing had she been more credulous than I: although calling myself John's wife, I had never any idea of actually wedding him.

It will probably amuse you, Dear Reader, if I say that at that era I was saving myself for marriage. Perhaps a better way of putting it is to say that I hesitated to marry a poor man when I might later have a chance at a rich one. More than one Medium has succeeded in bettering herself in this way. I had seen it done myself, by women no more attractive than I was, and at that time I had no higher aspiration. To have all the ease of wealth without more labour than is entailed by murmuring "I will" in front of a clergyman was a bargain I was quite prepared to make.

Since then, of course, my thinking has evolved a bit. It takes most of us a while to question the precepts we grew up with. In my youth, it was taken as a matter of course that a girl must marry if she could, since any fate was better than being left an old maid. But as the years went by, I met many women who had married for money and lived to repent their bargain. Not only that, but plenty of the ones who married for love seemed to repent it, too. If I had but thought of it, I had a personal example of that in my own parents' marriage. There is a great deal to be said for independence, when all is said and done.

I had only reached this conclusion through age and experience, so it was hardly surprising that Miss Waring did not share it. She might have the wealth and beauty I had never possessed, along with the freedom of a more progressive age, but just like me, she saw marriage with the eyes of youthful idealism.

Worse yet, she was idealizing a man who was certain to make her a hellish husband. But how best to open her eyes to that reality? There was nobody who was in a better position than I to tell her the true facts of the case, but only a very little thinking convinced me that I would have to tread carefully. Having been so grossly imposed upon by her fiancé, I was almost too nearly concerned in the matter.

Miss Waring might point out, with perfect justice, that I was incapable of viewing him and his behaviour with anything like impartiality. Had I been a judge, I would have been obliged to recuse myself.

Moreover, I could see that Miss Waring might choose to censure my own behaviour as much or more than John's. I had, after all, been living with him without the benefit of marriage. Society does not look kindly on that sort of thing. I was posing as a respectable woman nowadays, and to reveal I had ever been anything else was to risk losing all I had worked so hard to gain, with no guarantee of gaining anything in return. With great and growing ire, I realized that I had more to lose in the matter than John did.

Still, I had the advantage of him in other ways. Knowing who he was and what he was, I knew beyond doubt he was unworthy of Miss Waring. There must be some way to use such knowledge: if not directly, then indirectly. I found Susan's suggestion of blackmail kept returning to my mind. I put it from me as before, yet with the proviso that it might be worth considering if all else failed.

I had reached this point in my meditations when the doorbell rang. A glance at the clock showed me that somehow or other it had got to be late afternoon. The visitor was probably Inspector Harper, and here I was still clad in my mousy brown church-going dress and bonnet—not at all a suitable ensemble in which to receive him. Even more than my clients, I would rather he saw me only in my working guise. It was not mere vanity on my part, you understand, Dear Reader. Someday, I might wish to pass him inconspicuously in the street, and I would rather he not know how well I could do it.

With this in mind, I rose precipitately and hurried out into the corridor. I met Susan on her way to the door.

"Susan, if that is Inspector Harper, please show him in and tell him I will be with him presently," I said, and retired to my bedroom to dress myself in more seemly attire.

When presently I met him, I took care that my brow was as smooth and unwrinkled as my jet-trimmed sateen dress. "My dear Inspector," I said, "I do apologize for keeping you waiting."

"Not at all," he said cheerfully. "I hope I find you well, Madame Fox?"

"Very well, thank you." We exchanged a few more such conventional remarks, eyeing each other like fighters circling in the ring. Normally I let him make the first move in broaching serious topics, but I was afraid he was going to mention Captain Ingram. The secret I now knew about that gentleman made the whole subject dangerous, not to mention a bit painful. I thought I would buy time by discussing our other business first.

"I have been thinking a great deal about that anonymous letter you showed me last week," I said. "I still cannot conjecture what might have prompted it. Have you had a chance to investigate the matter?"

"Yes," said the Inspector. "I visited Waterloo House this week and spoke with the old lady and some of the servants. It *seems* as though there was nothing in it." He paused.

"But you're not sure?"

Slowly he shook his head. "The old lady—Miss Emily, as you call her—laughed to scorn the idea that anyone would poison her. At least, she tried to. But something in the situation didn't seem natural. I couldn't help wondering what she might have said if that woman wasn't there with her the whole time."

"Hilda, you mean?" I said. I assumed he must be speaking of Miss Emily's companion, Hilda Schmidt. It was true that Hilda seldom strayed far from Miss Emily's side, but I was surprised that the

Inspector should see anything amiss in the fact. I expressed my surprise by saying lightly, "I don't think there's any harm in Hilda. In fact, I'd be surprised to hear she took her eyes off her knitting."

"Oh, the companion woman—Miss Schmidt? Yes, it's true she never stopped knitting, the whole time I was there." The Inspector smiled reminiscently. "She didn't seem interested in anything else. Even the idea that someone might poison her mistress didn't make her look up from her work. To be honest, I wondered if she was half-witted." Returning to a more serious manner, he added, "But it wasn't she I meant, when I was talking about 'that woman.' I meant the niece, not Miss Schmidt."

"Lady Frost?" I said, with surprise. "Was she there?"

"No, Lady Frost is the younger niece, isn't she? It was the elder niece I meant—the unmarried one. Miss Morton, that's the name. The one who lives there."

"Lives there!" I exclaimed. "Miss Morton doesn't live at Waterloo House. Or does she?" I added, seeing the expression on his face.

"Yes," he said, looking at me curiously. "So I gathered."

"But this is something new! She did not live there before. I am sure of it." I shook my head with decision. "And you are certain she lives there now? She was not merely visiting?"

"No, she said she lived there, and Miss Emily agreed that she did."

"Poor Miss Emily, then!" I said. "I am sorry to hear it."

I heartily disliked Miss Morton, Dear Reader, and the feeling was, I believe, mutual. I was glad I never had to meet her above the one day a year. Of course, Miss Emily might feel differently about her—Miss Morton was, after all, the daughter of Miss Emily's beloved sister. Yet I had often noted that despite this family tie, Miss Emily did not seem to enjoy Miss Morton's company much more than I did.

I explained all this to the Inspector, who listened carefully. "I cannot think why Miss Emily would have taken that woman into her home. It's not as if she were alone and needing company. She has Hilda, after all—though to be sure, that is not necessarily *intelligent* company. But at least Hilda is good-humoured."

"Perhaps Miss Emily thought it her duty to give Miss Morton a home?" suggested the Inspector.

"Perhaps, but it still seems odd to me. By all accounts, Miss Morton was glad to shake the dust of Waterloo House from her feet at the earliest opportunity. She's lived with the Dinwiddies since her debut—cousins of her late father and people of fashion. Why should she have decided to abandon them and return to her aunt's now?"

"Perhaps the family thought Miss Emily needed someone to look out for her," said the Inspector. "Poor lady, she seemed very frail."

"Frail?" I repeated with dismay. Miss Emily had been as lively and energetic as a woman of her years well could be, the last time I had seen her. "You thought she appeared unwell?"

The Inspector looked sorry to be the bearer of bad tidings. "Yes," he said. "But remember I don't know her as you do. Perhaps it was merely a bad day for her."

"I don't think she used to *have* bad days. She always boasted about her health—how she dusted the valuable pieces in the drawing room herself, every day, just as she was brought up to do as a girl."

"People do sometimes have a sudden falling off of health, when they reach her age," suggested the Inspector.

I admitted this to be true. "But it's very sudden, if so. I saw her a couple of months ago, and she seemed as well as ever then."

"And she said nothing about taking Miss Morton into her household at that time?"

"Certainly not. If she had, I would have counseled against it. Or the Duke of Wellington would have. He was a sensible man who knew the value of a quiet home life."

The Inspector's eyes twinkled. "I suppose the Duke's opinions always coincide with yours?"

"Not necessarily," I said with dignity. "He has his own opinions, of course." After a moment's pause, I added, "I must say, this looks rather bad. Miss Morton coming to live at Waterloo House, and Miss Emily looking suddenly frail, and your getting a letter saying she is being poisoned. One cannot help wondering if there is a connection."

"Yes," said the Inspector. "It seems a suspicious series of events. But if this Miss Morton is as unpleasant as you say, that letter might be merely someone trying to stir up trouble at her expense—one of the servants, perhaps."

I had to admit this was perfectly possible. Miss Emily's servants were all of the old-fashioned sort, as devoted to their mistress as they were set in their ways. I had no doubt they would resent someone coming into the household and upsetting the quiet, well-ordered routine of their days. Equally, I had no doubt that Miss Morton would do just that, in any household she inhabited. If I were a servant, I would detest taking orders from her. To write an anonymous letter to Scotland Yard, in order to get her into trouble, would be a natural way to retaliate.

"At any rate, I will keep my eyes open when I am there for the Waterloo Dinner," I said decidedly. "Miss Emily is one of my best clients. I won't allow anyone to take her away from me prematurely if I can help it."

"A very public-spirited attitude," approved the Inspector with a smile. "I will appreciate hearing your opinion on the matter." Drawing his notebook from his pocket, he added, "Now, about that other matter we were discussing last week—the fellow you were wanting me to make inquiries about . . .."

"Oh, yes," I said. "Captain Ingram."

As I spoke the name, I braced myself inwardly, but found it did not evoke as much painful emotion as I feared. The distraction of discussing Miss Emily's affairs with the Inspector had done more to settle my feelings than all my solitary reflections.

"I did make inquiries, though there's not a lot known about the fellow," said the Inspector, consulting his notebook. "He lives alone, keeps himself to himself for the most part, but enjoys a certain popularity with the ladies."

I nodded grimly. All that was known to me, of course.

"I looked into his war record, and it appears to be perfectly genuine," continued the Inspector. "He served with distinction in the Zulu War, but left the service not long after. Emigrated to Canada— seems to have knocked about the North American continent a bit, before coming to London a year or two ago."

I heard all this with an unmoved expression, though my feelings were acute enough. It wasn't at all what I wanted to hear. "So he appears to be . . . respectable?" I said, enunciating the word with difficulty. "Since the Zulu War, at any rate?"

The Inspector looked at me a little curiously. "Not entirely. Apart from whatever he might get in the way of army pension, he has no visible means of support. You probably know what that means, for a man in his position."

"Gambling," I said at once. "And women." I tried not to say the last word bitterly.

"Mostly gambling, but some women," agreed the Inspector. "He's in debt to his landlady, for one thing. And he's been involved in one or two other little affairs that seem a bit smoky, besides this business of getting engaged to Miss Waring on the sly. But gambling's chiefly how he supports himself, as nearly as I can find out. Of course, it's possible to make a living gambling, but hard to do it honestly. I don't think the captain's ever been caught cheating, but he's been guilty of some sharp practice that's caused him to be looked on askance at the better sort of club."

I mulled this over for a minute or two. It didn't sound enough to make Miss Waring break the engagement, and I said so. "But I appreciate your efforts," I said. "Thank you very much."

"Do you want me to talk to the young lady?" he asked. "It's possible I might make her see reason. In my profession, I see enough of that kind of man to know he's not likely to make a good husband."

"Would you do that?" I asked. I was surprised and rather touched by his offer, Dear Reader, but after a moment's reflection, I shook my head. "I am afraid it would serve no purpose. Not without our having something more to go on, at any rate. Miss Waring is the sort of young woman who only becomes more determined with opposition. And already her mother has set her back up." Without going into too much detail, I explained to the Inspector that our strategy at present relied more on delaying tactics. "I'm hoping in time she might meet someone else—someone more eligible. There's nothing like the expulsive power of a new affection."

"I suppose not," said the Inspector, looking amused. "But I'm afraid I can't help you there. As a policeman, I wouldn't be considered much more eligible than your captain. Not to mention my being a bit old for the young lady!"

"You're no older than he is," I said without thinking.

Of course it was a slip, and of course the Inspector caught it, as is his inconvenient habit. "How would you know that?" he asked. "Have you seen this Captain Ingram?

There was a pause. "Just a glimpse," I said at last. "But it was all I needed to tell me his true character."

## CHAPTER 7

After the Inspector left, I remained in the Sitting Room thinking. Miss Emily's affairs had distracted me for a time, but the longer I sat, the more my thoughts returned to the subject of John, alias Captain Ingram. I still had to decide what I was going to do about him. More specifically, I had to decide if I were going to tell Susan and Jenny about my past dealings with him. I found I shrank from doing so, not so much because I had transgressed conventional morality (I still do that pretty regularly, after all) as because I felt I had behaved like a fool. That I do *not* do regularly. In fact, I pride myself on having something more of cleverness than most people. It's one of the reasons I took the name of Fox.

Now I felt I had let my pride show a little too openly and was about to be punished. I would have to confess, to two of the people whose opinion I valued most, that I had been taken in by a handsome rascal like any fool of a girl.

I did it, Dear Reader. I put my pride in my pocket and told them all about it. There is no use having intelligent assistants if you do not give them a chance to assist you.

Both Jenny and Susan were staggered to hear who Captain Ingram was, and what my past dealings with him had been. I may say, however, that my fears of being twitted about my youthful folly were unwarranted. They were entirely sympathetic and even bloodthirsty on my behalf. It was very touching.

"He left you without a penny, in a strange town and with no friends or family? I'd say he deserves a thrashing at the least," said Jenny, folding her lips grimly. "Just you point him out to me, ma'am, and I'll give him one. Sam'll help, too; see if he don't."

"No, that would give the game away," disagreed Susan. "What we want to do is queer his engagement with Miss Waring first. *Then* we can see about punishing him on *your* account, ma'am," she said, turning to me.

Having them so warm in my behalf gave me the most wonderful feeling. It entirely dispelled the chill that had lain over me since seeing that spectre of my foolish past made flesh.

And at the same time, my confidence, which had been at low ebb, also began to return to me. I recalled that the Duke of Wellington had condemned want of confidence as an evil which led to other evils. I had been on the verge of falling into that evil, but now I felt ready to assume command again and win against all odds. In any case, I calculated that the odds were still in my favour.

"Knowing what we know about him, it would be surprising if we could not find a way to use that knowledge somehow," I said. "It's a shame the Inspector didn't find anything more damning about his recent activities than that he gambles and has had a love affair or two."

"He's probably already told Miss Waring about all that," said Susan, pulling down the corners of her mouth. "Making it sound as romantic as possible, of course, and assuring the poor girl that she's reformed him entirely."

"Yes," I said. "The wretched thing is that no amount of past misbehaviour is likely to put her off, if she's really in love with him. What we need is to find he is somehow deceiving her *now*—about his army career, for instance. But it seems that was genuine. According to the Inspector, there isn't much doubt he did fight in the Zulu War." Suddenly I laughed aloud. "At any rate, I know one thing that isn't genuine, and that's his war wound. That limp wasn't acquired in Africa! He had it back when we were working together, and he was lying about it even then."

"Lying about it?" asked Susan.

"How?" asked Jenny.

"It depended on whether we were north or south of the Mason-Dixon Line," I said reminiscently. "The period John and I were working together was right after the War Between the States—that is to say, the American Civil War. And when we were in New Orleans, he claimed he got it taking in part in Pickett's gallant charge at Gettysburg,"

"Which would impress your Southerners," explained Susan to Jenny in an aside.

"Precisely," I said. "But when we were in Boston, he claimed he got it taking part in Sherman's fabled March to the Sea."

"Which would impress your *Northerners*," Susan told Jenny.

"Precisely. But to my certain knowledge, he got it in Cincinnati, jumping out of a second-floor window to escape a jealous husband," I said. "And the only service he actually saw during the Civil War was to enlist for the bounty a couple of times and then desert a few days later." I paused, transfixed by a sudden realization.

Jenny had had the same realization. "That's odd," she commented. "Him being a deserter in the States, and then getting a reputation for fighting brave-like in Africa."

"It *is* odd. In fact, it doesn't add up at all. The leopard does not change his spots—does he?" I looked at them both. "Can John have done all that, not to mention robbing me of all my worldly goods, and then fought nobly for the British Crown?"

"He might," said Susan, looking thoughtful. "But it doesn't seem likely."

"Still, the Inspector said his record was genuine. And he *was* English by birth—or at least, had an authentic-sounding English accent. Possibly he was willing to fight for his mother country and not his adopted one." I shook my head dubiously. "I suppose I can't rule out the idea that he might have turned over a new leaf. People do, sometimes. But everything else Inspector Harper told me sounded exactly in his old character. Cozening his landlady, and his tradesmen, too, by the look of the unpaid bills in his desk."

We argued the matter back and forth without being able to decide what, if anything, were best to do in the matter. But we agreed there was no immediate need to do anything. It was still over a month till Miss Waring would be of age, and in that time, something might happen that would make our best course of action clear.

More urgent was the situation at Waterloo House. I told Susan and Jenny what Inspector Harper had told me, and we all agreed it was very suspicious that Miss Morton should have moved into Miss Emily's home just about the time an anonymous letter appeared saying she was being poisoned. "And the Inspector said she looked very frail, too. Susan, you wouldn't have called her frail, would you, the last time you saw her?"

Susan shook her head with decision. "No, I wouldn't. She's a little slip of a thing, but so quick and lively that you'd take her for a girl if you only saw her from a distance."

"That's exactly what I would have said, too. I must say, I almost dread going to Waterloo House now. Miss Emily in a decline, and her odious niece riding herd over the household if I know anything about the matter. It doesn't bear thinking about."

"Not to mention that someone might be putting poison in the food," put in Susan, for whom this idea obviously held a ghoulish fascination.

I said firmly that I trusted this would not be the case. "But it might be my last appearance there anyway, if Miss Emily's health is so precarious. I must take care to give her an extra-good performance."

"If you're planning to sit for her at Waterloo House, then I suppose you won't be using your Spiritograph?" asked Jenny.

"No, on Waterloo Day I always summon the Duke to speak in person. Trance-speaking, we used to call it. It's not my preferred method nowadays, but I can still do it when I have to."

Jenny giggled. "It seems funny," she said. "You a lady, pretending to speak like you're the Duke of Wellington."

"Damn your eyes, d'you think I can't do it?"

Jenny recoiled, then burst into breathless laughter. "Oh! Well, I must say, ma'am, that was rather *impressive*."

"Thank you," I said complacently.

"But I can't see how you know what to *say*," she continued, with a perplexed look. "If they ask you questions, I mean."

"It's not much different from the usual kind of séance," I said. "Some questions are easy—a matter of public record. If they're matters of opinion, that's easy, too. I know the Duke's opinions pretty well from all the reading I've done." I thought back over the many Wellington séances I had presided over here and at Waterloo House. "People like to ask his opinion about present-day politics. I'm always tempted to have him advocate for woman suffrage, though that wouldn't exactly be in character!"

"Maybe a stay in the Summerland's enlightened his views," suggested Susan, grinning.

"But what if people ask questions you can't answer?" persisted Jenny.

"Then I just say, 'Don't be a damned fool!' That was his favourite response to questions he thought silly or impertinent."

"Or 'Don't be a croaker,'" put in Susan. "I've heard you say *that* more than once, when you've been sitting for Miss Emily here."

"Yes," I agreed, "though I use that more when someone's making difficulties about nothing. Hanging back rather than making what the Duke called 'a dash at the enemy.'"

"And you say those things to lords and ladies?" said Jenny, looking deeply impressed. "I don't see how you dare!"

"It's all part of the business," I explained. "They don't expect the Duke of Wellington to be mealy-mouthed."

"Besides, it gives her such a lot of satisfaction," put in Susan dryly.

"Some satisfaction," I conceded, smiling.

"I believe you, ma'am," said Jenny respectfully. After a pause, she added, "So what will you do at this séance Wednesday?"

"Probably just relive the great battle. That's what we typically do on Waterloo Night. I could do it in my sleep at this point." I rose, signaling that our conference was over. "The only thing I am nervous about is whether my dress will be ready in time. Mrs. O'Meagher said it ought to be done tomorrow. I hope it will be, for otherwise it will be cutting it rather fine to have it by Wednesday evening."

I went next morning to see Mrs. O'Meagher, and found, as I feared, that my dress was not quite done. "But if you've time, ma'am, and are willing to wait, I can have one of my girls finish it up in a trice," she told me.

Feeling that a dress in the hand was worth two delivered on the morrow, I said I would wait. She directed me to a bench in a corner of her shop, and there I sat leafing through *Myra's Journal of Dress and Fashion* and paying no particular attention as she and her attendants went about their business. All at once, a furious voice cut through my meditations on puffs, box-pleats, and kilting.

"You stupid girl! You've spoiled my glove, too—just look at it."

"Oh, I'm sorry, milady," said a second voice, sounding frightened. "I do beg your pardon. I'm sure I didn't mean to."

Looking around, I realized the voices were coming from the curtained recess where Mrs. O'Meagher's customers were fitted with their new raiment. "That's all very well, but it doesn't mend my glove, does it?" said the first speaker in a scathing tone. "Or my hand, either."

At this point, I heard the refined accents of Mrs. O'Meagher enter into the exchange. "I beg your pardon, my lady," she said. "Is there something amiss?"

"I should say so! This stupid girl of yours scratched my hand when she was trying to pin up the cuff on my new dress. And now there is blood on my glove—and on the dress, too. It is ruined, quite ruined."

I could not hear Mrs. O'Meagher's response, spoken in a soothing murmur, but the first speaker was clearly not to be soothed. "I don't believe it. Bloodstains on silk are quite indelible. And there is my glove, too, all stained. What of that?"

Again came the soothing murmur. "Very well," snapped the voice. "I shall send the glover's bill to you. And you must see that the stain doesn't show at all, or I won't pay for the dress."

A moment later the curtains parted, and Mrs. O'Meagher emerged, looking distressed. She was closely followed by another woman, who was railing at her in the voice I recognized as the first speaker's. "You are fortunate I am willing to take the dress, even at a discount. Upon my word, if it were not that I needed it for my aunt's little affair on Wednesday, I would be tempted to take my custom elsewhere."

"I am very sorry, my lady," said Mrs. O'Meagher in an abject voice. "It shall not happen again. After this, I will wait on you personally."

I looked to see what manner of woman could treat an honest tradeswoman in such a way, and was astonished to find I knew her. It was none other than Lady Frost, Miss Emily's younger niece. She is a slender, flaxen-haired woman with an ethereal, almost angelic appearance. Angelic-looking or not, however, I find her quite as unpleasant as her sister. Instinctively, I ducked my head to hide my face beneath my hat brim as Mrs. O'Meagher escorted Lady Frost to the door, still apologizing.

Once the door had slammed behind her, I ventured to look up again. Mrs. O'Meagher was standing there, looking after Lady Frost with an unhappy expression. I could not but feel for her. Being a tradeswoman myself, I could appreciate how vexing it was to lose a share of the profits before ever receiving payment for the goods.

"What a hateful woman," I remarked.

Mrs. O'Meagher started at the sound of my voice. It was clear she had forgotten I was there. From her face, I thought she would have liked to agree with me, but with her usual well-bred manner she merely said it was a sad business, and she supposed Lady Frost had reason to be upset.

"As for that, it's very much of a piece with her usual behaviour," I said. "I was sorry to hear her making such a fuss about a trifle."

"Ah, well—in her position, it is very natural," said Mrs. O'Meagher. "For a lady of her rank to employ me at all is a great condescension, I am sure."

I wasn't so sure, myself, but since Mrs. O'Meagher chose to take it that way, I didn't dispute with her. Inwardly, however, I reflected that no title could compensate for such disagreeable manners in *my* book. I also reflected that it was something of a coincidence that I should meet Lady Frost here, bent on the same errand as myself.

Obviously, she had been referring to the Waterloo Dinner when she spoke of her aunt's little affair. It was curious the way Miss Emily's business kept intermixing with mine. Just last night I had been discussing the behaviour of one of her nieces, and now here was the other one obtruding herself on my notice.

At this point, it occurred to me that the coincidence was even more curious than I had first thought it. Mrs. O'Meagher was a skillful needlewoman, but most of her clientele was, like me, solidly of the middle class. Lady Frost, on the other hand, was not only a peeress, but a woman of fashion. I would have assumed she obtained her dresses directly from Paris, or at least from one of the great London fashion houses. What was she doing buying a dress here?

I decided to ask Mrs. O'Meagher about it when presently she appeared to tell me my dress was ready. "Does Lady Frost order many of her dresses from you?" I inquired casually.

"Of late she has given me the majority of her custom, yes," said Mrs. O'Meagher.

She spoke with a pride I felt to be misplaced, Dear Reader. But since I was trying to extract information from her, I merely congratulated her on acquiring such a good customer. "So many of these society women cannot be depended upon to pay their bills in a timely fashion," I added with a shake of my head.

Just as I expected, a flash of pain appeared in Mrs. O'Meagher's eyes. "Yes," she said. "I would rather it were not so. But many women do think nothing of letting their bills run from month to month."

"It puts one in such a difficult position," I continued. I may say, Dear Reader, that no client of mine is suffered to put *me* in such a position. I insist upon receiving my payments regularly, and preferably in advance—but then I am lucky enough to be able to pick and choose my clients.

It was evident that Mrs. O'Meagher was not. "It is difficult," she agreed with a stifled sigh. "Flattering as it is to have Lady Frost's patronage—but there, I should not speak of it. The prestige of having such a customer is worth a good deal."

This told me all I needed to know. Lady Frost was clearly in debt to her dressmaker. That, in itself, might not indicate financial difficulties, for it is sadly true that even very wealthy women cannot be depended upon to pay their bills on receipt. But since the dressmaker was Mrs. O'Meagher rather than, say, Worth of Paris, it was certainly suggestive.

On the way home, I pondered the significance of this new information. I had taken a cab rather than walked, since I was burdened with my new dress and hat. When the driver set me down at the Temple, I rang the bell, and Susan came out to help me with the bandboxes. We had just hauled them into the house, leaving the door standing open behind us, when the doorbell rang again.

"I wonder if I left something in the cab?" I said.

Turning toward the doorway, I saw it was not the cabdriver who had rung the bell. It was a taller man—dark, and florid-faced, but still undeniably, strikingly handsome. "Madame Fox?" he said, advancing through the open door.

With a sinking heart, I recognized John Colley, alias Captain Francis Ingram.

## CHAPTER 8

It was an unfortunate situation.

By the time I realized it was John, he was already in the house. And I was standing practically face to face with him. My hat had a veil, but I had pulled it back on entering the house, and the whole business happened so fast that I had no time to pull it down again, even had I had presence of mind to think of doing so. As it was, I did not. I could only stand there, staring at him.

In the event, his shock was much greater than mine. I at least knew he was in London, even if I did not expect to see him on my doorstep. But it was evident he had no idea at all I was on this side of the Atlantic. His eyes bulged, and he took an involuntary step backwards. "*Mary?*" he gasped.

I pulled myself together, Dear Reader. I might have lost most of the advantage I had possessed before, but I still had some. "I beg your pardon?" I said, with an expression of well-bred puzzlement.

"Mary Marion," he said again. "Good God." He took another step backward and seemed inclined to beat a hasty retreat—not surprising, considering the circumstances under which we had parted. But satisfying as it would have been to drive him from the house (preferably with a horsewhip), I could see it would not answer. Even as I watched, a half smile appeared on his lips, and a speculative gleam in the dark eyes.

"I am afraid you have made a mistake, sir," I told him, with false civility. "There is no one named Mary Marion residing here."

He laughed. "Come, Mary," he said, "this to me! You haven't changed so much." He looked me up and down in a manner I strongly resented. "A little stouter, perhaps."

I opened my mouth to reply indignantly, realized my mistake just in time, and spoke with admirable restraint. "I don't know who you are, or what you are looking for, sir. But it's obvious you have come to the wrong place. I must ask you to leave now."

He looked amused. "Ah, but I haven't come to the wrong place. I came on purpose to make the acquaintance of Madame Seraphina Fox at the Temple of Spiritualism. And what should I find but that I am already *acquainted* with her?"

It was odious, the emphasis he put on the word "acquainted." I was sure he was trying to provoke me. No doubt he wished to make me admit I knew him, thus acknowledging our joint past. He had already seen that, positioned as I was, I could not afford to publicly acknowledge that past—not even to address my past grievance with him.

My only hope was to flatly deny all acquaintance. If I had no proof of his past wrongdoing, at least he was equally devoid of proof regarding mine. It all came down to words, as it so often does. "I am afraid you are mistaken," I said calmly. "Indeed, you are quite a stranger to me."

I was pleased to see that he looked a little irritated at this, although the smile did not leave his lips. "Very well," he said. "If that's the way you want to play it, Mary. Or Madame Fox, as I *should* say. My name is Captain Francis Ingram."

As he spoke the name, he threw me a laughing look, as though daring me to dispute it. I merely nodded in reply.

"I know it is a name you have heard before," he went on, his eyes fixed on mine. "I have it from my fiancée, Miss Julia Waring, that you have been—how can I put it? —meddling in my affairs."

I said nothing, but gazed back at him expressionlessly. "Of course I can see now," he continued, "why you have been working against me." He gave me the frank, manly look that had always served him so well in his dealings both personal and professional. "It is entirely understandable, given the circumstances. But I think you would do well to work with me, instead."

Still I said nothing, and his expression became again a little irritated. "I am sure you understand me," he said. "You must know I have had the whole story from my dear Julia. Apparently, the spirit of her father has warned her to be on her guard and to trust no one. Poor girl! She has been in such distress of mind. It took me a considerable time to get her to confide in me, but confide she did in the end, and of course felt much the better for it. I convinced her that if she is in danger, it is all the more desirable that we should be married as soon as possible, so that I am in a position to protect her."

This was a blow, Dear Reader, though I took care not to show it. Inwardly, however, I reflected that I might have anticipated such a turn of events. What so likely as that a woman in love should confide her worries to her lover?

Still, I said nothing aloud. Having waited in vain for some response, John shrugged and went on with his narrative. "Having heard the whole story of Madame Fox and her wonderful séances, I thought I would come here and talk to her, and perhaps succeed in winning her to my side of the question." He shot me another laughing look. "I have had dealings with Spiritualistic Mediums in the past, and I was sure that if I put it in the right light, the spirit of Mr. Waring might be prevailed upon to give his parental blessing to the match."

He paused again, but still I said nothing. His manner became abruptly much less friendly and much more forthright. "Be warned, Madame Fox," he said. "It will do you no good to oppose my marrying Miss Waring. I am sure her mother is paying you something handsome to do so, and of course you have a score of your own to settle. But it will not serve You had much better join forces with me. I tell you in confidence that the marriage is as good as accomplished. I have already won my Julia's consent to have our engagement publicly announced, despite her mother's objections."

Although discretion might be the better part of valour, still I could not resist opening my mouth at this point. "Creditors becoming pressing, are they," I said, "*Captain?*"

Just for a moment, I surprised a wary look in his eyes. He recovered quickly, however. "Just so," he said affably. "Creditors are always a bother."

After a pause, he continued. "About that military title—you'll find it's all right and tight. All since your time, but fairly earned. I've the papers to prove it, and photographs, too. My Julia can tell you all about it. She is never tired of hearing about my African exploits. In the words of the Bard, 'she loved me for the dangers I had pass'd.'" He threw me a wicked smile. "If I'd known a military career would have served me so well in that direction, I'd have enlisted twenty years ago."

Once more he waited, but I had nothing to say to this. "Ah, well," he said. "Think my offer over, Madame Fox. I have no doubt you will think better of it when you have had a chance to reflect a little. I know you for an intelligent woman, and it's evident you've prospered in the years since we parted." There was greedy appraisal in his eyes as he looked down the corridor to where the open doorway of the Sitting Room gave a glimpse of brocade and shining wood and exotic bijouterie.

You may imagine, Dear Reader, that I had a hard time restraining myself at this point. And indeed Susan, who knows me well, stepped forward hastily and stationed herself between us. "Do you want me to show the gentleman out, ma'am?" she asked.

"If you please," I said icily.

He shook his head at Susan, his expression one of smiling re-proof. "You may show me out in a minute, my good woman," he said. "But let me finish first." Addressing me again, he continued, "As I was saying, it's evident you've prospered, ma'am. You shouldn't begrudge me the chance to prosper likewise. If you do, you might find it affected your own livelihood. There, that's plain enough, isn't it? Good day, Madame Fox. No doubt I will be seeing more of you, now we both find ourselves in London."

After Susan had closed the door behind him, we looked at each other. "For brass, I never saw the like," she said. "I do apologize, ma'am. If I'd been quicker with the door—"

"Not your fault," I said. "It was purely an accident. I could wish it had been otherwise, however."

Susan shook her head. "It's trouble however you look at it," she prophesied. And look at it how I would, I could only agree with her.

I had hoped to keep John ignorant of my identity while I looked for something to use against him. That hope was gone now, of course. I talked the matter over with Susan and Jenny that evening, and we agreed it was a ticklish business. Even if he had not learned who Madame Fox really was, the fact that Miss Waring had decided to defy my Spiritual advice and confide the whole business to him would have told against me.

I did not see any good that could come from holding another séance for the Warings. The séances John and I had staged in the old days had not included such refinements as Spiritographs and phosphorescent oil, but I had no doubt he could guess enough of the techniques involved to destroy his fiancée's faith in me. Worse yet, he could also destroy the faith of others.

It was, indeed, now I who had more to lose than he did. Reputation is a fragile thing, and mine was key to my livelihood. John had something to lose in that respect, too, but once he married Miss Waring, his position would be secure. What would he do then? Somehow, I could not believe he would leave me to go my own way while he went his. No matter how large Miss Waring's fortune might be, it would not be enough to prevent him from extorting a little more from me, his ex-lover. Even in our brief interview today, it had been easy to see how much he relished having the whip hand of me. That is Human Nature at its worst, Dear Reader. If we injure someone unjustly, it is quite easy to convince ourselves that the injury was merited—and even that further injury might be called for. Entire wars have been started this way.

"In any case, it's blackmail," I said bitterly. "Blackmail!"

You will appreciate my bitterness, Dear Reader. I had nobly refrained from using such a weapon myself, only to find it now used against me.

"If I was you," said Susan, "I'd go to Felicity."

I knew what she meant. Felicity, though not participating directly in such business, could put me in touch with people who would warn John against interfering in my affairs—or even place him where he would be permanently unable to do so. It was a cheering thought. Still, that kind of help comes at a heavy price. There was, as I observed to Susan and Jenny, no guarantee that in getting rid of one blackmailer, I wouldn't leave myself open to another.

I had another objection, too, that was less easy to voice. Just as one cannot touch pitch without being defiled, one cannot consort with the lower sort of criminals without being drawn down to their depth. It was the same feeling that had always held me back from blackmail.

And this same feeling would have made me unwilling to assist in John's matrimonial schemes even if I had not had a grievance against him. I am not an honest woman, as the world counts such things, but I have my own code of honour. My unlikely friendship with Inspector Harper was based on the fact that he recognized this. I had come to prize our friendship and did not care to do anything now to endanger it. That meant I was debarred from some of the more rough-and-ready methods with which I might have dealt with John.

Mind you, I did not rule them out entirely, Dear Reader. Desperate situations do call for desperate measures sometimes. If John pushed me too far, there was no saying what I might not do. I already owed him a grudge for his past behaviour, and the balance was growing.

This trend of thought made me sigh and wish aloud that the Law had some method of dealing with blackmailers that did not rebound upon the victim.

"I'll bet the Inspector would help if you asked him," said Jenny. "He owes you a favour, doesn't he?"

"Not that much of a favour," I said, repressing a shudder. If I had been reluctant to confide the story of my youthful indiscretion to Susan and Jenny, I was utterly opposed to telling it to Inspector Harper. I presumed he might guess there were such episodes in my past, seeing that he had some idea of what my past actually was. But it is one thing to assume generalities, and quite another to be confronted with the specifics in such glaring form as Captain Ingram (as I supposed I must now call him).

It is easy to be wise after the fact, Dear Reader, but I had had time to look the captain over thoroughly during our conversation today. He might be attractive in a flashy way (though his attractions were looking a little shopworn, I thought), but it was perfectly obvious that he was also an unprincipled blackguard. His charm, such as it was, was entirely superficial. I was ashamed to have ever been taken in by it. How much worse, then, to expose the whole discreditable business to Inspector Harper, who could not help thinking less of me for it?

"Indeed, I am surprised I recognized John at all, now I have seen him at close hand," I said, pursuing another grievance. "His face is quite red, and he's at least a couple of stone heavier. And yet he has the nerve to say that *I* have grown stouter!"

"He's still a fine-looking man, though," said Susan. "I can see where women'd fall for him. A handsome, laughing devil. He's got that way of looking at you, like he was daring you to say what you really think of him."

"Good God, I hope *you're* not falling prey to his charms?"

"No fear of that," said Susan grimly. "But it don't do to underestimate the enemy." With a flash of mischief, she added, "I expect the Duke of Wellington said some such thing, if we only knew it."

The mention of the Iron Duke reminded me of something I had forgotten in the stress of late events. "Speaking of that," I said. "When I was at Mrs. O'Meagher's, I witnessed a strange little incident."

I told them all about Lady Frost and her fit of ill temper and how I had discovered that she was in debt to her dressmaker.

"That's interesting," said Susan. "And I can see what you're getting at. Lady Frost might have a motive for poisoning Miss Emily, too."

"Perhaps both of 'em are doing it," suggested Jenny. "They might be in it together—her *and* her sister."

"That would be a natural assumption," I said, "except that Miss Morton and Lady Frost can't stand each other. They squabble like children every time they are together."

Our discussion then returned to Captain Ingram, and it was late when we finally adjourned, having come to no more solid conclusion than that I dared not work openly against him as matters now stood. "There's no help for it. I must put Mrs. Waring off next time she asks me to sit for her, and hope Felicity is eventually able to find something we can use against him."

"Or else hope Miss Waring comes to her senses all by herself," suggested Jenny.

"But in that case, I wouldn't get paid," I said.

We all thought about this for a while. It was a dismal prospect, but I told the others I felt I could endure it. "At this point, I'd pay a thousand pounds myself, simply to put a spoke in that man's wheel."

It was with a melancholy feeling that I unpacked my new dress and put it away that night, Dear Reader. I had expected to wear it with such pleasure, and now, thanks to the day's events, it was associated with painful sensations instead. If you are female, you will understand it added yet another grievance to the balance against Captain Ingram.

## CHAPTER 9

I had expected Mrs. Waring would object when I put off our next sitting. I was prepared with all kinds of excuses, for she was a good client, and I did not want to lose her permanently if I could help it. I only wanted to fight a delaying action (as the Duke of Wellington might put it), until I found a weapon that might put our common enemy to rout. Once that was accomplished, I hoped we might resume our former, profitable relationship.

To my surprise, however, I learned Mrs. Waring was retiring from the field of battle. She called upon me the very next day—the day after the captain's visit—to tell me so.

"The truth is, Madame Fox, that I dislike the match as much as ever. But what can I do? Julia is resolved to marry the wretched man, and there's an end of it."

I already knew this, but patted her hand and said it was a great shame. "She may yet change her mind," I said. "If she can only be persuaded to wait—"

"Ah, but that's what no one seems able to do," said Mrs. Waring. "I had thought her father's words at our last sitting had convinced her. Indeed, his message was so clear!"

I agreed it had been very clear.

"And Julia was quite struck by it," continued Mrs. Waring. "The idea that she was in danger quite possessed her. She scarcely left the house for the next few days. But somehow that man got to her and talked her over. I am afraid they must correspond."

I knew only too well that they did, but tried to make light of the matter. "Of course, it is natural that they would correspond," I pointed out, "seeing that Miss Waring considers herself engaged to him."

Mrs. Waring sighed. "Yes, and now she is set on announcing the engagement. I am sure he is behind that. He thinks once it has been announced publicly, his position will be secure."

This, too, I knew to be the case. "Can you delay the announcement somehow?"

"I have delayed as long as I can. But now Julia says she will announce it herself if I do not." Mrs. Waring sighed again, dolefully. "We are holding a party next week—the first since Howard died. It has been two years now, and we are both out of mourning. Julia says it will be the ideal occasion to announce her engagement. I don't know how I am to bear it. I am certain it spells ruin for my poor daughter."

Once again, I was in a position to confirm this, but there is no point in being a Job's comforter. "Even if she does become engaged to him, the engagement can still be broken," I pointed out.

Mrs. Waring said grimly that if matters went that far, she feared there would be no drawing back. "I would pay a thousand pounds to anyone who could make her see reason at this point," she said, as she had often done before. "Indeed, ten thousand would not be too much!"

I pricked up my ears at this, but suspected she was only expressing the depth of her desperation. People say such things in the heat of the moment, but one cannot rely on their remembering them when it comes time to produce the cheque-book.

In any case, I was as far from earning the reward as ever. In fact, I was farther. Now that John knew my identity, I could not risk warning Miss Waring against him in my professional capacity. And to make matters worse, we had a new problem at the Temple. Jenny's relations with Sam, which had been progressing steadily for a period of months, overnight reached a state of crisis.

It was a scene of high drama I encountered when I innocently stepped down to the kitchen that evening to inquire about supper. I found Jenny in tears, Susan looking grim, and supper nowhere in sight. Naturally, I inquired what had produced this state of affairs.

"Sam has asked me to marry him," Jenny informed me through her tears.

"Oh," I said blankly. Of course, Susan and I had been expecting this for weeks. Sam was an honourable young man who was courting Jenny in an open, aboveboard manner, and marriage is the usual termination of such courtships. "Well, I will be sorry to lose you, Jenny—very sorry indeed. But I'm sure I wish you both very happy."

This produced a fresh effusion of tears. "Oh, ma'am, I don't believe I *can* marry him. He doesn't—he hasn't—he thinks I'm a *good* girl."

"Oh," I said again. This inadequate response caused Susan, who had her arm around Jenny's shoulders, to glare at me. "But you *are* a good girl, Jenny," I said, regrouping quickly. "I am sure Sam must think so, or he wouldn't want to marry you."

Jenny shook her head. "That's not what I mean, ma'am," she said. "What I mean is, he thinks I'm a maid—a virgin. And I'm not. You know I'm not."

I frowned. I did know it, but I also knew it wasn't Jenny's fault. I tried hard to convey this to her. "My poor girl! As if anyone in their senses could hold that against you. You were only a child at the time—and you were forced against your will."

"Yes, but that don't matter," said Jenny bleakly. "What matters is I'm not a maid. And Sam wouldn't want to marry me if he knew it."

"Nonsense," I said sharply. "If Sam felt that way—which I don't believe, mind you—then he wouldn't *deserve* to marry you."

"Exactly what I said," approved Susan.

Jenny shook her head. "He's a good man," she said. "I don't doubt he'd be sorry for me. But I don't believe he'd feel the same about me if he knew. And as it is, I don't dare tell him."

Susan and I exchanged despairing looks. I racked my brain for an idea that might help. "Perhaps you *shouldn't* tell him, then," I suggested.

Jenny looked at me with reproach. "But he'd be sure to find out, ma'am. You know yourself that he'd find out on our wedding night, if I didn't tell him afore."

As delicately as possible, I suggested that the illusion of virginity was a particularly easy one to create. As I expected, however, she rejected the idea indignantly. She wanted a marriage based on complete openness and honesty. "I'd rather not marry at all than fool him in such a way," she wept.

"Well, then," I said, "it appears you must risk telling him."

"But if he should draw back, ma'am, once he knew the truth? And then he might go telling people, and I couldn't bear that. I could never hold up my head again."

The idea of her going about in shame, for a crime in which she had been the victim, made me furious. "If you really think he would do such a thing, then you are well rid of him," I retorted.

All this earned me was another burst of tears. "Jenny, you haven't done anything wrong," I pleaded. "You are completely innocent of any wrongdoing."

"It don't matter."

"It does matter. You act as if a maidenhead were the only thing a man might value about you —and that without one, you have no value at all."

Unfortunately, this reasoning was above her head. She reiterated stubbornly that virginity was important to men.

"The more fools they, then," I said. "I wish you would think a little better of yourself, Jenny. You are a woman any man might be lucky to marry. Susan and I can see it if you can't."

This caused her to fling her arms around us both and bawl like a child. It was very affecting. I believe Susan cried a little, too, and I know I did. But in the end, we found ourselves no further along than when we began. Jenny did not dare trust Sam with the truth, and she would not marry him while he was in a state of ignorance. "I just told him I couldn't marry him. He kept asking why, and I couldn't tell him. He was so hurt."

I could not help feeling sorry for poor Sam. From all I had seen of him, I thought he might have been trusted with the truth. Still, I reasoned that she knew him better than I did. I could not urge her to go against her own judgment when it might have such disastrous results.

Even as it was, the results were dismal enough. She went about her work the next few days valiantly trying to seem as usual, yet it was easy to see from her reddened eyelids and sorrowful face how badly she was feeling.

You will note, Dear Reader, that I now had three sets of difficulties to contend with: my own, the Warings', and Jenny's. It was enough to make me welcome the prospect of being poisoned as light relief, as I told Susan on the evening of the Waterloo Dinner. I had come down to the kitchen to show her my new dress, and she was kind enough to admire it and say she didn't doubt I would fit right in with all the Nobs.

"At any rate, I will fit in with Lady Frost. For we both have the same dressmaker!" I said, admiring the effect of my feather-trimmed toque in the kitchen glass.

"And you're all ready to speak for the Duke, I've no doubt."

"Yes, even if we depart from the usual script. I always think it's a shame I can't use some of the anecdotes in Harriet Wilson's memoir," I said with a shake of my head. "But Miss Emily would never believe her hero had dealings with a woman of that sort."

"Ah," said Susan. "*That* kind of woman?"

"Yes, a courtesan, and very famous in her day. Frankly, I don't believe everything Miss Wilson says about the Duke, but I do think she must have had some basis for her claims.[9] Even a brazen creature like her wouldn't have tried to blackmail him otherwise."

"Blackmail," said Susan with a short laugh. "There's a coincidence for you. Don't tell me the Duke was blackmailed, too?"

"He wasn't blackmailed, but it wasn't for want of trying," I said. "Miss Wilson's publisher sent him a letter, saying that if he paid two hundred pounds, she would leave him out of her book. And as the story goes, his response was, 'Publish and be damned!'"

Susan said it was a good pithy response, and I agreed, though noting that Miss Wilson's scandalous anecdotes about the Duke had passed into the historical record as a result. "It's a high price to pay for a principle," I said, sighing.

"Aye, but once you start dealing with blackmailers, there's no end to it," observed Susan.

I said I was still fighting a delaying action in that respect, and that Felicity and I were planning to make another search of the captain's rooms on Sunday. "We didn't have enough time to finish last time. Possibly a second search will turn up something that might turn the trick."

---

9 Harriet Wilson's memoirs, published in 1825, gave details of her amorous liaisons with many gentlemen prominent in Regency society. Although there are serious inaccuracies in Wilson's narrative, the relationship she describes with the Duke was admitted by him and undoubtedly had a basis in fact. *–Ed.*

Jenny came in just then, sad-faced as usual. She brightened when she saw me and my dress, however. "Oh, how lovely, ma'am! You look fine as a queen. What a pretty stuff." She touched a fold of black taffeta, admiring the sheen of iridescent green that flickered under the light. "Just like a raven's wing."

The doorbell rang then, and Susan put down her ladle to answer it. "I'll get it, Susan," I said. "It's probably just someone wanting the dentist's next door." This was a perennial problem for us, as the dentist's rooms were in the same building as ours. Since my own entrance is clearly labeled with a sign reading "Temple of Spiritualism" and the dentist's with a set of enormous false teeth, you might imagine it would have been hard to mistake one for the other, but apparently toothache sufferers are often unobservant.

When I opened the door, however, I found not a toothache sufferer but Inspector Harper. It wasn't his usual day to call, but I was happy to see him nonetheless. This was not least because I felt I was looking extremely fetching in my new finery. I do not pretend to be superior to my sex in this regard, Dear Reader. Susan and Jenny's compliments had only made me hungry for more.

I welcomed him in and wished him many happy returns of the day.

"Oh, yes. It's the day of your Waterloo Dinner, isn't it?" he said, looking me over rather morosely. "If fine feathers make fine birds, you ought to be right at home among all the lords and ladies."

"What a gallant speech," I said admiringly.

He laughed and coloured a little. "I beg your pardon," he said. "You are looking very handsome, Madame Fox. I have no doubt you will be much admired tonight by men more skilled at gallantry than I."

"As to that," I said, "I'm more likely to be snubbed by their wives. But it's a pleasant thought."

"I won't keep you long," he continued, his manner becoming a little more cheerful. "But I thought I'd come by and tell you we had another of those anonymous letters. This one's the same as the other: letters cut from a newspaper—the *Times*, by the look of it—saying Miss Emily Randall is being poisoned, but giving no other detail."

"I will let you know if I see any sign of it tonight," I promised.

"I wish you would. There's probably nothing in it, but I still don't feel quite easy about the situation."

"As to that, I have a piece of information that may or may not bear on it," I said. I told him about my encounter with Lady Frost and how I had come to suspect she might be in financial difficulties.

"Lady Frost—she was the younger of the Miss Mortons, wasn't she?" he queried. "Sister to the one I met at Miss Emily's?"

"Yes, Lady Frost was the younger sister. She married Lord Frost only a few years ago. Her older sister never married."

"And you think she may be in financial difficulties?"

"Her behaviour would seem to indicate it. For a woman of fashion like her to go to a common dressmaker would be a terrible comedown."

"And as niece to Miss Emily, she might expect to inherit something when she dies?"

"That would be the natural assumption," I said. "But it may have no bearing on your anonymous letters, of course."

"I'll make a note of it just in case," he promised me. Having done so, he departed, saying he did not want to make me late for my grand dinner.

## CHAPTER 10

An hour later, I was at Waterloo House, facing an impressive array of silver knives, forks, and spoons, and awaiting the opening course of Miss Emily's Waterloo Dinner.

The place looked just as it always did. The dining room, a square, paneled apartment, was furnished with the same sideboard and table of heavy mahogany that had stood there for the past hundred years. The same pictures of dead game decorated the walls, and the same lavish display of china, crystal, and silver glinted beneath the light of a hundred candles.

The company was much the same as usual, too. Miss Emily's friends were, for the most part, as elderly as she was, or nearly so. They were a mixed bag of older men and women, both titled and untitled, with a scattering of younger people.

Her nieces were among the latter. Lady Frost, resplendent in a dress of white silk (whose secret history I was privy to), was seated diagonally across from me at the table. Her husband, Lord Frost, was at my right. Miss Morton was a seat or two farther down on my left side. As usual, she had been outshone by her younger sister. Miss Morton laboured under the disadvantage of a short, stout figure, which appeared yet shorter and stouter thanks to an ill-chosen dress of brown-and-blue striped summer velvet. Her fair hair tended toward mousy rather than flaxen like her sister's, and her face was drawn into its usual peevish scowl.

Hilda was there, too, unwontedly idle since the exigencies of dinner prevented her from knitting. Miss Emily's companion was a sturdy woman in her sixties, with fair hair turning to grey and a face singularly devoid of expression. Inspector Harper had opined that she was half-witted, and I could understand why he might think so, but she had always seemed perfectly competent to me within the limited range of her duties. I suspected she was simply one of those people lacking imagination or sensibility. Since slights and snubs are the usual lot of the paid companion, this might be accounted a blessing.

Looking around at all these people, I might have fancied it was last year, or the year before. Everyone appeared as usual in manners and appearance, with one exception. That exception was our hostess, looking sadly diminished in her place at the head of the table.

Even with Inspector Harper's words to warn me, I had been shocked by Miss Emily's appearance. As far as I could tell, she was not actually smaller or thinner—she had always been a tiny, bird-like woman. But her former brisk energy and bubbly manner were entirely absent tonight. Without them, her small figure seemed shrunken. She had greeted me kindly on my arrival, but since then had lapsed into silence. When she did speak, it was in a die-away voice quite unlike her usual chirping speech.

It seemed unlikely that this was the effect of poison, but I could not doubt she had suffered some kind of physical decline.

Once we were all seated at the table, however, she seemed to regain something of her old manner. "Dear friends," she said, with an echo of the flutelike tones of yesteryear in her voice, "my dear friends, I am so glad you can be with me tonight, as we celebrate once again the Great Battle and the Great Man who saved the world from," she lowered her voice, as though loath to mention such an indelicacy at the table, "the Corsican Monster."

We all murmured our approval of these sentiments, and she beamed around the table at us—not quite the beam of past years, but showing a spark still unextinguished. "I hope my cook will give us a good dinner. And then afterwards, as usual, dear Madame Fox," she bowed toward me, "will call upon her Spiritualistic powers that we may speak to the Great Man himself."

"Such foolishness," said Miss Morton, quite audibly.

I bowed and smiled back at Miss Emily, ignoring Miss Morton. I had found to my dismay that she did indeed now live at Waterloo House. It also appeared that she was steadily gathering the reins of the household into her hands. As the footmen were bringing in the first course, she adjured them sharply not to be clumsy, and when they had poured out the wine to accompany it, she scolded the butler for chilling it insufficiently.

It was a dinner not, perhaps, in the latest style: Miss Emily did not care about style, but rather about treating her guests with the open-handed hospitality that accorded with her old-fashioned notions. Abundance was the keynote of the feast. We started with soup and worked our way steadily through twelve full courses, a different wine served with each one.

It is the fashion to deplore this kind of meal, Dear Reader, but I seldom have the luxury to eat dinner at all, let alone a dinner of this sort. My work typically runs so late into the evening that I make do with tea beforehand and some kind of simple supper afterwards. Thus, I enjoyed the meal immensely. Even the presence of Miss Morton could not spoil it. Since I was going to have to work later that evening, I tried not to drink too much wine, but with the footmen refilling the glasses at every sip, it was easy to lose track.

I believe it was midway through the fish course (fried sole, and turbot with lobster sauce) that I noticed Miss Emily was looking better.

She was not very near me at the table. I was placed about half-way down, with Lord Frost and several others between. But when I looked at her, I saw she was chatting easily with her partner on the left, Lord Cecil Hazelton, a longtime friend of hers. Moreover, there was a lift to her head and an energy to her movements that had not been there before. I stared, wondering if I were imagining it. Just then she caught my eye and turned to me with an impulsive eagerness that was entirely in her old manner.

"Madame Fox, I was telling Lord Cecil how much I am looking forward to our sitting tonight. I never grow tired of hearing of the Duke's exploits from his own lips."

There was a snort from Miss Morton, which we both ignored.

"It's as if I were really there, on the field of Waterloo," she continued. At this point her voice was strong enough to be heard all the way to the other end of the table, where it caught the attention of the Honourable Daniel Fowler, Member of Parliament for Westminster.

"Ah, it's not like it was in the Duke's day," he said, shaking his head. "But still worth a visit, mind you. Every Englishman ought to see Waterloo."

"I wish I could have seen it," said Miss Emily wistfully. "It was the dearest wish of my life, but of course quite impossible."

She spoke with sad decision, and everyone at the table nodded, and murmured what a shame it was, and seemed to accept her decision as final. I looked at them, and at her, in wonderment. Here she was, a wealthy woman with no husband or parents to say her nay. She might be getting on in years, but at the moment she looked quite sound and healthy. Yet she spoke as though she were not merely an invalid but a prisoner. As far as I could see, there was nothing that would have kept her from going to Belgium any time these past fifty years.

I did not say as much as this, Dear Reader, but I had drunk enough wine to make me bold enough to say something.

"But it's not too late, is it?" I asked. "If you want to see Waterloo so badly, Miss Emily, perhaps you ought to go."

At my words, she seemed to shrink again—not quite as she had been before, but it was evident I had shocked or even frightened her. "Oh, but I couldn't," she said.

"Why not?"

"It would be impossible. I wouldn't know how to go about it."

"I daresay Mr. Cook's agency could help you with that."

"But at my age, Madame Fox! I am afraid I am too old to go traipsing about battlefields. I am not as . . . as *strong* as I was."

"As for that, surely you would not need to go on foot. Such a popular place of pilgrimage must have arrangements for invalids and the elderly. You could afford to hire people to assist you—an attendant with a wheeled chair, perhaps—"

"Nonsense," broke in Miss Morton, unable to contain herself any longer. "You oughtn't to encourage her in such folly, Madame Fox." She glared at me. "At her age, such goings-on would likely kill her."

Miss Emily drooped so much at this speech that I feared she had lost all the ground she had recovered. "That would be a pity, of course," I said, not looking at Miss Morton, but rather fixing my eyes on her aunt. "But it would be for her to decide if it were worth the risk. If it were me, I think I would risk a good deal to see a place that was as important to me as the field of Waterloo is to Miss Emily."

This speech elicited agreement from some of the guests and disagreement from others—chief among the latter being (of course) Miss Morton. Lady Frost, too, expressed her disapprobation in the fashionable drawling voice she affected when among her social equals.

"My poor aunt would do better to stop safely at *home,* I am sure," she said. "She has taken altogether too many *risks* in her life as it is."

Miss Emily cast her a swift look and nodded, her lips trembling. "Yes, it is impossible, of course. But it is very kind of you, Madame Fox, to be so—so encouraging."

It took a while before she recovered from this exchange, but by the game course (quails, and a haunch of venison) she was chattering away again to her neighbours. I was pleased to see her looking and acting so well. The food and drink appeared to have restored her to her old health and spirits. I could not imagine why she had been so weakened in the first place. Had she been half-starved, perhaps, though some misguided economy practiced by Miss Morton? But Miss Morton did not seem inclined to practice economy, in the matter of food and drink at any rate. She ate and drank quite as much as I did, and I was feeling so full as to be slightly unwell by the time we reached the sweet courses (Charlotte Russe, pastries, and ice cream, followed by fruit and bonbons). When the footmen had filled the champagne glasses, Miss Emily rose and held her glass aloft.

"A toast," she said, her voice as clear and flutelike as it ever was. "A toast to His Grace, the Duke of Wellington, on this most *historic* day."

We drank, and then someone proposed another toast to the brave British soldiers who fought with the Duke. Someone then proposed the brave allied troops and their leaders, and the usually phlegmatic Hilda raised her voice enthusiastically to her countryman Marshall Blücher. And so it continued, if not *ad infinitum,* at least until I felt not altogether steady on my feet when it came time for us ladies to retire from the table.

Because these matters are settled by rank, I was one of the last to enter the drawing room. I arrived just in time to hear Miss Morton telling Mrs. Fowler, "I would not have invited the creature if it were left to me. But of course it is one of my poor aunt's obsessions, and one must humour her."

I was pretty sure I was the creature under discussion. It was obvious from the embarrassed way Mrs. Fowler glanced at me, and from Miss Morton's unctuous tone as she said, "Oh, here *is* Madame Fox."

This was the part of the evening I always enjoyed least. Dear Reader. At the dinner table, and in the company of men, we ladies were on much the same footing, or at least were distinguished only by such material characteristics as age, wit, and beauty. But in the drawing room, all pretensions to equality were stripped away. It is here that the British Upper Class Female shows her mettle, and here, as I knew well from previous years, that I might look to be systematically snubbed by Miss Morton, Lady Frost, and their ilk.

Ignoring Miss Morton, I went over and sat down by Hilda. She was already absorbed in her knitting. Unless she was eating, or engaged in some other activity that occupied her hands, it was rare to see her without a piece of worsted in her lap and her needles clicking away. Early in my dealings with her, I had been obliged to put my foot down and forbid her to knit during séances, or she would have sat there knitting all the while and quite put me off my game.

"What are you making, Hilda?" I asked.

"Is a muffler," she replied briefly. She spoke English perfectly well, but her speech had still a German flavour in its accent and phrasing.

I admired the muffler, though between you and me, Dear Reader, it was very ugly: all muddy greens and murky blues. Hilda's projects always seemed wrought in these sort of unattractive hues. It could hardly be coincidence. Taste is a curiously individual thing.

At that moment, my attention was drawn by another sally from Miss Morton.

"Madame Fox," she cried, "Mrs. Fowler wants to know if you will tell her fortune if she crosses your palm with silver."

Mrs. Fowler, looking embarrassed, immediately disclaimed any such desire. I smiled a cool, distant smile. "You must forgive me, Mrs. Fowler," I said. "My talents do not lie in that direction. Miss Morton has mistaken Spiritualism for Chiromancy."

"But it's all fortune-telling, isn't it?" said Miss Morton aggressively. "And for my part, I think it is all nonsense."

"I must say that I *agree*, my dear Honoria," drawled Lady Frost, who was reclining decoratively on the sofa. "I have attended séances, and received messages *purported* to be from some deceased friend or relative, but they never seem to be anything to the *purpose*."

"Purest mummery," snorted Miss Morton.

I had often reflected, Dear Reader, that the difference between the two sisters was the difference between the bludgeon and the stiletto. Neither was pleasant; Lady Frost was only a little subtler and more sophisticated.

"I daresay Spiritualism is *harmless* enough," she continued, with a wary eye on her aunt. "It may be there is even something in it, when practiced by persons possessing a *genuine* gift."

Unfortunately for me, Miss Emily was deep in conversation with another lady guest and had heard nothing of this exchange. If she had, she would have flown to defend me. As it was, however, Lady Frost was emboldened to carry her taunts a step further.

"I assure you, Madame Fox, it would give me great *pleasure* to be converted into a true *believer*," she said, smiling maliciously and leaning forward on the sofa. "Do you think you could summon up one *tiny* little display of your powers for me here and now? Something really *convincing?*"

Could you have resisted, Dear Reader? I could not. I came over and sat down opposite her and stared her in the eye. She held my gaze steadily enough. There was even a smile lurking on her lips. "Blood," I said.

She blinked at that, although her smile did not waver. "I don't think—" she began.

"Blood on your hands," I said in a quelling voice.

She went quite still, but continued looking at me.

"No, on your *hand*," I said, shaking my head as though seeking to clear some inner vision. "You have injured your hand, my lady. Have you not?"

She did not answer the question. It was her sister who cried, "Nonsense," and came over to pull away the fall of lace that half-covered Lady Frost's hands. "You can see she has *not* injured—" she began and then stopped.

We all looked at the scratch, slight but unmistakable, that disfigured Lady Frost's left hand. She immediately twitched the lace back over both hands and leaned back on the sofa. "Very impressive," she said coolly.

"I daresay she saw it earlier, at dinner," said Miss Morton with a snort. "At any rate, it is some trick, you may be sure."

It was, of course, but I merely smiled mysteriously and drifted back over to my seat beside Hilda. I hoped I might get through the rest of the evening without further provocation. And so it proved, for once I was out of the line of fire, Lady Frost and Miss Morton turned on each other and were soon engaged in one of those sisterly exchanges that typically enlivened these soirées.

"My dear Honoria, I did not like to see you take so much *pudding* this evening," purred Lady Frost. "Persons who eat a great many sweets are so prone to becoming *stout*."

"Yes, and people who starve themselves to stay thin are so prone to become ill-natured," snapped her sister.

"I always think that, had you not been so stout, you might not have ended up a spinster, dear Honoria," continued Lady Frost in a sweet, pensive tone.

"I am sure I would prefer to remain a spinster, dear Catherine, rather than take another woman's leavings." This was an allusion to Lord Frost's having been a widower when the younger Miss Morton married him. She only smiled, however, and shook her head.

"Dear me! But I think you would have been only too *happy* to accept *any* man, dear Honoria, had he *offered*. I fear these must be *sour grapes*."

"At any rate, I didn't lower myself to become a man's mistress as a stepping-stone to matrimony," said Miss Morton with a crack of laughter. "If Frost did marry you, it wasn't before time, to *my* way of thinking."

I could hardly forbear smiling at this home thrust, Dear Reader. I had myself heard rumours that the younger Miss Morton had been Lord Frost's mistress even before the death of his first wife. She received her sister's words with composure, however, only smiling and shaking her head again as she got up from the sofa. "Sour grapes indeed," she murmured, disappearing into the adjoining parlour with a rustle of silk skirts.

Since this had very much the appearance of a strategic withdrawal, I considered Miss Morton to have got the better of the engagement. It was apparent she thought so, too, for she turned again to Mrs. Fowler and began elaborating on the scandalous accusation she had just made.

"Is jealousy," said Hilda in my ear.

This made me jump, for it was rare for Miss Emily's companion to make an unsolicited remark. "You mean Miss Morton is jealous of Lady Frost?" I asked.

She shook her head, her expression serious. "They both are jealous," she explained. "Always it was so. When their brother was alive, it was of him they were jealous. Still they are jealous of his memory, I think."

I knew, of course, that Miss Emily had once had a nephew as well as two nieces. Christened Arthur Wellesley, young Mr. Morton had pursued a military career like his namesake, but not so fortunately. He had died in India years ago, and his mother and aunt had never ceased to mourn him. There was a sort of shrine to him in this very room. I could see it from where I sat: an oval miniature of a handsome young man in regimentals, with a vase of flowers set beneath it.

"I suppose his sisters might have some reason for resentment," I said, trying to be fair-minded. It was a fact that when Lady Morton had been alive, she had often spoken of her fallen son but seldom of her living daughters. Miss Emily had always shown the same preference, prefacing many a speech with the words, "If only dear Arthur had lived!" There is, sad to say, a tendency among many people to value their male offspring higher than their female. It might explain in part why Miss Morton and Lady Frost were such nasty pieces of work, though it could not wholly excuse them.

In any case, Hilda did not dispute my statement. She merely nodded in a non-committal way and continued knitting. At that moment, Miss Emily came over to us. Her face—an amazingly youthful face for an eighty-year-old woman—was aglow with smiles, and she seized my hand like an excited child.

"The gentlemen should be joining us soon," she said. "Will you come with me to look at the room, Madame Fox? To see that all is as you want it?"

"Of course I will," I said. Bidding Hilda farewell (she acknowledged this, too, with a nod), I accompanied Miss Emily into the parlour next door.

## CHAPTER 11

The parlour next to the drawing room was to serve as our séance room. Miss Emily, with a mixture of pride and anxiety, showed me the preparations that had been made: the round table with chairs set about it; the single candle in its brass candlestick; the fire shielded by a fire-screen (although it was June, the room had the chill that so often pervades English homes, and a fire was very welcome).

"This should do perfectly, Miss Emily," I said, smiling at her eagerness. "Of course, you know my requirements very well by this time."

"Indeed I do, Madame Fox! But it is well to make sure."

Seeing her so much her normal self was a great relief. I told her so, mentioning that I had been concerned by her appearance earlier in the evening.

"Have you been unwell?" I asked. "I thought you did not seem quite in your normal health and spirits before dinner."

"No," she said, her face shadowing a little. "I have not been entirely well of late."

"I am very sorry to hear it," I said. "I hope you have consulted a doctor?"

"Oh, yes," she assured me. "Sir Stanley has been my doctor for years, though up till now I have been fortunate enough to have little need of him."

"Not Sir Stanley Heron?" I exclaimed.

She nodded, confirming my worst fears.

I have no opinion of doctors in general, Dear Reader. Like the Iron Duke, I might say that they are all more or less quacks. But Sir Stanley was something worse even than the usual quack practitioner. In a sense, he performs my own function in reverse: whereas I help bring dead souls to the world of the living, he helps hurry living ones into the world of the dead

"I hope Sir Stanley was able to help you," I said, making the statement a question.

Miss Emily shook her head, trying to smile. "No, I fear there is no help for me. It is simply a matter of *anno Domini*, as Sir Stanley puts it. At my age, I must expect a few infirmities."

"But what infirmities are these? You appear perfectly well to me."

"Yes, and I *feel* perfectly well, at the moment. But of late I have been suffering from—well, I can only call them sinking spells. The most peculiar sensation! And—and—my mind doesn't always seem to be clear."

I looked at her in alarm. "I think you should see another doctor, Miss Emily. I wouldn't trust Sir Stanley to relieve me of a splinter in my finger, let alone anything serious."

She only shook her head, however, and took refuge in religious platitude, saying she was resigned to suffer whatever ills the Lord sent her. I told her that was nonsense. If the Lord helps at all (a question open to doubt in my book), He assuredly helps best those who help themselves.

Again, she only shook her head. "I know you mean well, Madame Fox. And I thank you—indeed I do. But there is nothing anyone can do, and I am resigned to it."

She then changed the subject, saying she wanted to show me something else while she had me to herself. I followed her out of the parlour and along the hall to her bedroom. This was on the house's main floor along with the dining room and drawing room and other reception rooms.

In the doorway of her room, she stopped short. "Oh!" she said. Then after a moment, "Ah. Now I wonder—but there, never mind."

She gave no explanation for these words, but entered the room, beckoning me to follow. It was a large, old-fashioned chamber. The bed was one of those enormous canopied affairs that would sleep six at the very least. I could imagine Miss Emily's tiny form would be quite lost in it. There were two doors close together on the far wall. Probably they led to a dressing room and a closet or sitting room.

Miss Emily went over to a cabinet that stood between these two doors. She turned a key in the lock, opened the cabinet, and produced a bundle wrapped in scarlet silk. This she unwrapped with great reverence to reveal a single boot, much scuffed.

"It was His," she said in a hushed voice. "The Duke's. I was able to obtain it from his former manservant."

I admired it with suitable solemnity. "Should we have it in the séance room?" she asked, surveying her treasure with pride. "As it was His, perhaps it would assist the Spirit Energy?"

I suggested that so valuable a relic ought to remain safely locked away, but she thrust it into my arms. "If it assists at all, I don't begrudge it. You may carry it, Madame Fox. And while I am here in my room, I'll just take my tonic."

"Tonic?" I asked, clutching the boot to my chest and watching as she made for a washstand near the head of the bed.

"Iron tonic," she said, displaying a bottle of patent medicine that stood there. "I have taken it ever since I was a little girl. My dear mother always swore by it. A couple of spoonfuls after dinner, to aid the digestion." She swallowed the dose, then grimaced. "Such a nasty flavour! I always have a sweet afterwards, to take away the taste."

She popped a sweet into her mouth, then offered the box to me. It was a fancy box, frilled and beribboned and nearly empty. There was only one sweet left in it, and I took it to be polite (for I was certainly not hungry, after that gargantuan dinner). As she tossed the empty box down on the table, I observed there was a new box standing ready beside it.

The sweet proved to be mint-flavoured. I have never cared for the flavour of mint. I spat it into my handkerchief when Miss Emily wasn't looking. As I followed her out of the room, I reflected that it was just like her to go on swallowing a tonic she disliked for eighty years, simply because her mother had prescribed it. On the other hand, she had enjoyed eighty years of excellent health, so perhaps there was something in it. At any rate, I felt I would trust her mother's tonic further than Sir Stanley Heron.

We carried the Sacred Boot to the séance room, placed it with care in the centre of the table, and stood back to admire the effect. Miss Emily said again how much she was looking forward to the séance, especially reliving the climactic encounter of the Foot Guards with Napoleon's *Garde Imperiale* ("Now, Maitland! Now's your time!"), and I resolved it should be all she hoped for.

We then returned to the drawing room.

The gentlemen had begun to filter in by now. Miss Emily headed for the table where the tea tray stood. Before she had got halfway there, however, she stopped suddenly and looked about her in a bewildered way. An instant later, I saw her sway on her feet. I rushed forward and caught her as she fell, then helped her to a nearby chair.

"Miss Emily, are you unwell?" I asked.

She stared at me—or through me. "Shadows," she whispered.

Her expression was so fearful that I felt gooseflesh prickle on my arms. "Are you unwell?" I repeated. "Should I send for your maid?"

Before she could reply, Miss Morton came bustling over. "What's the matter?" she demanded. She looked at her aunt, then shook her head. "It's one of her spells. I was afraid of it. This business has been too much for her." Going over to the bell-pull, she rang the bell sharply several times.

"Is there something we can do for her?" I asked.

"Nothing but get her to her room," said Miss Morton. "*You* have done enough."

This was so unjust that for a moment I was too stunned to speak. "I beg your pardon, but I have done nothing," I protested, as soon as I had recovered from my shock. "I cannot think what has caused this. She was quite well up till a minute ago."

"Very likely. These spells take her suddenly, as a rule." Miss Morton spoke off-hand, not even looking at me. Her eyes were on her aunt. Miss Emily turned her head restlessly from side to side, murmuring under her breath. Then, for an instant, her eyes met mine, and she spoke aloud, her voice suddenly panic-stricken.

"Shadows," she cried. "Oh, help me!"

I tried to go to her and was roughly pushed aside. "You had better go. You can do nothing here," said Miss Morton.

"But—the séance," I said.

Miss Morton turned a furious face upon me. "Do you think she is in any condition for that?" she demanded. "If you ask me, it was you and your morbid nonsense that brought this fit on."

"She was quite well until a minute ago! She was looking forward to it."

"Your services will not be required tonight, *Madame*," hissed Miss Morton. "You may show yourself out. Or do you prefer that I have the servants throw you out?"

A footman arrived just then, in answer to Miss Morton's summons. Paying no further heed to me, she instructed him to help get Miss Emily to her room.

As they assisted her to her feet, however, she made a sudden dart forward and caught me by the hand. "Help me!" she cried. "Save me!"

It was horrible to be thus appealed to, and to be powerless to help. I had no idea what to do. Before I could do anything, Miss Morton had wrenched her away from me, almost lifting her from her feet.

"She ought to have a doctor," I said.

"You may be sure we will do all that is necessary," said Miss Morton.

"Someone other than Sir Stanley Heron," I urged.

Miss Morton did not even reply. She only looked at the butler, who had come hurrying up with an expression of concern. "Wilton," she said. "Show this person out, please."

The butler looked at me, then at her. He was plainly shocked. "But the séance?" he said. "Miss Emily's instructions—?"

"You fool, that's all off now. We must get her to her room."

"Yes, Miss," he said, doubtfully. "But what of the party?" He glanced around the drawing room, where the guests were all standing frozen, watching this drama.

"Never mind the party. Miss Emily is ill."

"Yes, of course, Miss But what shall I do? There is still the supper to be served—and the fireworks." He turned to the guests, as though appealing to them. "There were to be fireworks after. Miss Emily particularly desired it."

Miss Morton made an exasperated gesture. "Do whatever you like. It hardly matters at this point." Nodding to the footman, she took one arm and he the other, and they hurried Miss Emily out of the room.

The butler stood looking after them, his brow furrowed. Lady Frost came drifting up. "You may as well have the fireworks, Wilton," she drawled. "I daresay the servants were looking forward to them."

"Yes, my lady. But the supper?"[10]

"Go ahead and serve it now," she said. "And then we will go. That will be the best way. No one will care to stay, since our hostess is ill." She glanced at me, her brows raised. "Don't you agree?"

I did agree, Dear Reader. In fact, I did not even care to wait for supper. For all I knew, Miss Morton would have me ejected from the house anyway, once she returned.

The Duke of Wellington once observed that the highest military talent lies in knowing when to retreat. This looked like a moment when retreat was prudent. So I left quietly by the side door without even saying farewell to the company.

I had hired a carriage for the evening, so I had then to find a stableman, send him in search of my driver, and wait for my carriage to be brought around. No sooner had I stepped inside than I realized I had left my shawl in the drawing room. For a moment I hesitated, wondering if I should go back for it. In the end, however, I decided to let it go. I felt shaken and not entirely myself. A shawl was the least of my concerns.

Susan was surprised to see me home so early. "I didn't look for you for hours yet," she exclaimed. Then, looking at me more closely, she demanded, "What happened?"

"I'm not quite sure," I said.

"Miss Emily?" she said at once. "Don't tell me they *did* poison her?"

---

10  Unbelievable as it may seem, a hostess like Miss Emily would have served supper to her guests later in the evening, even after giving them such a dinner as Madame Fox describes. It would normally have been served some hours later, after whatever entertainment the hostess had provided—in this case, a séance. –*Ed.*

"She's ill enough, at any rate," I said. "Or so they say." I stood a moment, thinking. "Susan, I don't think they are poisoning her. I think they are *drugging* her."

I told her all about it, and her calm good sense was like a balm to my wounded feelings. Not only that, but in telling her everything that had happened, I was able to make sense of my somewhat disjointed impressions. "It was the tonic," I said. "I'm sure of it. She was perfectly well until then."

"You think her tonic was drugged? What kind of drug?"

I thought back, trying to remember the details as accurately as possible. "Opium, perhaps. No, her pupils were dilated rather than contracted like an opium-eater's. In any case, she was having hallucinations. She kept talking about shadows."

Susan shook her head in disgust. "That's a nice thing, that is. Drugging an innocent old lady! Do you think it was the niece who's responsible?"

"Yes. It would explain why Miss Morton was so offensive to me—even more than she usually is. She wanted me out of there at any price. If I had stayed, I might have guessed what was going on."

Jenny came in just then, and I was obliged to repeat the whole story over to her. She listened with absorbed interest and many a shocked exclamation. "Such wickedness!" she said. "What are you going to do, ma'am?"

Now it is a fact, Dear Reader, that until that moment I had not thought of doing anything. I had been shocked and distressed by what I had witnessed at Waterloo House, but I had not felt I had any right to intervene. Jenny's words, however, with their implication of boundless confidence and simple trust, awoke something in me. "Do, ma'am?" I said, getting briskly to my feet. "Why, rescue her from that den of vipers."

I paused. I had the sense of a martial echo reverberating through my words. Jenny and Susan were both staring at me. I frowned. "This state of things cannot be allowed to continue," I said with emphasis.

"No," said Susan, in a careful voice. "But when you say you are going to rescue her, surely you don't mean you are going to do it yourself?"

"Nobody else will do it. So I must."

"But you can't break into her home and take her away in the middle of the night! That would be kidnapping."

"No, it won't," I said firmly. "She *asked* me to rescue her. And," I added with satisfaction, "there was a whole roomful of witnesses who heard her!"

"But still, if you break into her house, you are sure to get into trouble," protested Susan.

"I won't have to break in," I said. As I spoke, I had the strangest sense of certainty: of being led purposefully down a preordained path. "There are to be fireworks. All the servants will be out front, watching. I can go in through the side door. It was unlocked when I left, and chances are it still is."

"But if they catch you in the house—"

"I can say I came back to fetch my shawl."

"It might pass," agreed Susan, after a moment's thought. "But I'm still afraid you'll get yourself in difficulties."

I told her not to be a damned croaker. This seemed to temporarily deprive her of speech, and to cause her and Jenny to regard me again with strange expressions.

"How will you get Miss Emily away, ma'am?" asked Jenny.

I turned my attention to this detail. I had already dismissed my hired carriage, but in any case I did not like the idea of a strange coachman privy to what was a delicate (though not actually illegal) affair. "Not a hansom," I said. "But we will need some kind of a conveyance."

"Sam's van," said Jenny, then looked stricken.

"The very thing," I said approvingly. "Much less conspicuous than a hansom."

"Oh, but I forgot, ma'am! I forgot that I—that he—"

Kindly but firmly, I advised her not to let her personal feelings enter into the matter. "Miss Emily's life hangs in the balance. We must try to save her. The question is whether Sam would lend himself to such an enterprise?"

Jenny nodded at once, resolutely. "He will, if I ask him. And if I tell him it's for you. I've told him some of what you've done for me, ma'am—not all, but some. He thinks you're a regular right one. We both do."

"Then run around this minute and fetch him," I told her. "We haven't a moment to lose. We must get there before the fireworks are over."

"Yes, sir," said Jenny, and then paused, looking disconcerted. "I mean ma'am."

Waving this aside, I emphasized once more the need for haste. Susan, with unaccountable levity, told her she had better follow orders, and that it would probably mean a court-martial if she disobeyed.

This frivolous utterance had the effect of drawing my attention back to Susan. I told her sternly that Miss Emily would need a doctor when we returned and that her job would be to fetch one. "Not a Harley Street quack like Sir Stanley. We need someone competent—and someone discreet. You'd better go ask Felicity. I daresay she knows someone suitable."

"Yes, sir," said Susan cheerfully, and departed on this errand. I ran upstairs to change my taffeta dress for simpler attire and was ready by the time Sam and Jenny returned with the milk van.

CHAPTER 12

Waterloo House, with its grounds and gardens, comprised one whole side of a city square. Like most London squares, it had a park area surrounded by railings as its central feature. This park was where the fireworks were to be set off, and the first rockets were already exploding overhead as we approached from the side street. I had Sam draw up near the house's side entrance. Stepping down, I drew the hood of my cloak over my head, unlatched the gate, and entered the side yard.

As I anticipated, I met no one. All the servants were out front watching the fireworks. The side door was still unlocked. As swiftly and noiselessly as possible, I made my way to Miss Emily's room. Her door was locked, but the key was on the outside. I turned it and opened the door, calling softly, "Miss Emily?"

"Yes," came her voice at once. It was so dark that I could not see her, and it took a moment for my eyes to adjust. When they did, I could just make out a small figure huddled in the corner near the washstand.

Under the circumstances, perhaps it was not surprising they had not trusted her with a light. But to see her huddled in the dark that way, like a lost child, set me aflame with indignation. I came over and extended my hand to her, speaking as gently as I could so as not to frighten her.

"You must come with me, Miss Emily. It is not safe for you here."

"No," she agreed obediently.

"I am going to take you somewhere safe."

She put her hand in mine at once. "Yes, your Grace," she whispered.

Clearly she was still having hallucinations. Thankfully, they did not seem to be frightening ones. Hoping devoutly that this state of affairs might continue, I helped her to her feet and drew her close to me, putting my arm around her for support and drawing my cloak over her shoulders.

In this way, I got her out of the room and halfway down the hall without too much trouble. But just as I was congratulating myself that my mission was as good as accomplished, a woman's sturdy figure suddenly stepped out of the gloom and stood barring our path.

It was Hilda.

For a moment, Hilda and I looked at each other. My brain was busily considering plans of action. I had just decided that my best option was to lie and hope she was simple enough to believe me, when she leaned forward and addressed me in an urgent whisper. "You must hurry," she said. "You must take her away from here."

"Yes," I agreed, staring at her with amazement.

"Should I come with you? She is used to me. If I can be of service, I will come."

I thought this over as rapidly as possible, conscious that time was pressing. "No, I think you'd better stay here, Hilda. They will blame you for her disappearance if you disappear, too. Besides, if you stay, you can keep us apprised of what happens when they discover she's gone."

She nodded. "I will stay, then. But tomorrow you will let me come see her? She will need clothing and other things. I can bring them."

"Yes," I said, astounded to find such unexpected depths in a woman I had always imagined insensible. "If you can do so safely, that would be very helpful. But don't come near us if they seem to suspect you. We can manage without the clothing."

She nodded, and went ahead of us to open the side door. "Wait here," she whispered. "I will see that all is safe."

She returned presently to say it was. "Gott bless you," she added, looking from me to Miss Emily, "Gott bless you all."

"Thank you, Hilda," I said with gratitude, then hurried Miss Emily across the side yard and toward the waiting van.

It would have been a trick getting Miss Emily into the milk van by myself. The cargo area was high off the ground—almost as high as she was tall. With Sam and Jenny to help, however, there was not the least difficulty. I scrambled in first; Sam scooped Miss Emily into his arms as if she were a child, and Jenny, inside the van, reached out and drew her in. "Don't be alarmed," I told her. "These are friends."

She smiled wanly. "Yes, your Grace."

I was relieved by her docility. If she had begun to scream or cry, I might have been obliged to gag her. Happily, she fell into a doze on the way home and did not wake even when we arrived at the Temple. We were able to smuggle her inside, wrapped in my cloak, in a manner entirely inconspicuous.

Once inside, with her laid carefully on the Sitting Room sofa, I thrust out my hand to Sam. "Thank you," I said. "I am greatly obliged to you. *We* are greatly obliged to you."

He shook my hand in the careful manner of a man who seldom practices the social niceties. "Glad to be of service, ma'am," he told me. With a glance at Miss Emily's still figure, he added, "Will she be all right?"

"I hope so. We have a doctor coming."

"That's good," he said.

As he spoke, his eyes slid toward Jenny rather wistfully. She gave him no encouragement to linger, however, so after saying a couple of times that he would be glad to oblige if we needed anything else, he took himself off.

Susan arrived soon after, in company with the doctor Felicity had recommended. Rather to my surprise, the doctor was an American— and female. She was a spare young woman with short-cropped hair and an utterly no-nonsense manner. Although it developed that gynæcological matters were her specialty, she admitted to having some acquaintance with drugging as well. After examining Miss Emily, she gave it as her opinion that she had been administered datura, perhaps in combination with some kind of sedative.

"Jimsonweed, we call it in the States. That'd account for most of the symptoms you describe. But I wonder how she came by it. You don't see much of it in this country. Has she any Indian connections? It's pretty common in India, by all accounts."

Thinking of the deceased Arthur Wellesley Morton, I said there was an Indian connection, though I wasn't sure how it fit in. The doctor accepted this without question, merely advising us to watch Miss Emily closely until the drug wore off, and to call her if any more alarming symptoms developed. She then accepted her fee (which she stipulated for being in cash) and left, without our ever learning her name.

By the next morning, Miss Emily was more or less herself again. She moved and spoke languidly, but as the day wore on she improved. By dinnertime she was almost fully recovered. I guessed this to be the usual pattern, assuming she had been taking the drugged tonic after her evening meal.

Although I was eager to question her now that she was rational, I had a séance scheduled that evening. You will understand, Dear Reader, that to have Miss Emily wandering about the house at such a time would be inconvenient for more reasons than one. Before I was obliged to make Jenny her jailer, however, Hilda appeared with a valise full of clothing. So I deputed her to keep Miss Emily upstairs in my bedroom while Susan and I were busy in the Spirit Parlour.

As soon as I had seen my clients off the premises, I summoned everyone to a meeting in the Sitting Room.

Susan and Jenny were already there when Hilda appeared, leading Miss Emily by the hand. "Please sit down," I invited them both. "I know it is late and Hilda must leave soon, but I must speak to you both first."

Miss Emily, looking appealingly sweet in a lacy cap and shawl, seated herself on the sofa and fixed her eyes on me. Hilda, sitting beside her, merely looked stupid, but I wasn't fooled by that any longer. I addressed her first.

"Hilda, what happened at Waterloo House this morning when they discovered Miss Emily was missing?"

She shook her head. "Nothing," she said. "Nothing happened."

"Nothing?" I repeated incredulously. "But there must have been some outcry at finding Miss Emily gone?"

"No," said Hilda, shaking her head again. "Miss Morton told the servants her aunt had had a bad night and was not able to leave her room."

This was the last thing I had expected, Dear Reader. I could not imagine why Miss Morton would conceal her aunt's disappearance. "Surely that will not answer for long," I said. "Won't the servants guess Miss Emily isn't there?"

"No," said Hilda. "Miss Morton said her aunt was too unwell to see anyone but her. She has kept her bedroom door locked, and she takes her meals in herself."

"And does no one think this odd?"

Hilda shrugged. "The servants do not like it. But they do not like Miss Morton anyway. I do not think they suspect anything, except that she is above herself and perhaps keeping her aunt in subjection as she is wont to do."

Glancing at Miss Emily, I surprised an anguished look on her face. "Miss Emily," I said, "I don't know how much you remember from last night, but after we brought you here, I called in a doctor to look at you. And it seems you were drugged."

Her lips made a soundless "oh," but she did not speak. Hilda squeezed her arm encouragingly.

"I think probably the drug was in your iron tonic," I went on. "And I think that you have been taking it for some time without realizing it. That is why you have been having sinking spells, and why your mind isn't always clear."

Her eyes filled with tears, but still she did not speak. Hilda, clucking her tongue, got out her handkerchief and would have wiped away the tears as if she had been a child, but Miss Emily shook her head, took the handkerchief, and did it herself.

"Do you know who is doing this to you?" I asked.

She opened her mouth, shut it again, then looked at Hilda. Hilda seemed to understand the unspoken appeal. "Miss Morton," she said with a nod. "Assuredly it is Miss Morton. It is of a piece with her behaviour. You must know she has a great wish to rule the household. It would suit her well if her aunt were incapable."

"Do you think Lady Frost played a rôle as well?" I asked. This was an idea that had occurred to me in the night, Dear Reader. Lady

Frost had seemed to side with her sister in keeping Miss Emily down, though admittedly not in much else.

Hilda shook her head decisively. "No," she said. "I cannot see it. She and her sister detest each other."

"And you, Miss Emily?" I asked. "Do you think Lady Frost might have had a hand in drugging you, or do you think it was only Miss Morton?"

"I do not know," said Miss Emily, in a very low voice. "Indeed, I cannot believe either of them would do such a thing. Why, I have known Honoria and Catherine since they were children."

"They were vicious children," said Hilda bluntly. "Always."

"Not *vicious*, Hilda," pleaded Miss Emily. "*Difficult*, perhaps. But you must know the circumstances of their upbringing were less than ideal." Turning to me, she explained, "Sir Oliver, their father, died when they were both little more than babies. And my sister married late—she was well along in years when they were born. It must have seemed staid and dull to them, poor things, growing up in a house with only a couple of old ladies for company."

"They had their brother, surely?"

Miss Emily shook her head. "Arthur was quite a bit older," she said, in the sad voice she always used when speaking of her nephew. "He was born within a year of my sister's marriage. The girls were born almost a decade later. Arthur was already at school when Honoria was born."

This was interesting, Dear Reader, but I did not see that growing up without a father or brother entitled Honoria Morton to poison her aunt—and I said so. "Miss Emily, you cannot let this go on," I told her. "What your niece has been doing is criminal. Drugged like that, you might have done yourself an injury and died. People do sometimes."

She shook her head. "No," she whispered. "No."

I took this more as an expression of disbelief than of objection to my words. "I think you should tell the police," I continued.

"No," she said, and her voice was stronger now. "No, I can't do that."

I had been afraid she would object to bringing the police into it. Indeed, I could hardly blame her. Even now, it is not easy for me to overcome my own prejudice against police involvement. "Then you must make Miss Morton leave Waterloo House," I said. "At least you can do that. Obviously, she can't be allowed to stay after this."

"No," said Miss Emily.

I mistook this for capitulation. "Then you will send her away?"

"No," she said, hanging her head and speaking in a voice barely above a whisper. "I can't do that either."

I looked at her, then at Jenny and Susan. They both looked as nonplussed as I felt. "In God's name, why not?" I demanded.

She embarked on a disjointed explanation, saying that it would make a great scandal, and that she could not bear the shame, and that she would rather die.

"But if you let your niece stay, she will very likely go on drugging you. And then you might indeed die!"

Tears were coursing down Miss Emily's cheeks. "If Heaven wills it, I must bear it," she said, speaking with an effort. "I daresay it is no more than I deserve." Wiping her eyes with the handkerchief, she added, "If only Arthur had lived! Oh, I am sure it would have been different then. But as it is, there is no help for it."

This speech irritated me so much that I could hardly forbear shaking her. "I don't think you should confound Heaven's will with that of your odious niece," I retorted. "And whatever your nephew might or might not have done, he is not in a position to help you now. You must help yourself, ma'am. For heaven's sake, do you *want* to be poisoned?"

She shook her head mutely, with a fresh burst of tears. I looked at Hilda, seeking enlightenment. She merely shrugged.

"Well," I said, "I'm not going to sit tamely by and see you poisoned, Miss Emily. I don't believe you've given this matter enough thought. Perhaps you ought to stay here a few more days and see if you don't change your mind."

"Oh, *may* I?" she asked, her tears changing to smiles in an instant.

Apparently her instincts of self-preservation were not entirely absent, Dear Reader. It was clear she did not want to return to Waterloo House. Yet she seemed stubbornly opposed to sending away the niece who was imperiling her existence there. I exchanged mystified looks with Susan and Jenny, and later, after Hilda had gone home and Miss Emily was safely in bed, the three of us discussed the matter.

"I can see that she wouldn't want a scandal," said Susan. "Her sort don't. That would explain her not wanting to call in the police. But for the life of me, I don't see why she can't send the niece away, quiet-like. All she'd have to do is tell her she knows she's been drugging her tonic. Ten to one, the niece would take *herself* off after that, and pretty quickly, too!"

We all agreed this was the heart of the mystery. "Though to my mind, Miss Morton's behaviour is even more mysterious than Miss Emily's," I said. "Why the devil is she trying to conceal the fact that her aunt has disappeared? It doesn't make sense. For all she knows, Miss Emily might be dead. She could have drowned in the Serpentine, or been run over by a cab, or had some other accident very easily while her mind was befogged."

"Yes, and it'd look pretty bad for the niece if her aunt's body turned up, when she's been pretending to take care of her," said Jenny shrewdly.

"For some reason or other, she must be fairly sure her aunt's not dead," I agreed. "But then why wouldn't she tell the servants that

Miss Emily has disappeared? The natural assumption would be that she wandered off during one of her spells. And that would fit in very well with the idea that Miss Emily is senile and incapable and needs Miss Morton to run her household for her."

"It would," agreed Jenny.

"Then why isn't Miss Morton taking advantage of the situation? There must be more to this matter than appears on the surface."

We looked at one another. "Hidden Knowledge," suggested Susan with a grin. "'Hidden Knowledge will emerge.'"

"I hope it emerges sooner rather than later," I said.

Discuss it as we would, we could make nothing of this mystery. Nothing happened during the next couple of days to make it any clearer. I searched the newspapers in vain for any mention of Miss Emily's disappearance. Apparently, Miss Morton was still keeping it a secret. Finally, after much inner argument, I ventured to call at Waterloo House and make a few inquiries in person.

Of course, to call on one's hostess after a party (however abortive) is proper anyway. But I had an even better excuse in the form of my shawl. I had been reluctant to claim it initially, feeling it might look suspicious for me to revisit the scene of my crime; then it had occurred to me that it might look even more suspicious if I didn't. After all, a woman in my station of life does not typically abandon a twenty-guinea shawl without making a push to recover it.

I did get my shawl back, but I didn't get much else. Miss Morton was not At Home to me. She was too busy caring for her ailing aunt to receive visitors, according to the butler. "Is Miss Emily very unwell?" I asked him.

"I am afraid so, Madame," he said regretfully. "Since the Waterloo Dinner, she has been unable to leave her room. And she scarcely eats a thing—not enough to keep a bird alive, Cook says."

I thought this very inartistic of Miss Morton. She ought to have made sure Miss Emily's trays went back to the kitchen with enough eaten to look natural, even if it meant choking down a second dinner. Unless—and it was a sinister thought—unless she was wanting to suggest Miss Emily was at death's door. But what would she do when it came time to deliver the body?

These thoughts, and others like them, kept Susan, Jenny, and I in a state of suspense as the week wore to a close. Suspense was not the only thing we had to try us. Although I did not regret my impulsive action in rescuing Miss Emily, I did find myself wishing now and then that I had given more thought to the consequences.

Having her resident in my place of business required some major adjustments for us all. When the daily women arrived to do the heavy cleaning, she had to be kept out of sight. When I met with the agents who bring me confidential information about my clients, she had to be kept out of sight. When I was holding séances, she had not only to be kept out of sight, but to be kept as far distant from the Spirit Parlour as possible, lest she see or hear something that might destroy her faith in my abilities as a Medium.

What was more, she could not be depended on to stay out of sight by herself. She had lived so long as mistress of her own household that she was quite oblivious to the differing requirements of mine. Someone had to stay with her all the time, lest she come fluttering heedlessly into a room where some confidential matter was being discussed. Thankfully, Hilda was of help here. She seemed able to come and go from Waterloo House without anyone paying heed, and she took to spending evenings with us—the time when we most needed help with Miss Emily.

Still, this could only be a temporary solution. Miss Emily had been a good client for nearly a decade, and she had also paid me in advance for the séance on Waterloo Night. Thus, I reckoned I owed her a debt. But I felt strongly that the best way I could repay that debt was to make it possible for her to return to her own home, and this she could not do so long as Miss Morton remained there.

So far I had had no luck convincing her that she must get rid of her niece. Her objections were vague but apparently insuperable. I made up my mind that if I had not convinced her by Sunday afternoon, I would take Inspector Harper into my confidence. I did not care to tell him I had been high-handed enough to remove Miss Emily from her home, but I could at least disclose my suspicions about Miss Morton and the datura. Perhaps he would have an idea how to proceed.

## CHAPTER 13

It was a relief when Sunday finally arrived. Not only did I expect to see Inspector Harper that afternoon, I was also scheduled to meet Felicity to make a second search of Captain Ingram's rooms.

I was glad to turn my attention to the captain, even despite the problem he represented. Earlier, I had embraced Miss Emily's problems as a distraction from my own, but now hers were assuming such a serious aspect that the prospect of blackmail (for me) and an injudicious marriage (for Miss Waring) appeared light matters in comparison.

Sunday morning, I put on the same brown church-going costume I had worn the previous week, supplemented with a heavier veil. There was no point in donning servant's garb like Felicity. John would recognize me if he saw my face; therefore, it was essential that he not see it.

Happily, he did not. Felicity and I spent more than three hours in his room, prodding the mattress and cushions with a hatpin, inspecting the floor for loose boards, removing the pictures from the walls, and otherwise subjecting the place to the closest examination. But we found nothing—or rather, nothing we had not found on our previous visit. The letters from Miss Waring and the unknown Miss Tate were still in the table drawer; the pornographic pictures were still concealed between the pages of an innocuous novel.

Still, it was not a wasted trip. I was relieved to find, after a thorough search of John's possessions, that he had no letters or photographs or other evidence to identify me as the former Mrs. Erasmus Brooke. This was an undoubted positive. On the negative side, I also found none of the keepsakes like my mother's wedding ring and my father's watch that he had stolen years before and I had been hoping against hope to recover. No doubt he had sold them long ago, before he ever left the States.

Having gone carefully through his papers, I spent some time scrutinizing his army photograph, hoping to detect it as a fraud. I had brought a magnifying glass with me to inspect it more closely. Alas, even without the glass I could see it was no fraud. Now that I knew the figure on the far left was John, there was no mistaking him. The wonder was that I had not recognized him before, even with the mustachios to disguise him.

"Damn it," I said aloud. "I felt sure he was lying about that. He made such a point of telling me that his army career was genuine. It struck me afterward that it might be a case of protesting too much. But that is he, all right." Morosely, I gazed at the little mustachioed figure, standing beside the rows of uniformed men and flanked by a pair of natives with spears and shields.

Felicity did not reply. She had been flipping through the pornographic pictures again. "Here's a thing," she said. "Come and look at this, my dear."

Glad to abandon my unprofitable study, I came over to see what she had found. She had gathered a few of the pictures into her hand. "Look," she said, fanning them out. "What do you make of this?"

The photographs were all the same: a plump brunette with a coy smile, her legs widespread and her drawers unaccountably missing. "Duplicates?" I said with interest.

"I didn't notice it last time, we were in such a hurry. But I think there are some more." We went through the stack together and found duplicate copies of several of the pictures. What was more, we also discovered that the same women appeared in all the photographs: the plump brunette, a lanky girl with fair hair, and a little swarthy one with pop-eyes and a rosebud mouth.

"What do you make of that?" said Felicity with relish.

I was not sure what to make of it. "I suppose a man might conceivably want duplicates of his favourites," I said doubtfully. "But it seems a little odd."

Felicity nodded. "If you were to ask *me*, I'd say he's selling them," she said.

I saw at once that she must be right. "Of course. He probably takes them around to the clubs. Allowing other men just a peek, with an offer to sell them for a consideration. It would help eke out his income from gambling."

"Anything doing?" said Felicity hopefully.

She meant, by this, to ask whether the vending of pornographic pictures would be enough to make Miss Waring jilt him. I shook my head regretfully. "I don't believe so. We can't prove that he's selling them. We can't even prove they are his. I don't think Miss Waring would believe him capable of doing such a thing without more proof than we have here."

Unfortunately, there did not seem to be any more proof to find. Since Esther, the maid, had already poked her head in once or twice to warn us that her mistress was due to return very soon, I told Felicity that we might as well go. I took one last, long look at the army photograph before I left, hoping to see something I had missed. By this time, I felt I could have drawn the whole thing from memory.

There was nothing new to be seen in it, of course. But I knew a momentary impulse to take it away with me. This impulse I suppressed, for the captain would certainly notice its absence, which might rebound upon our ally Esther. I did not want to get her in trouble, because we might want to come back another time. Over the course of my career, I have learned that it pays not to burn one's bridges behind one.

⸙

We had taken so long going through the captain's things that it was late in the afternoon by the time I arrived back at the Temple. As I came through the side door, Susan met me with the news that Inspector Harper was waiting for me in the Sitting Room.

"I'm glad he waited," I said, pulling off my veil and bonnet. "I'll just run up and change my clothes before I see him."

"He *insisted* on waiting," said Susan. "He and the other policeman."

This brought me up short. "He brought another policeman with him?"

"Yes," said Susan. "*And* the Inspector looks upset-like."

We looked at each other. "Miss Emily?" I whispered.

"I'm afraid so," she whispered back. "Jenny has her in the kitchen. We've been taking turns watching her, as Hilda hasn't got here yet. Mercy, I hope she won't come while the police are here!"

With this awful prospect to drive me, I made short work of changing my clothing, Dear Reader. When I walked into the Sitting Room, however, it was with a smiling face and unruffled brow. "My dear Inspector Harper! I do apologize for keeping you waiting."

He rose from the sofa, and I could see at once that Susan was right. His face was grimly set and his eyes more than usually searching as he looked me over. "I was obliged to wait," he said. "Smith and I need to talk to you, in an official capacity."

This was the natural moment for my eyes to flicker to the other policeman. He was a uniformed officer, middle-aged, with a red, truculent face. I did not much like his looks, but I smiled at him as I said, "Oh, I beg your pardon! I did not realize you had a companion."

"Sergeant Smith," said the Inspector shortly. "Sergeant, this is Madame Fox."

We nodded to each other, and I bade them both sit down, disposing myself on a chair that faced them both. "How may I help you, Inspector?"

"It's about this business at Waterloo House," he said. "Things have taken an unexpected turn."

I looked concerned. "I hope nothing has happened to Miss Emily?"

"Miss Emily has disappeared," he said.

I made shocked noises. "Disappeared?"

"Yes," he said grimly. "Very mysteriously. What's more, we have reason to believe the allegations in those anonymous letters were true."

I thought this was the moment to put in my own contribution. "Ah, yes: about those allegations, Inspector. You know I was there for the Waterloo Dinner—"

"I do know," he interrupted. "I want to know everything that happened that night."

"Be sure I will tell you," I said soothingly. He was rather spoiling my story, making me broach the subject flatly, without a suspenseful build-up. Still, I did my best. "There were several circumstances that struck me that evening," I told him. "Rather *sinister* circumstances. What with one thing and another, I now strongly suspect that Miss Emily's niece, Miss Morton, may be poisoning her aunt."

Both the Inspector and Sergeant Smith looked at me—strangely, I thought. "You suspect that, do you?" said the Inspector.

"I'm almost sure of it."

"Then would it surprise you to hear that Miss Morton has herself been poisoned?"

You may believe it surprised me, Dear Reader. In fact, it surprised me into indiscretion "Poisoned with datura?" I exclaimed.

The Inspector gave me a long look. "With arsenic," he said. After a pause, he added, "She died this morning."

I could only stare at him.

"I think you'd better explain," he said.

At this point, I hardly knew where to begin. Sergeant Smith, however, suggested helpfully that I start by describing the events of the Waterloo Dinner. "We know you was there, ma'am," he said. "And that you had words with the deceased."

To hear Miss Morton described as "the deceased" did nothing to put me at my ease. Neither did the recollection that she and I had exchanged words, thus giving me a possible motive for her murder. Still, I composed myself as well as I could and gave an account of my evening at Waterloo House that avoided all the more obvious pitfalls. I was careful to underplay my observations in regard to Miss Emily. I said that the spell she had suffered had distressed me so much that it was not until long afterwards that it had occurred to me to connect it with her tonic.

"I had decided to tell you about it today and see what you thought," I told Inspector Harper with wide-eyed sincerity.

"I wish to God you had told me about it earlier," he snapped.

I was stung by his reproach. "I doubt it would have helped," I retorted. "I thought Miss Emily was being drugged by Miss Morton with datura or something like it. Now it seems she was being poisoned with arsenic, and that it wasn't Miss Morton at all."

The Inspector was frowning. "We *think* it was arsenic," he said. "It will need looking into, but there doesn't seem much doubt. You thought the tonic was to blame?"

I described again the scene in Miss Emily's bedroom: how she had swallowed a dose of the tonic, saying she took it every night after dinner. "She said it was very nasty-tasting. She had a sweet afterwards, to take the flavour out of her mouth."

"A sweet," he repeated.

He looked at Sergeant Smith, who nodded. "That's it," he said. "I'll bet anything you like."

"The sweets were poisoned?" I said.

The Inspector exchanged another look with Sergeant Smith before replying. "It may be," he said guardedly. "The servants confirm what you say, about Miss Emily keeping sweets in her room. They came in boxes, which she kept there near her washstand. She had usually two boxes at any given time: one open, with a new box to replace it when the first was gone. She didn't go through them very fast—about a box a month, which would equate to one sweet a day, more or less."

I nodded to show my comprehension.

"But both boxes were empty when we found them. It looks as though Miss Morton had eaten them all in one go. If the servants are telling the truth, she didn't eat or drink anything else yesterday that could have poisoned her."

"I looked into all that thoroughly," broke in Sergeant Smith, with a self-important air. "There was nothing sent to the dining room that wasn't eaten in the servant's hall, one way or another."

"The presumption is that Miss Morton ate or drank something the others didn't," continued Inspector Harper. "When we found the empty sweet boxes, there where she had been staying in her aunt's room, it seemed logical to suspect she ingested the poison that way."

"Good God," I said. An even more shocking thought occurred to me. "I ate one of those sweets myself!"

They both stared at me. "Only I didn't," I recollected. "I spat it out in my handkerchief. And it was the last one in the box. I remember that, because I saw the new box there, too. I remember thinking that she would have to open it next time."

The Inspector was scribbling away in his notebook. "That's very helpful," he said. "So Miss Emily ate one, and you took one, but didn't eat it? And those two sweets accounted for the contents of one box?"

"Yes," I said.

"And you say Miss Emily became unwell afterwards—as if she had been poisoned?"

I hesitated. "More as if she had been drugged," I said. "I wouldn't say poisoned, *per se*, though I suppose it's a matter of degree."

Sergeant Smith shot me a look of suspicion—or perhaps he was merely puzzled by the Latin. The Inspector, however, leaned forward intently. "You don't think it was arsenic?"

"I don't know," I said, and explained that the little I knew about arsenic poisoning had been gleaned from the sensationalist press, hardly a reliable guide. "What symptoms does arsenic produce?"

"In small doses, it doesn't cause any symptoms at all. In fact, some people take it as a tonic or a beauty aid. It's supposed to improve the condition of the hair and skin among other things. You've probably seen arsenic complexion wafers."

I had seen them, Dear Reader, though I had never been tempted to try them. For a woman of my age, my complexion is in excellent condition, probably as a result of having spent so much of my life in darkened rooms.

"If you take the stuff regularly, you can build up a tolerance," continued the Inspector. "You can take larger and larger doses, until eventually you can swallow a fatal dose with no ill effects.[11] Without

---

11  Inspector Harper is voicing a belief common in his day (c. 1882), but medical opinion in the present day considers arsenic unhealthy in any quantity, both in the short term and the long. Although it is easy to jeer at Victorian notions of health and beauty, historical probability suggests that our descendants will jeer quite as much at our own. —*Ed.*

a tolerance, however, arsenic in large doses causes gastric problems—vomiting and so forth. And convulsions. And of course, it can result in death, if the dose is large enough."

"Well, I didn't see that Miss Emily was suffering any gastric problems," I said. "Just hallucinations and weakness."

"You said she only ate the one sweet, though," pointed out Sergeant Smith.

"Yes, only one," I agreed.

"One mightn't have been enough to cause the other symptoms," he said. Again he exchanged looks with the Inspector.

"Perhaps the other symptoms developed later?" suggested the Inspector. "But then you wouldn't have been in a position to know, would you, Madame Fox? For you left immediately after and didn't see Miss Emily again."

I was beginning to feel very uneasy, Dear Reader. I did not like to lie, but it was hard to know how much trouble confession might get me into at this point. "I did leave, though I didn't like to," I said carefully. "But Miss Morton said she would do all that was necessary for her aunt."

"And she did, too, by all accounts," said Sergeant Smith, shaking his head. "All that was necessary and then some. Keeping the old lady shut up alone in her room, and not letting anyone else see her."

The two men exchanged looks again. "I wonder," said the Inspector. "But where would she get arsenic?"

"Complexion wafers, like you said. You can buy 'em at any druggist's."

I looked from one to the other. "Are you talking about *Miss Emily?*" I demanded.

"Everyone says she's wonderful young-looking for her age," continued Sergeant Smith, disregarding me. "If she'd been taking the stuff right along, that'd explain it."

"That would mean she had been planning this for some time."

"Well, she'd got a motive. From what the servants say, the niece was riding the old girl rough-shod from the time she moved in."

"But then why has she disappeared?" said Inspector Harper. "If she took the trouble to dose herself with arsenic beforehand, it can only have been because she was planning to poison her niece with some food or drink they would share. She'd have an immunity to the arsenic and live; her niece wouldn't, and she would die. Why, then, would she run as soon as her niece ate the poisoned sweets and died?"

"Because the niece ate the whole box," said the sergeant triumphantly. "She wasn't supposed to. She was supposed to eat one or two at a time—get sick—recover—and then eat a few more. After a while, everyone'd say the niece had a sensitive stomach, or some such thing. And then, when she finally died of it, it wouldn't look suspicious."

"Yes," said the Inspector, considering this with a judicial air. "It could be."

"It could *not* be," I said, finding my tongue at last. "Miss Emily Randall is not a cold-blooded murderess!"

The Inspector considered my statement dispassionately, then shook his head. "You can't know that," he said. "From what you yourself have told us, she had a motive for murdering her niece. And where is she, if she is innocent?"

"She may have been poisoned, too," I shot back.

The Inspector shook his head again. "Doubtful," he said. "Quite a lot of her clothing is missing."

He let me think about that for a moment. You can believe I *was* thinking, Dear Reader: thinking desperately how to escape the web of deceit I was now tangled in. Miss Emily's missing clothing was upstairs right now in my own bedroom, and she herself was down in my kitchen. "But what does it prove that Miss Emily's clothing is missing?" I argued. "She still might have been poisoned."

The Inspector responded to this kindly enough, but I had the sense I had disappointed him. "All the signs point to her having left the house voluntarily," he explained. "Besides her clothing being gone, none of the servants heard any outcry during the night, or saw anything suspicious. And you know what a household that is. You can't walk ten paces without bumping into a servant."

"Yes," I said, because I couldn't think of anything else to say.

"It seems to me unlikely in the extreme that any outside person would have known how to contrive such an inconspicuous escape," he continued. "Mind you, we may yet discover that some or all of the servants know more than they're telling. It's evident that they disliked Miss Morton intensely, and that their sympathies were all with Miss Emily."

I could only nod, thinking how bad all this looked for Miss Emily. The Inspector, seeing my expression, sought to reassure me. "Although it looks suspicious, you must know we are not seeking to arrest Miss Emily," he said. "Certainly not without more evidence than we possess. But we do need to question her, to determine exactly what happened last night. At present, we are questioning her friends and relatives, hoping to gain more information about where she might be. That is why I am here, for you may be counted one of her friends, I think. She hasn't tried to communicate with you in the last twenty-four hours?"

"Not through Earthly Channels," I told him, looking as sincere and soulful as I could. "Do you want me to consult the Spiritograph?"

This might have been overplaying my hand a little, Dear Reader. The Inspector shot me a suspicious look, but finally said that wasn't necessary. "I do trust Miss Emily is still in the land of the living, Madame Fox," he said. "Just keep your eyes and ears open."

## CHAPTER 14

After the police had gone, I waited hardly an instant before summoning Susan. To my relief, she had taken the sensible precaution and eavesdropped on the whole conversation. I had no need to explain what a pickle we were in. She mentioned it herself, several times, until I was obliged to tell her she wasn't being helpful.

"I know we are in a pickle. The question is, what's to be done about it?"

Susan merely shook her head and said Miss Emily was a deep one. "Do you think she did it?" she asked. "Do you think she poisoned her niece?"

I started to say "certainly not," then hesitated. "God knows she had a motive," I said. "She had even more of a motive than the police realize."

"And the niece is actually *dead*," marveled Susan. "That's a twist and no mistake. I'd say good riddance, except if they think Miss Emily did it—"

"I can't believe she did, Susan. Putting arsenic in her own sweets, in some convoluted plot to get Miss Morton to share them? I simply can't see it. Miss Emily's not a murderess. There's more to this than we know."

"Hidden Knowledge," said Susan portentously.

"Yes, damn it. Let me think." My instinct was to protect Miss Emily, even to the extent of keeping her niece's murder a secret from her, but Susan pointed out very logically that she had borne up under the knowledge that she herself was being poisoned. This was knowledge she needed still more.

"It's a case of murder now, not just drugging," said Susan. "Whether she's responsible or not, she has to know. It might make her more willing to tell us what's been troubling her."

That seemed reasonable, so I called everyone into the Sitting Room again and broke the news to Miss Emily that her niece was no longer inhabiting our Earthly Sphere. I would have liked to wait until Hilda was there to support her, but we couldn't be sure Hilda would be coming that evening—or ever again, for that matter. Now that Waterloo House was the scene of a murder, her comings and goings would probably be scrutinized much more closely, and she was quite intelligent enough to know it.

In the event, Miss Emily took the news quietly enough. Her eyes opened wide, and she gasped, "Dead? Oh, no, no! No, I cannot believe it. Honoria is dead?"

"Yes, I'm afraid so, ma'am. The police think she has been poisoned." I let that sink in for a moment, then added, "They think she was poisoned eating the sweets in your bedroom."

"The sweets in my bedroom?" repeated Miss Emily, looking bewildered. "But how—*why?*" With increasing bewilderment, she added, "Did you not say it was my *tonic* that was poisoned?"

"Yes, that's what I thought. And I still think so. You appeared to have been dosed with something like datura. The police seem pretty sure that Miss Morton was poisoned with arsenic."

"Arsenic," she repeated blankly. "Arsenic."

I could have sworn she was as puzzled as I was. Yet I could not help being affected to some degree by Inspector Harper's suspicions.

"My theory is that the datura was in the tonic," I said, watching her closely. "And the arsenic was in the sweets. The sweets you take *after* the tonic, to take away the taste."

"Oh," said Miss Emily. And then she said, "Oh," in quite a different voice and jumped as though someone had poked her with a pin.

"What?" I said urgently. "What is it?"

Her expression was still bewildered, but there was a look of dawning comprehension on her face as she turned to answer me. "That is why," she said. "I saw her, that evening."

"Saw her? Saw who? What evening? Who'd you see?" The three of us pelted her with questions. Miss Emily opened her mouth to answer, then shut it again.

"No," she said heavily. "No, it's no use. I see it now, but it doesn't matter."

And to our very great frustration, she would say no more than this. When pressed, she dissolved into tears and gave the same kind of disjointed speech she had given before about not being able to bear the shame and not wanting to cause a scandal.

I pointed out that murder was, by itself, a pretty scandalous proceeding. She acknowledged it, but in a distracted manner. "Poor Honoria! I don't know what to do. It's all too dreadful—too shocking."

"The police want to talk to you," I said.

She considered this with a bewildered air. "Yes? But I can't tell them anything—not about this."

"Can't or won't?" I asked.

She evaded this question with a shake of her head. "I have been very wrong, very culpable," she said. "Oh, whatever shall I do?"

"Tell the police. Tell them the truth," I urged. "If you are innocent, you have nothing to fear."

Susan snorted at these words, and I saw Jenny roll her eyes. Indeed, I tend to doubt myself that innocence provides much of a safeguard against police suspicion. But my words were wasted in any case, for Miss Emily merely shook her head again and said, "But I am not innocent. Not in the least. And I am a coward besides." With a fresh burst of tears, she added, "If the police wish to punish me for this crime, I shall have to bear it."

And that was that, as I told the others later. Misguided goose she might be, but I was willing to stake my life that she was not a murderess. For now, at least, I felt obliged to protect her from herself.

"You're not going to be able to do it forever," Susan pointed out. "Keeping her here is like sitting on a volcano that might explode any minute."

"Yes, I do realize that, Susan. But the police are surely investigating other people besides Miss Emily. Perhaps they will find out who really did put arsenic in those sweets, and then it will be safe for her to reappear."

"*If* they find out," said Susan, looking skeptical.

"As to that, I have been thinking," I said. "It's pretty certain someone knows the truth. Remember those anonymous letters?"

"But the police never found out who wrote them, did they?" asked Jenny.

"No," I admitted. "But we ought to be able to narrow it down. According to my calculations, there can only be two reasons for sending those letters, now that we know they aren't a joke. Either someone wanted to help Miss Emily, or someone wanted to hinder her would-be murderer."

"That doesn't narrow it down much," said Susan.

"It might. Because for my money, the person with the very best motive for putting arsenic in the sweets is Lady Frost."

Jenny stared at me, open-mouthed. "But if you're right about Miss Morton putting datura in her tonic, that would mean both sisters were poisoners!"

"Yes, and it would also mean that they tried to poison their aunt at the same time," added Susan. "*And* that both their methods involved their aunt's tonic. Too much of a coincidence for my taste."

"I agree it would be a coincidence, but coincidences happen all the time. Think of my visiting the same dressmaker as Lady Frost on the same afternoon. Indeed, this is less a coincidence than that, if you allow there is anything in heredity. Hilda said both sisters were vicious from childhood."

Susan hesitated. "As to that, are we sure Hilda didn't have something to do with it?" she said. "I know she's been pretty helpful with Miss Emily, but it's odd the way she took that whole business of your bringing her here without hardly blinking an eye. She's another deep one if you ask me."

I admitted that Hilda was a deep one and that it would not hurt to keep an open mind on the subject. "But I can't see that she has a motive, and Lady Frost most certainly has. What's more, Miss Emily's reluctance to speak out about whoever or whatever is behind this seems as though she is protecting someone. In the case of Miss Morton and Lady Frost, that would make sense, as they are her sister's children. She might think it was her duty to save them from the consequences of their actions, even at the risk of her life."

"What are you going to do?" asked Susan. "She doesn't seem apt to change her mind."

"It wouldn't hurt to look into things at Lady Frost's," I said. "I will ask Felicity to make a few inquiries."

"Don't you suppose the police are already doing that?"

"I hope they are. But I'm afraid that as long as Miss Emily is missing, they will focus most of their attention on her."

"You'd better hope they don't find out you've got her here," observed Susan.

"Yes," I agreed, shuddering at the idea. "But as long as they believe Miss Emily left Waterloo House last night, there shouldn't be any trail to lead them here."

"You forget Sam helped bring her away," said Susan, staring at Jenny. "What assurance have we that he won't tell the police the whole story?"

Jenny, flushing brick-red, said that Sam would never open his mouth. "I'd trust him with my life," she cried.

"But not with the truth about—"

"That's enough," I said hastily. "We must trust Sam will not give us away. Or the doctor, either," I added, as an afterthought. "But I have an idea she avoids police notice even more than we do."

I went on to say that, assuming the doctor and Sam did not give us away, there should be little to connect us with Miss Emily's disappearance. "If the police ask questions of our neighbours, they will be questions about what happened last night, not what happened on Waterloo Night. Last night was business as usual, and so they will learn if they start nosing about. They will be on the wrong track completely." I felt a pang for Inspector Harper, wasting his time on a false trail, but that could not be helped. In this case, we were adversaries and must remain that way until something happened to free Miss Emily from suspicion.

Pensively, I added, "I still wonder why Miss Morton concealed her aunt's disappearance all these days. If we knew that, I feel we would know everything."

At present, it seemed we knew nothing—or at least nothing but what Inspector Harper had told me. The newspapers were full of the story in the days that followed, but since they accepted the idea that Miss Emily had disappeared the night of Miss Morton's murder, there was no help to be gained from their theories and speculations.

I was interested to see that these theories and speculations fell into two groups. One group embraced the idea that Miss Emily might have been responsible for her niece's death, but they were definitely in the minority. She benefitted from a widespread public prejudice against the idea that a sweet old lady could be a murderess. More often she was mentioned as a likely second victim, with much dramatic speculation about her fate.

Perhaps it was merely that the idea of a double murder sold more newspapers. But I was glad to think Miss Emily was generally held innocent of wrongdoing—at least, until I recalled that the police are not above using journalists to serve their own ends. They might themselves have promoted this theory, hoping Miss Emily might be lulled out of hiding by if she believed she was not suspected of murder. As things stood, we simply couldn't take the chance.

I fretted a good deal during those days, wishing I knew whither Inspector Harper's thoughts were tending. It was not until I got around to emptying the reticule I had used the night of the Waterloo Dinner that I realized I might have a pretext for asking him. I flew down to the kitchen to display my find.

"Look," I said, holding out my hand triumphantly. "I had forgotten."

"What is it?" demanded Susan, staring at the half-eaten sweet reposing in the midst of my best handkerchief.

"It's the sweet I took that night at Miss Emily's. I had forgotten I still had it."

Jenny and Miss Emily came over to inspect my prize. "Do you think it really is poisoned?" said Jenny in a hushed voice. Miss Emily made a little inarticulate sound and gazed at the sweet as if it might leap out of my hand and bite her.

"I don't know. But I expect the police would be interested in it, don't you?"

We all agreed the police ought to be interested in it. "Will you take it down to Scotland Yard?" Susan wanted to know.

"I could. Or I could summon Inspector Harper here to give it to him."

"But Miss Emily's here!" objected Susan.

"Exactly," I said.

She was quick enough to catch the idea. "I see. A way to throw him off the scent, if he has any suspicions."

"Yes, that's what I thought. He wouldn't imagine I would ask him here if I had anything to hide. Unless—"

"Unless?" prompted Jenny.

"Unless he might guess I had something to hide simply because I *did* invite him here?"

Susan opined that this was over-thinking the matter. "You've worked together before. He knows you're a friend of Miss Emily's—"

"Yes, indeed," chirped Miss Emily, with a warm smile.

"—and it'd be natural for you to do what you could to help her. I'd say ask him here. Jenny and I'll take care Miss Emily's out of sight."

⁓⁓⁓

The Inspector arrived post-haste, less than an hour after I had sent off my message to him. I was glad to see Sergeant Smith was not with him. I felt we could very well dispense with his presence, which had had rather a dampening effect on our last interview.

Inspector Harper himself was looking a little dampened, I thought. His face had the wan look of a man who has been dispensing with regular meals and sleep. I insisted he have a cup of tea and a sandwich to recruit his energies before getting down to the (alleged) reason I had summoned him.

"Have you had any success in finding Miss Emily?" I inquired as he drank his tea.

He shot me a look. "No," he said. "It's been much like the Langley affair.[12] Every lunatic and fool in England claims to have seen her, and I've wasted I don't know how many hours following leads I know very well are false." He laughed mirthlessly. "In fact, the best evidence I've found seems to indicate she never left Waterloo House at all!"

"Indeed?" I said encouragingly.

"Indeed, yes." He shook his head. "According to the servants, it's impossible that she should have left the house that night without anyone's seeing her. The butler and the porter and the footmen and the maids and that companion of hers—between them, they've accounted for all the times and all the ways she might have left. Their stories interlock like a Chinese puzzle. *Ergo*, she didn't leave at all. But she's not there." He made an exasperated noise. "It's as if she simply vanished into thin air."

"Like a spirit," I said, much struck.

He accorded this a perfunctory smile. "Like a spirit, yes. Normally when you get a situation like that—a *reductio ad absurdum*— you keep chipping away at your witnesses and their stories. Sooner or later, you find that some of them are lying—or all of them are. But I don't see any sign of it this time. I'd swear they're all telling the truth." He shook his head wonderingly.

---

12  See *Ghost in the Machine*.

"A difficult case," I observed.

"You're right there." He gave me a weary smile. "Don't tell me you called me here just to tell me that? I was hoping you might have a lead that doesn't end in a stone wall."

"As to that, I can't say," I said cautiously. "But I have something." I produced the handkerchief, which I had enclosed in an envelope for hygiene's sake, and told him what it contained.

He was interested at once: took charge of the nasty thing with great care and promised to have it analyzed. "I may say that all the evidence does point to the arsenic being in the sweets," he said. "An examination of Miss Morton's stomach contents made it pretty clear."

"Have you analyzed the tonic as well?" I asked.

He contemplated me for a moment before shaking his head. "We didn't find any tonic," he said.

This took me aback momentarily, but I soon realized that it made perfect sense. "Of course! Miss Morton got rid of it. She was the one drugging it, so she made sure to destroy the evidence before anyone could find it."

The Inspector frowned. "When she was dying of arsenic poisoning?" he asked incredulously. "I doubt her thoughts were concerned with destroying evidence at that point. And we've found no such bottle as you described. I'd be more likely to guess her aunt took it with her when she left."

I realized that, in my zeal to be helpful, I had nearly given myself away. I clicked my tongue. "Of course, I was forgetting. We don't know if Miss Emily left before or after her niece ate the poisoned sweets."

"No, we don't," said the Inspector, scrutinizing me more closely than I liked. "In fact, we don't know that she left at all, except that we don't seem to be able to find her body!"

He left himself soon after that, and I hoped I had given his thoughts a different direction. The news about the tonic was disheartening, however. I could see that without evidence to prove someone had been trying to poison Miss Emily prior to Miss Morton's murder, Miss Emily herself must remain a strong suspect.

⁂

I was not given long to ponder these events, for the very next day I received a call from Mrs. Waring. Wearing a look of tight-lipped endurance, she dropped down on my sofa and practically flung a rectangle of pasteboard in my direction. "I cannot bear it," she said.

Looking at the card, I saw it was an engraved announcement of an engagement between Captain Francis K. Ingram and Miss Julia Anne Waring. "Oh, dear," I said.

"I have prayed and prayed that this might be averted," said Mrs. Waring, looking at me reproachfully. "I have begged my dear Howard to use his influence from the Other Side. But Julia is still determined, and so there appears nothing to do but accept it."

"You have sent out these announcements, then?"

"Not yet. The engagement will be announced at our party, and the cards go out after. I may say that I am still hoping for a last-minute miracle to save us."

"I see," I said. "And the party is tomorrow night?"

"Yes, and I am at my wits' end. If only there were some way of preventing this disastrous marriage. It will ruin the rest of Julia's life: I know it."

I was pretty sure she was right, but there was no point in making her feel worse. I said what was soothing and sent her away, then called my assistants together. Miss Emily came, too, perforce. We were obliged to watch her by turns, since Hilda was not there to help us. I saw no harm in her taking part in this meeting, though of course we were obliged to speak a little more discreetly than usual with her there.

Miss Emily was very interested to hear of Miss Waring's plight. "Poor girl, she would not be the first to be deceived by a handsome scoundrel," she said, shaking her head.

"No," I agreed morosely.

"Of course a scarlet coat is always attractive to women."

"Some of us don't even require a scarlet coat."

"But you think the army career is genuine?" put in Susan.

"Yes, unfortunately," I said. "He appears to have fought bravely in Africa."

"Then perhaps the marriage will not turn out so badly," said Miss Emily hopefully. "When I was a girl, it was often said that a reformed rake makes a good husband."

"I have heard that saying, too," I said. "But from my own observations, I would say that a reformed rake is likely to relapse back into his rakish ways immediately after marriage and make an abominable husband."

Miss Emily thought this over and reluctantly conceded that there was something to it. "What can we do?" she asked.

I was amused that she was taking such a personal interest in the matter. "I don't know that we can do anything. Miss Waring is deeply in love with the man, and blind to any hint of danger. She sees him as a hero. It overshadows everything else about him."

"Shadows," said Miss Emily.

We all looked at her. For a moment, I feared she had suffered a relapse, but she appeared merely thoughtful, her eyes distant and her lips a little pursed. "Shadows," she said again. "The past often does overshadow the present, doesn't it? And the future as well, sad to say."

She spoke as though there were some personal meaning to the words. "You spoke of shadows the night we brought you here," I said, watching her closely. "When you were drugged with datura, on the night of the Waterloo Dinner, you kept talking about shadows."

"Did I? Yes, I can just recall it—how dark and frightening everything seemed. And then the Duke of Wellington came and took me away."

Susan and Jenny exchanged looks. "*I* took you away," I said. "It was I, Miss Emily."

"Yes, you and the Duke of Wellington."

There did not seem anything to say to this, so I tried to recall where we had been before the conversation got diverted. "Shadows," said Susan.

"No, surely not," I protested. "We were talking about Captain Ingram. About his—oh!"

It was one of those chance remarks that makes the whole riddle clear. In my mind's eye, I saw again the photograph in the captain's room: the line of uniformed figures against the African landscape; the natives with their spears; the hut, like a beehive, in the background. I could see the shadows that the sun had cast of all these things: dark shadows, cast by a strong sun, lying black against the ground. But what I could not remember was a shadow of the captain's figure where he stood to the left of the others.

"The photograph," I said.

"Yes?" said Susan encouragingly.

"The captain's army photograph. It's not real. At least, most of it's real, but he altered it somehow."

"*Can* one alter photographs?" asked Miss Emily.

"Yes," I said. "Yes, if one knows something about photography, I daresay it is quite possible." I let out a whoop that made them all look at me in astonishment. "That's it. He must have taken up photography in the States, after he and I—after his other business fell through. I'll bet he took those other photographs himself—the naughty pictures of women without their drawers."

"Naughty pictures?" queried Miss Emily, looking lost.

"I'll bet anything you like he did Spirit Photography, too," I went on, thinking it best to skip over Miss Emily's question. "I've never practiced it myself, but I've heard of it. You take a photograph of the client, and when the plate is developed, there's a figure of their deceased wife or husband or child sitting beside them. That's probably how he learned to falsify photographs in the first place."

"Falsified photographs?" said Miss Emily, shaking her head. "What a very shocking thing, to be sure."

"There are a lot of unprincipled people about," Susan told her, with a wink in my direction.

"So you think he never fought in Africa at all?" asked Jenny.

"I'd be much surprised. I must get another look at that photograph, just to be sure—but it would make perfect sense. Much more sense than the leopard changing his spots."

Of course all this meant little to Miss Emily, but she seized on these last words to inform me that Napoleon ("the Corsican Monster") had often referred to the Duke and his men as leopards, as a term of insult.

"Sounds silly to me," said Susan. "What's insulting about being called a leopard?"

"It's an inferior cat to a lion," I explained. "At least in the Gallic mind."

"The Duke thought it silly, too," added Miss Emily.

"He was a sensible man," I said, patting her hand. "Miss Emily, I am much indebted to you—to you, and to the Duke. Between you, you have given me the weapon I needed."

"How will you use it?" asked Susan.

We discussed the matter at length and eventually agreed that it might be well to enlist real military aid in unmasking the false captain. This posed no great problem, for among my clientele are a number of retired military men. I decided that once I had determined for certain that the photograph was falsified, I would consult one of these to see how best to proceed in the matter.

"And the Warings' party is tomorrow?" said Susan. "The party where they're planning to announce the engagement?"

"Yes," I said. "You'd better reschedule my sitting for tomorrow night. It looks like being a busy day, what with one thing and another."

## CHAPTER 15

On the following day, I put my plan into operation. It was rather like a military campaign, involving a show of strength, the formation of alliances, problems of transport and communication, and culminating in the final confrontation with the enemy.

My first step was to call at the captain's lodging house. I did not disguise myself in dowdy attire this time, but rather strove to look imposing in a broad black hat laden with funereal plumes, black silk dress pleated and ruched and exceedingly *bouffante*, neat black kid gloves, and black button boots. On this occasion, I felt that rather than trying to sneak in with Esther's help, I would do better to confront John's landlady and make her an ally if I could. And for that, I needed all the authority dress could give me.

Esther opened the door when I rang the bell. Her face showed consternation when she recognized me. "You can't come in," she hissed. "Mrs. Marker's here. She'd catch you sure, if you tried to get in the captain's room."

"Thank you, but I wish to *speak* with Mrs. Marker," I said, and gave her my card. It was not my professional card, Dear Reader, but rather an alternate one, primly engraved "Miss Letitia Blackwood." I use this name when I wish to represent myself as a member of the upper classes, or on any other occasion when my professional name might not be appropriate. If my errand today prospered, John would shortly find himself in an uncomfortable position, and I would rather he never guess that I had anything to do with it. Much as I might wish to publicly triumph over my enemy, I am familiar enough with both Human Nature and the annals of history to know that this invariably leads to an endless cycle of retaliation.

Mystified but obedient, Esther accepted the card, allowed me into the house, and went off to find her mistress.

Mrs. Marker was a comely widow in her forties. Like many women of her age and occupation, she possessed a disarming air of gentility disguising an underlying core of steel. "You wished to speak to me, Miss Blackwood?" she asked, looking me over in a manner that made me glad I was wearing my best dress.

"Yes, ma'am," I said. "I understand you have a boarder calling himself Captain Francis Ingram?"

At these words, the steel in her character drew visibly to the forefront. "I beg your pardon," she said. "Captain Ingram is indeed a boarder here, but I don't understand your manner of referring to him. Or indeed, what your business with him may be?"

"My business is to prevent a great crime," I said impressively. "The man you know as Captain Ingram is an imposter."

"Nonsense!"

"I regret that it is so, ma'am. If you allow me into the so-called captain's room, I can prove it to you."

"I shall do no such thing," said Mrs. Marker. "The captain is well known to me, and I am quite satisfied in his character. I am afraid you have been grossly deceived."

I shook my head. "You say the captain is well known to you?"

"Yes," she said, in a tone that assured me she, like Miss Waring, was fully under his spell. "I may say I know him very well indeed."

"Then no doubt he has told you of his engagement?"

Opening my reticule, I produced the announcement Mrs. Waring had given me. Mrs. Marker read it through, then raised her head to stare at me.

"Where did you get this?" she demanded.

"From Mrs. Waring, the captain's future mother-in-law."

"I don't believe it," said Mrs. Marker. "It's a lie."

"Then go and ask her," I said with a shrug. "Or better yet, ask her daughter, to whom the captain is engaged. The Warings are holding a party tonight to announce the engagement to their friends and family."

I felt sorry for Mrs. Marker now. She was obviously reeling from these disclosures. "He never breathed a word of this to me," she gasped. "He said—he implied—oh, and he owes me for more than two months' rent!"

I shook my head in genuine sympathy. "He is an unprincipled man who makes a practice of deceiving women to defraud them. Miss Waring is another of his victims. She is a great heiress, and he is after her money."

Mrs. Marker nodded grimly. There was a look in her eyes that boded ill for the ersatz captain. "If this is true, he'll not set foot in my house again. I'll hold his belongings against the debt he owes me. It's payment in full or nothing."

I congratulated her on this businesslike attitude. "Will you please allow me into his room? He has a photograph in his possession that proves his imposture. With it, I believe I can convince Miss Waring to break the engagement."

She was *glad* to allow me into his room, Dear Reader, and quite willing that I should take away his army photograph. I went ahead and showed her the pornographic pictures, too, just to help cement her new attitude. While she was fulminating over these, I opened the desk drawer and abstracted the letters from Miss Waring. At the last minute, I decided to take Miss Tate's as well, for undoubtedly she was another of John's victims. I did not want the poor girl liable to blackmail in the future.

I was careful, however, to leave all his unpaid bills behind.

The army photograph revealed exactly what I had hoped. As I demonstrated to Mrs. Marker, there was a complete lack of shadowing to the captain's figure, alone of everything else in the landscape. It was so obvious that I wondered I had not seen it before, but of course we do not often look at the shadows of things, only the things themselves.

With photograph in hand, I called on General Fallon, one of my regular clients. He directed me in turn to Colonel Sir Cyril St. Simon, a veteran of the African wars residing in Aldershot. A short train ride took me there, and I was lucky enough to find him at home. I lost no time asking him if he were acquainted with Captain Francis Ingram.

"Dear me, yes," cried the colonel, beaming. I had a strange sense of *déjà vu* whenever I looked at him, Dear Reader. Whereas John had been an imitation, he was the genuine article: a British military man no longer young but still handsome and stalwart and gallant enough to set your teeth on edge.

"Francis was under my command, there in Zululand. A bad business, that." The colonel shook his head somberly. "Still, one does one's duty, what? He was one of my best men. A close-mouthed fella, but a damned good fighter—begging your pardon for the language, ma'am."

I graciously accorded him pardon for the language. "So you knew Captain Ingram well?"

"To be sure I did. To be sure I did. We were both in that business at Eshowe." The colonel made an expressive gesture. "Men dropping like flies from illness and starvation. And you couldn't so much as show your nose outside without a pack of Zulus setting on you. One doesn't soon forget a thing like that."

"Do you know what happened to Captain Ingram after the war?"

"Heard he'd sold out and gone to Canada. Going to try his hand at farming, I believe."

"Would it surprise you to learn there is a man calling himself Captain Ingram in London right now?" I asked.

There was no doubt but the colonel was surprised. "Francis in London?" he exclaimed. "Why, how is this? I haven't heard a word of it."

"So you are surprised?"

"Dear me, yes. I can't think why he wouldn't have called on me. He must know he'd find me here at the old shop."

By this time, Dear Reader, I was feeling very foolish. If only I had looked up Colonel St. Simon earlier, I might have managed the whole business even without the photograph. Knowing I had that as my trump card, however, I sought to strengthen my hand.

"If you know Captain Ingram well," I said, "then no doubt you are aware he was wounded in Africa?"

The colonel nodded. "Aye, we both were—there at Eshowe. Precious few of us came through that business unscathed, I can tell you!"

I was a little taken aback by this, but a moment's thought served to reassure me. I knew John had not acquired his limp in Africa. "Do you recall *where* Captain Ingram was wounded?" I said. "In what part of his body, I mean?"

"Shoulder," said the colonel at once, touching his own shoulder reminiscently. "Remember it well, poor fella."

"Not his leg?"

"Certainly not. Remember it like it was yesterday." The colonel stared at me. "Why do you ask?"

"Because the man who calls himself Captain Ingram claims to have been wounded in the leg."

The colonel thought this over, plainly puzzled. "Doesn't make sense," he objected. "Dash it, a fella would remember whether he was wounded in the shoulder or leg, wouldn't he?"

"That is what *I* think," I said. "And that is why I have come to you, Colonel. I fear this man may not be Captain Ingram at all, but an imposter."

The colonel was much struck by my words. "An imposter!" he exclaimed. "You don't mean it, ma'am."

"I do. We can settle the matter beyond any doubt, I think, if you will only look at this photograph."

I laid the photograph in front of him and my magnifying glass as well, in case he was short-sighted enough to need it. But he did not seem to need it; his face brightened as he looked at the photograph. "By Jove, yes," he said. "Remember those fellas, all right. There's Francis right there." He pointed to a figure standing among the massed men.

"So that is *not* Captain Ingram?" I said, pointing to John's figure on the left.

"Certainly not," said the colonel. He frowned, squinting at John's figure. "Who *is* that fella? I don't recognize him."

"That is the man calling himself Captain Ingram."

"No!" exclaimed the colonel. Again he squinted at the figure. "Something odd about this," he announced presently.

"I think so, too."

"Dashed odd, ma'am. For one thing, who *is* that fella? I'm sure he'd nothing to do with Francis's company."

"I should be surprised if he had."

"For another, his uniform's wrong," the colonel went on. "Not in our regiment at all." He seized the glass and inspected the figure more closely. "Thought as much," he announced. "Old-style uniform—we'd the new. Tell you what, ma'am: this fella *is* an imposter!"

I was delighted to hear that John had made such an elementary mistake. The shadows were a point against him, but I felt this was an even stronger one. "Yes," I said. "I believe he was never in Africa at all." I then explained how I thought the photograph had been altered to support John's imaginary military career.

The colonel, of course, considered this tantamount to treason. "The scoundrel! But what could be his object, ma'am?"

This was my opening, Dear Reader, and you may believe I made the most of it. There are times when our purpose is best served by laying the facts concisely before our auditors, and other times when we do better to tell them a story. I adjudged this one of the latter times. It is my private opinion that men, as a sex, are more romantic than women. It was a thrilling tale I told, with Miss Waring an imperiled princess, her beauty and youth and trusting nature all menaced by a duplicitous villain. I represented myself as her godmother. There is a strong tradition of fairy godmothers in romantic tales, and it pleased me to think of myself in this rôle.

The colonel positively lapped it up.

"But we must do something, ma'am!" he exclaimed, at the conclusion of my story. "Dash it, can't let this poor girl be taken in by such a scoundrel!"

"But what can we do?" I asked in pretended despair. "Her mother and I have tried to reason with her. She will not believe this man is not what he claims to be."

"Only one thing to be done," said the colonel, getting to his feet. "That's to see the fella himself. He's got to be made to understand he can't get away with impersonating an honourable British soldier. Where can I find him?"

"*Not* at his rooming house," I said, with some satisfaction. "I daresay he may already be at the Warings'. They are giving a party tonight, to announce his engagement to Miss Waring."

"Lead me to him," said the colonel grimly. "And leave the rest to me."

It was evening by the time we arrived back in London. The only train had been a slow one, but I used the time to give the colonel a lot of extra detail about John's background and character. The idea that he was twice a deserter as well as a military imposter were naturally the things that most impressed him. He snorted like a warhorse and opined that hanging was too good for such a fella.

From Waterloo Station (I noted the coincidence with a smile), we took a cab to the Warings'. It was easy to identify their house by the awning and red carpet in front. Fortunately, we were early enough that the party had not yet begun.

We were admitted, rather reluctantly, by the Warings' butler. Although he was one of my informants, we had only communicated via intermediary, and so he did not recognize me. With a disapproving air, he informed us that the family and a select party of their guests were at dinner.

"Are they?" said the colonel grimly. "Would there be a fella calling himself Francis Ingram among 'em?"

The butler admitted that there would be.

"Tell him I'd like a word with him," said the colonel. "I'd send him my card, but—" he gave a derisive snort, "I daresay it wouldn't mean anything to him."

I thought it best to withdraw at this point, Dear Reader, but I did not go far. I merely stationed myself behind a convenient cluster of palms and settled down to enjoy what followed.

After the butler had gone, the colonel paced up and down, gnawing his mustache and glaring around at the garlands and vases of flowers that decorated the hall. Presently John appeared, looking wary. It was obvious he thought the colonel must be a dun come to collect a debt, for his first words were, "If it's about my account at Metcalf's, I'll be able to pay something down tomorrow. For God's sake, be a good fellow and take yourself off." He gave the colonel a conspiratorial smile. "Tonight's my engagement party, don't you know."

The colonel audibly ground his teeth. "Engagement, is it? By God, you make me sick! Who are you, fella, and what d'you mean by pretending you're Francis Ingram, one of the finest men who ever lived?"

At these words, the smile was wiped from John's face. "What do I mean?" he repeated, obviously stalling for time. "What do *you* mean?"

"I mean I *knew* Francis Ingram—and I know you're not him! Devil a bit of it!"

"Now look here," said John, in what was meant to be a conciliatory tone. "There must be some mistake. I assure you my name is Francis Ingram. Perhaps you are confusing me with someone else of the same name?"

"No," said the colonel with triumph. "Not if you're representing yourself as the Captain Francis Ingram who fought in Zululand. Do you dare tell me you're not?"

John clearly could not decide whether to accept the colonel's dare. Unfortunately for him, Miss Waring chose this moment to appear. She was wearing a cream-coloured satin gown with a string of pearls around her throat and more pearls set in a crescent in her dark hair. I was pleased to see what a beautiful, regal figure she made, quite the image of a fairy-tale princess.

"What is it, Francis?" she said, looking from John to the colonel in surprise. "Who is this gentleman?"

"I haven't an idea," said John, affecting nonchalance. "Some lunatic, I believe."

"Lunatic, is it?" growled the colonel. "By God, sir, you'd know my name well enough if you really were Francis Ingram—which you're not." Turning to Miss Waring, he addressed her with exaggerated courtesy. "Colonel Sir Cyril St. Simon, at your service, ma'am."

She gazed from him to John in bewilderment. "I beg your pardon, Colonel, but I don't understand," she said. "What are you doing here, and what have you to do with Francis?"

"I beg *your* pardon, ma'am," said the colonel earnestly. "Believe me, I wouldn't be here if it weren't a matter of the most solemn duty. This fella—" he indicated John with a contemptuous wave of his hand, "is a bald-faced imposter. He's been deceiving you about his military career and a good deal else besides if all I hear is true. I'm sorry if it gives you pain—"

"It's all nonsense, Julia," broke in John. "Don't believe a word of it."

It was clear, however, that Miss Waring had been swayed by the colonel's manner, even if she could not quite bring herself to believe his words. "I don't understand," she said again. "Surely there must be some mistake. This gentleman—" she glanced at John, "—is certainly known to me as Captain Francis Ingram. I have seen papers and photographs to prove that he fought in Africa."

"Yes," said the colonel, giving John a cutting look. "Stolen papers, I've no doubt. As for the photographs—doctored, ma'am! I give you my word! Most infamous thing. The fella was never in Africa at all. I was there, by God, and I can prove it right now." He looked fiercely at John. "Do you dare stand there and tell me you fought at Eshowe?"

John laughed uneasily. "I think you are overexcited, sir, and that this discussion can wait until another time."

He was looking at the colonel as he spoke, so he did not see the surprise and disillusionment on his fiancée's face. "Just a moment, Francis," she said. "I think such a serious allegation had better be addressed directly."

"My dear Julia, you must know there is no truth in it." Turning away from the colonel, John addressed her with a forced smile. "Don't you know me better than that?"

The colonel swiftly interposed himself between them. "You mustn't let yourself be deceived, ma'am," he told her kindly, before turning a fierce face to John. "You, sir! If you will step outside, we can settle this matter very quickly."

"I have no intention of stepping outside," said John coldly. "My dear Julia, will you tell the servants to show this person out?"

"Show me out, will you? Not before I've shown *you* how we deal with lying dogs and scoundrels in Her Majesty's service!"

It will ever be one of my fondest memories, Dear Reader: the colonel forcibly ejecting John from the house by means of a boot applied to his posterior. Miss Waring watched the whole thing with a stunned expression, obviously unable to decide if she ought to weep or applaud.

The colonel completed his rout of the enemy by shouting that he'd better not stick around London if he knew what was good for him. He then turned to Miss Waring and apologized gravely for subjecting her to a scene of such violence.

"There, there, little woman," he said, taking her hand tenderly in his and gazing down at her with concern. "I know all this must be a tremendous shock to you. I don't know what that fella deserves for deceiving you in such a way. Don't cry, little woman: 'deed, and he's not worth a single tear from such an angel."

It did not seem to me that my services were needed any longer, Dear Reader. When I left, the colonel was still murmuring clumsy endearments to Miss Waring, and she was sobbing quietly into his shoulder, obviously in a fair way to being consoled already.

## CHAPTER 16

It was one of the best day's work I ever put in, as I told Susan on returning home. She was both amazed and amused to hear of the captain's rout.

"I wonder what happened about the party?" she speculated. "Would the Warings go on and hold it, after that? The whole point was to announce the girl's engagement to Captain Ingram!"

"God knows," I said. "But I expect Mrs. Waring will be perfectly happy however they arrange it."

We were still discussing the matter when someone began hammering on the front door.

"What on earth?" exclaimed Susan.

I thought at once of our fugitive guest. "Where's Miss Emily?"

"Downstairs with Jenny. She's helping teach her to read."

"This might be the police. Go and warn them both. I'll answer it."

I was glad I was still wearing my best dress and hat. I rustled down the corridor to the door, waited a good minute to let Susan complete her errand, and then flung the door open in my grandest manner. "Yes?" I said. "What is the meaning of—oh, it's *you*."

It was John, looking grimly determined. "May I come in?" he asked. Not waiting for an invitation, he pushed past me.

"Get out," I said.

He smiled unpleasantly. "Not until I've had a word with you." He looked me up and down. "Very smart," he said approvingly. "Yes, indeed. Obviously you've prospered. You can afford to help me now."

I thought it best to pretend ignorance of the day's events. "Don't tell me Miss Waring has failed you?" I exclaimed with exaggerated surprise.

He scowled. "Yes," he said. "The most damnable thing. Some army fellow turned up and told her I wasn't Captain Ingram after all. Now the fat's in the fire."

"*Not* Captain Ingram?" I said with well-feigned puzzlement. "But what of that army record that was warranted genuine?"

He looked a little sheepish. "Oh, the record's genuine enough," he said. "It's just that it's not mine. I met Francis Ingram up in Canada, when I was prospecting for gold. We were partners for a time."

"Didn't he mind your borrowing his name and record?"

"Poor fellow wasn't in any position to mind. He had an unfortunate encounter with a grizzly up in the Cariboos. 'Exit, pursued by a bear.'" He laughed shortly. "That being the case, I decided to take advantage of the situation. I'd gotten into a bit of trouble back in the States, what with one thing and another."

He threw me a fleeting look. When I made no comment, he shrugged and went on. "With Francis gone, it was a chance to start fresh under a new name. He and I weren't unlike in appearance, and he hadn't any family left living. Damn it, what are the odds that I'd run across someone who knew him in Africa, after all these years?" Abandoning his grievance, for which I was showing small sympathy, he became abruptly businesslike. "I need five hundred pounds."

I lifted my brows. "And what has that to do with me?"

"Come, Mary, you can certainly spare it."

"My name is not Mary, and I certainly *cannot* spare it. I think you had better go."

"If five hundred is too much, I'll settle for three hundred," he said, with an air of doing me a favour. "Believe me, Mary, you'd do well to oblige me. I could do you a lot of harm, in your position."

For answer, I shouted, "Jenny," then fixed him with a cold stare. "You can leave now, or be . . . thrown out," I told him. I almost said "kicked out," before remembering that it would be better if he did not know my connection with that other business. He could still do me harm, but I was counting on his not being around long enough to do much of it. After all, I had the British Army behind me now.

"You don't dare throw me out," he shot back. "I know the kind of people you work for, and I know they'd be *extremely* shocked at some of the tales I could tell them about your past—Mrs. Brooke."

There's never a horsewhip around when you need one. Happily, Jenny arrived at that moment in answer to my summons. "You called, ma'am?" she said, eyeing us both in a questioning way.

"Show this gentleman out, Jenny."

She advanced on John in a businesslike way. Jenny is a formidable figure at any time, and she was looking especially formidable just then. He fell back a step, but kept his eyes on me. "You don't dare," he said again. "Surely you don't want the whole world to know about our little affair years ago?"

The words rose to my lips in the most satisfying way. "'Publish and be damned!'" I said, then turned on my heel and walked away.

Behind me, I could hear Jenny telling John he'd best be leaving now, in a voice that brooked no compromise. As I rounded the turn in the corridor, I almost ran into Miss Emily. She was standing stock-still with a dazed expression.

"Miss Emily," I said, lowering my voice. "What are you doing here?"

"I came with Jenny, when you called." She lifted her eyes to me and regarded me with a peculiar expression.

"Well, you'd better go back downstairs. Or—no, it's all right. He's gone now," I said, hearing the front door close. "Let's go into the Sitting Room."

Once seated in the Sitting Room, Miss Emily leaned forward in her chair. "Madame Fox," she said, her voice trembling a little, "who was that man? The man you were talking to a moment ago?"

I might easily have lied, Dear Reader, but somehow I felt I owed her the truth. "He was a man I knew years ago. We had some business dealings together—and some personal dealings as well. In fact," I said, "not to put too fine a point on the matter, we were lovers."

I wondered if I had shocked her, but she only nodded. "That is why he was threatening you? Threatening to tell?"

"Yes."

"But you told him . . . you told him to. . . .."

"'Publish and be damned,'" I said. "Yes, I did. It isn't an original expression, of course. I was quoting the Duke of Wellington."

She opened her eyes very wide. "The Duke said that?"

"He's supposed to have said it. On an occasion when he was being blackmailed."

Miss Emily looked astonished. "The *Duke* was blackmailed?"

Since she already knew about my own youthful peccadilloes, I went ahead and told her about the Duke's. It was a day of revelations all around. For when Miss Emily had listened to how the Duke had defied his would-be blackmailers, she nodded, pursed her lips, and said, "I see. Then that is what I must do, too. I can see it all clearly now." She nodded again, decisively. "You had better call the others together. I have something to tell you all."

It took a minute to bring Susan up from the kitchen. Jenny we could not find at all, but fortunately, before we could do more than speculate about her whereabouts, she came in through the front door looking extremely pleased with herself. I was too intent on hearing Miss Emily's confession to ask her what she had been doing.

Once the three of us were seated around Miss Emily, she shut her eyes for a moment, opened them, and began to speak.

It was the second time that day I had felt remarkably foolish.

I had always thought Miss Emily a sweet creature, Dear Reader—everyone did. Her fluting voice and fluttering ways made it easy to see her as a kind of stage character: the elderly spinster, sweet, sheltered, and perpetually virginal. She seemed so much the embodiment of that stereotype that it was difficult to realize she had ever been anything else.

Yet though she embodied that stereotype now, she had once been a woman with hopes and dreams and desires as powerful and unruly as any woman's. It is always a mistake to judge by appearances, Dear Reader. I of all people ought to know that, but on this occasion I was taken in like any greenhorn.

The gist of the matter was this: when Miss Emily had been in her late twenties—soon after her beloved sister had married—she had met a man whom she could not marry, but for whom she dared all for love, as the saying goes. She had ended up bearing him a son out of wedlock. And that son had been none other than the late Arthur Wellesley Morton—known to the outside world as her sister's son and Miss Emily's nephew.

"Did Sir Oliver Morton *know*?" I asked with awe.

Miss Emily shook her head. "No," she said softly. "No one knew but my sister. It was she who arranged the whole business. As soon as

I told her of my situation, she put it about that *she* was with child, but ailing, so that she needed to go into the country for rest and quiet. And I went along with her. It was a tiny village, very quiet and very far away from any of our friends and family. Arthur was born there. Once he was born, it was easy enough for her to claim that he was hers rather than mine."

Dear Reader, I had always thought the late Lady Morton a determined character, but I felt now I had underestimated her. "She passed off her sister's child as her husband's son and heir?" I said incredulously.

"Yes," said Miss Emily. "I felt guilty enough about it, you may be sure. But she was always stronger than I was. She was so very determined there should be no scandal in the family."

"Still, there must have been servants who knew the truth," I said, thinking the matter over. "And the doctor or midwife who attended the birth. They would have known you were the mother."

"Yes, but you see it was a small place, and we weren't known there. We simply pretended to be each other." Miss Emily looked down at her hands. "It seemed to answer. But I have always wondered whether I ought to have told the truth at the outset, hard as that might have been. All these years, I have carried this secret. Seeing my own son grow up, without being able to claim him as my own." She shook her head, tears running down her face. "That was bad enough—but then he died, and I had to accept that it was out of my power ever to set matters right. I felt it was a judgment on me."

At these words, Jenny gave a cry of protest. Miss Emily smiled through her tears and reached out to pat her hand. "You have a good heart, my dear," she said. "I know you pity an old woman's folly. But indeed, I have been very foolish and very wicked. Not so much in loving in the first place, for I cannot believe that I committed such a great sin there." Looking at us all earnestly, she said, "We would have married if we could. But we could not, for he was married already. It had been an arranged marriage, such as were common in those days, and it had not been a success. By the time I met him, he and his wife were living wholly apart."

"What a pity," I said. "I suppose divorce was out of the question?"

"Yes, for she was a victim as much as he was," explained Miss Emily, with a worldly-wise air that sat oddly on her sweet face. "And it would have made no difference to *my* situation. In those days, divorce was a terrible stigma—far worse than it is now. My people would never have heard of my marrying a divorced man. So it meant we could not marry, and I understood that and was willing to pay the price—I thought."

She paused a moment, seeming to gather her thoughts. None of us spoke to interrupt her. "Still, I have been punished for it," she went on. "And not only by guilt and regret. My sister took care that no one should suspect the truth while she was living, but she must have written the truth down somewhere—in her diary perhaps. She was always a great one for keeping a diary. And when she died, her daughters must have found it amongst her papers. At any rate, they learned of it somehow—of the deceit we had practiced. And I have not had an easy moment since."

I could fill in all the gaps now. "They have been blackmailing you?"

"It amounts to that, yes. Catherine—Lady Frost—has not been too demanding. It is only money she wants, and I can spare that easily enough. But Honoria—you have seen what Honoria was like. Nothing would do but that she live at Waterloo House with me. I would not have minded that in itself, but . . .."

"But she wanted to supplant you as mistress," I said.

Fresh tears filled Miss Emily's eyes. "I can still hardly believe it. That she would do such a thing! But I have no doubt it was just as you said. She wanted to make it appear I was incapable. Those spells—I could not think what was happening to me. I did not connect it with her being there."

To myself, I reflected that it was a pity that she had not had a more competent doctor, or the connection might have been established much sooner. Aloud, I merely observed that in being poisoned herself, Miss Morton appeared to have gotten no more than her just deserts.

"Desserts, rather," said Susan, with a grim smile. "Very appropriate, considering that she died of eating poisoned sweets. That's what the police think, isn't it?"

"Yes," I said, "and that is what we need to consider now, Miss Emily. For until we can solve the mystery of who poisoned those sweets, the police will consider you to have the best motive." I regarded her with anxiety. "It may grieve you to hear it, but I think Lady Frost is responsible."

To my astonishment, Miss Emily received this with perfect composure. "Yes," she said. "I know she is."

"You *know* it?"

"Yes," said Miss Emily. "I saw her—on Waterloo Night." She looked at me. "It was when I took you to see the Boot. Catherine was there in my room. She had the box in her hand."

We all stared at her speechlessly.

"I couldn't think what she was doing," continued Miss Emily. "When I opened the door, she looked around, then went out through my dressing room very quickly. It seemed odd, but I didn't think much about it at the time." She smiled wanly. "I supposed she simply wanted a sweet! She and her sister knew I kept them there, and they were always coaxing for them when they were children."

Thinking back to that night at Waterloo House, I could just recall Miss Emily pausing in the doorway with an exclamation of surprise. "And you actually saw Lady Frost with the box of sweets in her hand?"

"Two boxes," corrected Miss Emily. "She had just put one down. She took the other with her when she went."

"She must have been substituting a box of poisoned sweets for the ones you normally kept there," I said.

"Yes," said Miss Emily.

I paused again, trying to remember. "Of course! I remember Lady Frost left the drawing room by herself, some time before we did. I thought it was just to escape her sister, but I'll bet she was planning to go to your room all along."

"Did she have the sweets with her?" Jenny wanted to know.

"Not in her hand," I said. "But she could easily have had them concealed about her person. You know what dresses are like nowadays." I sketched an outline with my hand. "All that fullness behind, and supported by wire cages and pads and petticoats. And her dress had a perfectly enormous bustle—much bigger than any of the rest of us had. She might have carried a barrel of gunpowder back there, and we would never have known it."

That seemed to settle the question of means. But we had a larger question now to settle, concerning what Miss Emily ought to do to bring her niece to justice.

"Are you willing to tell all this to the police, Miss Emily?" I asked.

She sighed. "I suppose I must. But it will be very painful. I can hardly expect Catherine to spare my own secret, once I give hers away."

We could all see that this was true. "But she's bound to be arrested for murder, once you tell what you know," said Susan. "Would she want to kick up another scandal, just for spite?"

We considered this question at length and agreed it was hard to know what Lady Frost might do in such circumstances. "You say you have given her money already, Miss Emily, to keep your secret," I said. "That means you could charge her with blackmail as well as murder. But I'm not sure the threat of doing that would be any use in keeping her quiet, since murder is so much the more serious charge."

We could only agree that as matters now stood, Miss Emily would have to brave the risk of having her secret made public if she accused her niece of murder. "I will do it if I must," said Miss Emily, looking determined. "I am only sorry I did not do it sooner. As it is, I feel Honoria's death is my doing. If I had spoken earlier, she might not have eaten those sweets."

"Don't you go bothering your conscience about that," Susan advised her. "Serves her right for drugging you. And for being stupid enough to think she could cover it up when you escaped."

"That raises an interesting point, Susan," I said. "Of course the whole reason she tried to cover it up was because she had no idea what was going to happen next." To Miss Emily, I explained, "She probably hoped you might be found dead, or wandering harmlessly out of your wits. In that case, she could have claimed you got out without her noticing. It might have been awkward if they discovered you as a three-day-old corpse, but even then I don't believe she could have been charged with anything worse than negligence."

Miss Emily looked so distressed at the idea of herself as a three-day-old corpse that I hurried on without giving her time to speak. "What tied her hands was the uncertainty. For all she knew, you might be biding your time somewhere, just waiting your moment to accuse her of blackmail as well as poisoning. She had already taken steps to conceal her guilt, just in case. Inspector Harper said the bottle of tonic was gone from the house when he and his men searched it."

"So there is nothing to show she was drugging me?" asked Miss Emily.

"No, but that needn't concern us at the moment. It's the case against Lady Frost we must consider now."

Susan was looking thoughtful. "It appears to me she'd be feeling about like her sister right now," she said. "Not sure where her aunt is, or what she's likely to do next."

We all looked at each other. I could feel an idea forming, or at least the beginning of one. "Perhaps we ought to let her remain in a state of uncertainty a little longer," I said. "The police may yet find something that will let them act without Miss Emily's testimony. And so might we."

Although I did not say anything in front of Miss Emily, I was pinning a good deal of hope on Felicity's investigations. She might yet determine who the anonymous letter writer was, or at least discover the evidence on which the writer had based his or her accusations. There seemed no harm in letting the situation bide for a few days longer.

## CHAPTER 17

I visited the Calico Cat the next afternoon, on the chance that Felicity might have discovered something of interest. I was impatient to act on the new information Miss Emily had given me. I did not mind Lady Frost suffering a few more days of suspense, but the sooner I could put poor Inspector Harper out of his misery, the better I would be pleased. As it was, I felt a pang of guilt whenever I pictured him losing sleep and patience in pursuit of some idiot witness's false clue.

Felicity was dressed like a music hall actress today: hat broad as a cartwheel tipped over one eye, bunches of false brunette curls, and an awe-inspiring dress in variegated shades of fuchsia, amber, and cherry red. "I can see what you're thinking, dear," she said, as I contemplated this remarkable toilette. "But I hadn't the figure for a ballet-girl, so it was this or nothing."

She was very willing to tell me about her visits to Lady Frost's, but warned me she hadn't much to show for them. "You thought those letters might have been sent by somebody that wishes her ill," she said. "Well, as far as I can tell, every servant in the house wishes her ill. She's a hard mistress by all accounts, and rules over 'em with a heavy hand. Rules her lord as well, from what they tell me."

"It's almost certain that she's a murderess," I said.

Felicity was interested to hear this. "You wouldn't think it, would you?" she said. "Living in a great house like that, with a handle to her name and dozens of servants at her beck and call. What cause has a woman like that to murder?"

"Money," I said. "She wants her aunt's inheritance."

Felicity observed leniently that we all had to live. "Though it's outside of enough when rich folk don't know they're well off." Fixing me with a shrewd eye, she added, "Mind you, I did get a hint or two that the ready wasn't so plentiful as it might be in that house."

"Gambling, do you think? Or general extravagance?"

"Bit of both, I'd say."

I filed this away for later consideration. "But let us return to the letters," I said. "You've no idea who might have sent them? I'm assuming they were put together by someone with a bit of education, for there weren't any misspelled words. And the letters were all cut out of the *Times* newspaper."

Felicity shrugged. "Lord Frost takes the *Times*. It'd be easy enough for any of the servants to get hold of a copy. Or to buy one themselves, for that matter."

"What is done with the old papers?"

"They're burned every day with the other household waste."

This was disappointing, Dear Reader, but of course it had always been unlikely that we could discover any proof at this late date. "Have you any idea where Lady Frost might have gotten arsenic?" I asked.

"Arsenic? Is that what she used?"

"The police think so. But they don't know yet that she's responsible."

Felicity promised to do some more investigating, and to let me know if she learned anything that might be of use. "But if Lady Frost's really done a murder, I'm afraid we'll catch cold trying to prove it," she said. "They all may talk against her, but everybody seems to agree she's a very clever woman."

⁂

I spent the journey home weighing and discarding various plans of action. For a time, I toyed with the idea of composing my own anonymous letter and sending it to Scotland Yard. But I was afraid this would not be enough to prompt an investigation against a woman of Lady Frost's rank. Even if it were, I suspected Felicity was right, and Lady Frost was too clever to leave proof lying about. Like her sister, she had probably destroyed any evidence that implicated her as soon as she felt threatened by events at Waterloo House.

When I reached the Temple, I was astounded to learn that the mountain had come to Mohammed—or at least the mountain's spouse had come. "Lord Frost is here," Susan told me. "He's in the Sitting Room." In a lower voice, she added, "We've got Miss Emily down in the kitchen."

Nodding to signal my understanding, I directed my steps to the Sitting Room.

Lord Frost rose to his feet as I entered. We had met before at any number of Waterloo Dinners, but now that I knew him to be the husband of a murderess, I could not help regarding him with new interest. He was a handsome man in the traditional style of the English aristocrat: fair, with an aquiline profile and reserved manner. "Madame Fox," he said.

"Lord Frost," I returned. "How may I help you?"

He hesitated. "It's this business of Miss Randall," he said.

He was the only person I knew who called Miss Emily by her proper name. By all the rules of etiquette, she should have been Miss Randall from the moment her sister had married. But she had gone on being called by her childhood title all her life, until it was hard to think of her by any other. Indeed, it took me a moment to realize whom Lord Frost was talking about.

"Miss Emily," I said, "yes."

He bowed a cold acknowledgement of my words. "I may say I am very concerned," he said. "That is to say, *we* are very concerned. That is to say, my wife and I. Lady Frost, that is," he explained painstakingly.

I merely nodded, hoping to save time. At the rate he was going, it was going to take him hours to get to the point.

"Miss Morton's death, under such circumstances, would have been bad enough," continued Lord Frost. "Naturally it was a dreadful shock to Lady Frost that her sister should have died in such a way. Foul play," he explained in a hushed voice. "There does not seem to be any doubt that foul play was involved. I have it from the police inspector in charge of the case."

Again I nodded. I wondered how he would react if he knew that his own wife was, by my calculations, the perpetrator of said foul play.

"As I say, the death of Miss Morton was bad enough in itself," continued Lord Frost. "But in addition to that shocking business, we have also to contend with the disappearance of Miss Randall, under the most puzzling circumstances. I hardly need say we are very distressed."

"Of course," I said. "I am sure all of us who wish Miss Emily well have been shocked and puzzled by her disappearance."

Lord Frost received this coldly. "I daresay," he said. "But my wife and I, as Miss Randall's nearest family, naturally feel it *more*, Madame Fox."

Having thus put me in my place, he went on speaking. "The police seem unable to find the least clue as to where she has gone. I find it remarkable that this should be so. At her age, and in her state of health, it seems inconceivable that she could have gone very far."

I agreed that it seemed inconceivable.

"Lady Frost and I fear that she has met with some accident. It seems the only explanation."

I noted that Lord Frost did not quite meet my eye in making this statement. "That is possible," I agreed. "Although it may be that she has merely taken refuge with friends."

Lord Frost seemed taken aback by this idea. "I hardly think so," he protested. "If she had done that, surely she must have communicated with us before now."

"There might be circumstances to explain why she has not."

"Her mental incapacity, do you mean?"

I regarded him with interest. "You consider her mentally incapable?"

Lord Frost hesitated before answering. "At her age, it would not be wonderful," he said.

This sounded like evasion to me. I decided to prod him a little. "I have always thought Miss Emily very astute for a person of her age," I said. "Indeed, for a person of *any* age."

Again Lord Frost hesitated before answering. "It may be," he said. "But she seemed definitely failing, on the last occasion I saw her. That evening at Waterloo House, when we were all together— you yourself must recall how wildly she spoke and acted."

"After dinner," I agreed. "But did you not think she was perfectly rational and composed *during* dinner?"

Lord Frost frowned. "Now you mention it, yes," he admitted. "But that, too, is not wonderful. I believe such debilities often fluctuate from day to day and hour to hour." Having once again disposed of me and my pretensions, he forged ahead. "It seems to me very possible that in a state of mental incapacity, she may have left the house and been involved in some accident. Lady Frost and I would be very sorry to hear of such a thing, as I hardly need say. But at present, given the absolute lack of any information as to her whereabouts . . . ." His voice trailed off.

I thought I could see where this was going. "The uncertainty must be very trying," I suggested.

Lord Frost received this much more warmly than my previous offerings. "Indeed it is. Very trying," he agreed. "And that is why I have come to you, Madame Fox. I wish to arrange a—a sitting, is it? Is that the proper term?"

I assured him it was the proper term. "I wish to arrange a sitting," he repeated. "I am not necessarily a believer in Spiritualism. But I think anyone of intelligence must concede that there is much that is unknown to us on this Earth, and also much that may be learned through keeping an open mind."

Of course I agreed with him, Dear Reader. Such a general statement could hardly be disputed, even leaving my own interests out of the question.

"And then there is the fact that Miss Randall was herself a believer in Spiritualism," he went on. "It seems to me that might predispose her to—to—"

"Communicate through Spiritualistic means?" I suggested helpfully.

"Yes, exactly so. If she is . . . if she is in a condition to do so."

I regarded him thoughtfully. "Most Spiritualistic Communications come from those who have passed to the Other Side," I said. "But it is not unheard-of for Living Souls to communicate as well. Especially those who are in what we may call a—" I paused to choose my words carefully, "—what we may call a *shadow state*. That is to say, neither living nor dead."

To my surprise, Lord Frost grasped at this idea. I felt I had done him an injustice. Up till now, I had supposed that he, like his wife, merely wanted to ascertain Miss Emily's demise in order to get his hands on her inheritance. "That is very interesting indeed," he said warmly. "If only it could be so! Lady Frost has expressed some skepticism about consulting you, but as I told her, I don't see that it could do any harm. It will not hurt to explore all avenues."

"Certainly not," I agreed.

"Even the detective in charge of the case has conceded that assistance may sometimes be gained through Spiritualistic sources," he went on.

"I *beg* your pardon?"

"The detective in charge of the case," repeated Lord Frost. "Inspector—Inspector—ah, I cannot think of the name—"

"Harper," I said grimly. "Inspector Harper."

"Yes, that's the fellow. In fact, he said that if we decided to make the experiment, he would be interested in taking part."

"Did he indeed?" I said.

"Yes. I cannot say I have any objection. Already the police are involved, so we cannot hope to keep matters quiet. It is a dreadful situation—dreadful, dreadful. I would be glad to resolve it by any means."

There was so much genuine emotion in Lord Frost's voice that I awoke from my speculations concerning Inspector Harper and regarded him with renewed interest. "Yes," I said. "Well, let us set a date and time, and we will see what may be learned through consulting the Spirits."

Susan, of course, had not only been listening to this conversation, but had followed our usual practice of transcribing it onto paper. "This is very interesting," I said, tapping my fingers on the transcript. "I hardly expected such a request from such a quarter."

"Yes," agreed Susan. "Do you think he suspects his wife is responsible?"

"It's difficult to say. I wouldn't suppose he would seek my services if he thought she were, but one never knows."

Susan nodded. "It might be just to show willing," she suggested, "to allay suspicion that he himself might be involved. It would demonstrate to the police that—how did he put it? — that he had explored all avenues."

"And speaking of the police," I said. "What do you make of Inspector Harper's encouraging the idea?"

"The Lord only knows," said Susan frankly. "He's a deep one, if anyone is. Are you going to let him take part in the sitting, ma'am? After what happened last time?"

I informed her sternly that what happened last time had been an accident. "Besides, he really wasn't taking part in the sitting that time. He was merely watching from behind the scenes. This time it would be different, I presume. He would be attending as a guest."

"Still, you'd have to watch your step with him here," said Susan.

"Yes, and I don't like it. I am perfectly sure that he thinks the Spiritograph and I are both frauds. What is the point of his coming here and pretending to be seeking information from us?"

❦

Neither Susan nor I could guess what the point was, but it wasn't long before I had an opportunity to ask him for myself. Later that same day, Susan came down to the kitchen, where I was taking my turn with Miss Emily, and informed me that Inspector Harper had called and wished to speak to me.

Warily, I ascended the service stair and entered the Sitting Room. "How do you do, Inspector Harper?" I asked.

He said shortly that he was very well. I thought, however, that he was still looking a bit wan and weary. "I thought you'd be interested to hear," he said. "They analyzed the sweet you gave me, but there didn't seem to be any arsenic in it."

I was not surprised to hear this, Dear Reader. I was fairly certain now that Lady Frost had substituted a new box of poisoned sweets for the unopened box, leaving the partial box untouched. I would have done the exact same thing in her place. Knowing her aunt's habits, she could be sure that Miss Emily would not open the new box for at least a day or two.

By the time Miss Emily started to feel the effects of the arsenic, Lady Frost might reasonably hope that no one would suspect she had played any rôle in her aunt's illness. Once a pattern of ill-health was set, she could later introduce a fatal dose—or perhaps one of the sweets on the lower layer had contained such a dose. It was a clever enough plan, since only the mischance of being observed with the box actually in her hand proved her responsible beyond doubt. And even then she might hope her aunt would dismiss the circumstance, as indeed she had done at the time.

The Inspector's voice broke into my reflections. "You don't seem very surprised," he said.

I awoke to find he was regarding me with a distinct air of suspicion. "I beg your pardon," I said. "I am not entirely surprised, to be quite honest. But I am glad to have my suspicions confirmed."

"May I ask what those suspicions are?" said the Inspector. "Or do you find it more amusing to let me thrash around in the dark?"

He sounded a little bitter. I could not altogether blame him, but I felt the situation was not my fault—or at least only partly my fault. Certainly I had acted for the best. "You already know my suspicions," I retorted. "I believe Miss Emily is innocent. I think someone was drugging her tonic with datura, and that someone was Miss Morton. I think someone else poisoned those sweets, not realizing the tonic was also drugged."

The Inspector sighed. "Do you have any proof of that?" he said. "Apart from a sweet that *isn't* poisoned?"

I opened my mouth to retort, but before I could say anything, he passed a weary hand over his forehead. "No, forgive me, Madame Fox," he said. "I shouldn't have said that. Police work always relies heavily on the process of elimination. You have helped us eliminate something—I think. You believe that the open box of sweets was not poisoned?"

"That is what I believe."

"But the new box was?"

"That I believe also."

"And how do you explain this circumstance?"

"I believe the murderer wished to be out of the house before the poisoned sweets took effect."

The Inspector considered this statement from all angles and pronounced it sound. "That's the devil of poison as a weapon," he said. "That, and the fact that it can so easily be consumed by the wrong person. I take it you think that's what happened in this case?"

"Yes, I believe the poisoned sweets were meant for Miss Emily, not Miss Morton."

"I wish we could find Miss Emily and ask her what *she* thinks," said the Inspector.

"As to that," I said, "I had a call from Lord Frost today. He wishes me to hold a sitting to try to locate her."

"Ah!" said the Inspector.

I looked at him suspiciously. His expression was non-committal, but I thought there was suppressed excitement in his voice. "I was surprised to hear that you have been promoting the idea," I said. "*Very* surprised."

"I don't know why you would be," said the Inspector. "I have a very high opinion of you and your abilities."

"But you cannot think I can find Miss Emily where Scotland Yard has failed!"

"I might not go as far as that," he conceded. "But I have noticed you generally come through with the goods when it's a question of a paying client. So I thought if you didn't mind, I'd tag along, just on the off-chance you might discover something that would help."

⸜⸝

Put like that, it seemed reasonable, but I still had my doubts. "Can he possibly suspect we are concealing Miss Emily here?" I asked Susan, as soon as he had left.

"I think he'd get a warrant and search the place if he did suspect," said Susan with her usual common sense.

"True," I admitted, "but perhaps he is being—polite? Giving me a chance to produce her myself?"

"Then maybe you'd better do it," said Susan. "Miss Emily's got to come forward sooner or later, after all."

⸜⸝

I decided to go down to the kitchen to get Miss Emily's own opinion on the subject. I found her and Jenny with their heads together over *Lady Deirdre's Dilemma*, which Jenny was spelling aloud under Miss

Emily's tutelage. Miss Emily was addicted to novels of the romantic sort, and since coming to stay at the Temple she had introduced Jenny to this form of literature.

It was rather a sore point with me, Dear Reader. After all, it had been my idea to teach Jenny to read in the first place. I had gone about it in a sensible and logical manner, providing her with a beginning grammar and some of the simple books one uses to introduce children to the written word.

Jenny had applied herself to these works diligently, if not enthusiastically. Over time she had made a decent progress. But upon being introduced to the Romance Novel, her reading ability had improved by leaps and bounds. She was now often to be found, in her own time and of her own volition, puzzling out the adventures of some romantic heroine.

I felt it to be yet another misjudgment on my part. It made perfect sense that with her own unhappy romance weighing on her, Jenny should find relief in comparing her plight with that of some fictional heroine. There is much comfort to be found between the covers of a book, Dear Reader, and it is not always the best books (so-called) that provide the best comfort.

Both women looked up when I entered the room: the young and the old, misty-eyed alike over Lady Deirdre's romantic trials. "That's enough for now, dear," said Miss Emily, marking her place in the book with care.

"Lord Frost has been here," I told her.

Her brow creased. "Lord Frost?"

"He is very worried about your disappearance. He wants to hold a sitting to speak with you."

Miss Emily thought this over, and after a moment a sparkle of laughter appeared in her eyes. "But how funny! I should not laugh, of course, for it shows a very proper feeling in him. But to think of his wanting to hold a séance to speak to me!"

"It seemed a little odd," I said. "I could not determine if he had any suspicion of his wife."

The mention of her murderous niece promptly quenched Miss Emily's sparkle. "Yes," she said, looking apprehensive now. "What does Lady Frost think of the idea?"

"I gather she has no objection," I said. "But of course, I am rather at a loss how to proceed. Seeing that you are not a Spirit."

Miss Emily nodded.

"And seeing also that Inspector Harper wishes to be present. He, too, wants very much to speak to you."

Again Miss Emily nodded, looking a little scared. "I will talk to him, of course," she said. "I must."

"The question is how best we may bring that about. Since he does not know you are here—in the flesh."

"And if he did, it would make trouble for you," said Miss Emily with understanding. "I can see that, of course. And you have been put to a great deal of trouble as it is."

I assured her it had been no trouble, and Jenny seconded my statement with rather more sincerity. "Still, I am puzzled to think how we will explain ourselves, as explain ourselves we must, sooner or later," I went on. "It's this business of how—and when—you left Waterloo House that will be our chief problem."

Miss Emily misunderstood me. "I will not tell the inspector about the Duke of Wellington," she assured me. "I can see he would not be likely to believe it."

"No," I said inadequately. There was a little pause. It was Jenny who broke the silence. "Are you going to hold the séance for Lord Frost, then?" she asked.

I shot her a warning look. "How can I? It would be a charade under the circumstances—with Miss Emily here, alive and well."

"But you get messages from living people now and then, don't you?" persisted Jenny.

"Yes," I said, "yes, I do. That is an idea, to be sure."

She and Miss Emily both looked at me expectantly, in the manner of children expecting a conjurer to pull a rabbit out of a hat. "Miss Emily," I said, "the chief awkwardness we are facing is how to explain to Inspector Harper that you left Waterloo House several days before he thinks you did, and why we did not tell him of it before now."

"Yes?" she said.

"He has been devoting much time and effort to determine how you could have left the house without anyone seeing you. He told me it seemed as though you had vanished into thin air, like a spirit."

"Yes?" she said again.

"Perhaps it would be simpler if we just let him think you did."

She considered this with a pleased air. "Could we do that?"

"I think we could. And perhaps it would solve your other problem as well. You must, at some point, confront Lady Frost with her wrongdoing. You are the only one who saw her with those sweets in hand. If you make the accusation impressive enough, perhaps she will be too taken aback to accuse you in return."

"I will do whatever you say," said Miss Emily.

"Mind you, she may still threaten to disclose your secret. You must be prepared for that."

She nodded, looking determined. "Like the Duke."

"Yes," I said. "*And* like the Duke, we must take advantage of the element of surprise. Let me talk the matter over with Susan, and then we will all get together to plan our strategy."

## CHAPTER 18

Susan, predictably, was full of objections. "You've run mad," she informed me sternly. "How can you believe anyone would be taken in by such a plan? Let alone two hard-headed people like Lady Frost and Inspector Harper."

"You wait until you've seen it for yourself, my girl. You admitted yourself that our Spirit Lights were impressive. This will be more impressive yet."

"Impressive enough to make the Inspector believe in Spiritualism?" said Susan in a voice full of incredulity.

"It doesn't matter what he *believes*," I told her. "Only what he *sees*. Of course he will realize afterwards that it was a trick, or at least guess that it must be. But he won't be able to prove it, and that's the important thing."

"Yes, but you're forgetting Miss Emily."

"Nonsense—how could I? She is essential to the plan."

"What I mean is, your plan involves her taking part in a fraudulent séance," explained Susan. "And she is one of your best clients. Don't you suppose that will give her to think?"

That aspect of the affair had already occurred to me, Dear Reader. I told Susan I did not like it, but that I was prepared to take the risk. "In any case, this will be a séance unlike any other séance she has ever attended," I said. "Thank heaven I have never tried to materialize the Duke of Wellington!"

Susan, switching tacks, pointed out that I had good reason to eschew materializations, given my unfortunate past experiences. "You've told us often enough about that séance where the young newspaper reporter tackled you, while you were running around in the dark," she reminded me. "And you swore you'd never take such a risk again."

"Yes, but don't you see? That was a risk because the Medium and the Materialization were one and the same. But this time, I will produce a Spiritual Materialization that is not only entirely separate from me, but who looks, acts, and sounds exactly like the person I am summoning. Because it *is* that person. Whom we will subsequently unveil as such. It's foolproof, Susan. No Medium ever had such a heaven-sent opportunity. I'm damned if I will pass it up."

Susan said darkly that I was likely enough to be damned, but it was plain to see the plan held a certain appeal for her. One of the reasons she is such a good assistant is that she, too, takes pride in outstanding work. "I don't like it," she told me. "But of course I'll help if you're bound to try it. I'm afraid you'll need all the help you can get," she added fatalistically.

I told her she was worth a brigade to me, realizing only later that I was quoting the Duke of Wellington. Once again, he seemed to be obtruding into my affairs. His favourite rejoinder, "Don't be a damned fool," was on my lips more often than was polite in the days that followed, as I planned my campaign and put my troops through their drill. Susan accused me now and then of being high-handed, but in no very condemnatory spirit. As I had predicted, she was impressed by Miss Emily's Materialization when she witnessed it for the first time. After that, she gave no more than the most token remonstrance to my plan and indeed appeared to be looking forward to putting it into action.

Although I felt we had enough evidence against Lady Frost to carry the day, we received an augmentation at the last minute. The day before the séance, I received a visit from a new client: a woman in deep mourning, heavily veiled and weeping loudly, who (Susan informed me) was too distraught even to give her name.

There was nothing very surprising in any of this, Dear Reader. Given the nature of my business, I see a lot of grief-stricken people in mourning. When I entered the Sitting Room, however, the woman immediately stopped weeping, put her veil back from her face, and disclosed the familiar features of Felicity.

"As there's murder in the case, I thought it best to come in disguise," she explained. "I didn't know but the police might be watching your place again."

I told her I was surprised she was willing to come at all, under those circumstances. "Don't say you have discovered something important?" I asked hopefully.

"Haven't I, just! Just you listen, my dear, and see if you don't think I've done you proud."

In a nutshell, she had discovered the identity of the anonymous letter writer. "Lady's maid," said Felicity succinctly. "Been with Lady Frost since before she was married. I'd already spoken to her a time or two and thought there might be something there. It was plain enough she hated her mistress, but at the same time she seemed scared to say much against her. Well, your telling me Lady Frost was a murderess gave me a new angle to try. I put it to the girl direct and asked if she'd any suspicion, and after a bit of coaxing she broke down and told me the whole story."

That, at least, was no surprise. Felicity's abilities to coax amount to genius. When the occasion calls for it, she can exude a motherly warmth that draws even the most unlikely people to confide in her.

"It seems the poor girl got in trouble years ago," Felicity continued. "There's a child, which she supports with her pay and visits when she can. Lady Frost found out about it and has been putting the black on her."

"*Blackmailing* her?" I exclaimed. This was news indeed, Dear Reader. I felt Milverton ought to look to his laurels, for Lady Frost was bidding fair to overtake him on his own ground.

Felicity said the blackmailing of the lady's maid had been going on for about five years now. "You know how it is, dear," she said. "As a servant, she'd be dependent on her mistress for a character, if she was to go looking for another place."

"And it doesn't suit Lady Frost that she should do so?"

"Worse than that, dear. In fact, it suits Lady Frost very well to have a lady's maid who's got to follow orders and daren't quit and is obliged to accept whatever terms her mistress cares to give her."

"So the maid got even by writing anonymous letters?"

Felicity said she thought it was more a matter of conscience than revenge. "The poor girl didn't count on being a party to murder," she explained. "It's been bothering her something awful, all these years."

"All these years?" I echoed. "But surely . . . no, I can't believe Lady Frost has been plotting to poison her aunt as long as that. She's only had a motive this past year or so."

"It turns out we didn't know the half of it, dear! Just you listen to this."

In a voice that practically purred with satisfaction, Felicity disclosed that Miss Morton was not Lady Frost's first victim. "It seems she and Lord Frost were something more than friends, dear, while the first Lady Frost was still alive. And wanting her promotion like a sensible girl, she decided poison was the quickest way to get it.

"So she *murdered* the first Lady Frost?"

"So it seems, dear."

"I *will* be damned." I sat back to consider this amazing revelation. Presently a question occurred to me. "Do you know how she did it?"

"Arsenic," said Felicity, smiling. "Just like you supposed with the other. The girl told me all about it. Lady Frost—of course she wasn't Lady Frost then—got the stuff in Paris. It came from some kind of chemist's there. The girl was with her at the time, but since she don't speak French, she can't give too much detail about that part of it. But she remembers the name of the place all right. That ought to be enough to go on."

I agreed that it ought to be. "I wonder if it's the same arsenic she used for Miss Emily?"

"Yes, it is," said Felicity with authority. "I asked, and the girl said she'd a supply of it still left over from the first business. Keeps it hidden away in an old writing desk she's had since she was a child. One of those little ones you can carry about, with a slanted top that opens up to hold paper and pens." She held out her hands, indicating a box about a foot and a half square.

"Yes, I know the sort you mean," I said. "But I must say, it doesn't sound a very secure hiding place. Even if you locked it, anyone might pick it up and carry it off."

"Ah, but that's what it wouldn't occur to anybody to do. It's a shabby old thing, you see, and Lady Frost doesn't keep anything of value in it. She doesn't even bother to lock it. But it seems there's a false bottom. The girl said you'd never guess it. Of course it's not a very large hiding place. There's just space to slip in a letter or two— or an envelope with arsenic powder in it."

"Does the girl know how Lady Frost used the arsenic to poison her predecessor?"

"She put it in sweets, my dear." Felicity raised her eyebrows significantly. "The first Lady Frost was very fond of them  It was a drawn-out business, for our Lady Frost didn't want to send her off with the first dose. That would've looked suspicious."

"It's exactly the way she was proceeding with Miss Emily," I said with satisfaction. "Do you suppose she doctored the sweets herself? She must have, I suppose. It's not a task you could trust to anyone else."

"Aye, she did it herself—in the stillroom, after the other servants had gone to bed. The lady's maid knew about it, but she was the only one."

"That's everything, then. I *am* impressed, Felicity! If the police had you in their employ, they would have solved the case weeks ago."

Felicity disclaimed modestly, saying that she ought to have tumbled to it long ago that the lady's maid knew something. "But you'll find she's set against talking to the police," she warned me.

"She's afraid of being blamed for not speaking sooner?"

"That's part of it, but I think she's even more afraid of what her mistress might do."

These did not seem to me insurmountable obstacles. "She was not a willing accomplice. Lady Frost has been blackmailing her. Surely the police will take that into consideration. Plus, she has tried to prevent a second murder by writing those letters. That ought to count in her favour, too. As for being afraid of her mistress—well, if the police have sufficient evidence to hold Lady Frost even without the maid's testimony, I trust she'd feel safe enough to add her share to the balance. I think it will do, Felicity. Excellent work, upon my word."

Felicity appeared pleased by my commendation and even more pleased with the sum I gave her by way of compensation. Pulling her veil back over her face, she prepared to depart. "By the by, dear, when you're talking to that inspector of yours, you might just drop a word in his ear that it wouldn't hurt for him to watch the pawnshop in Holburn Street, near the Museum," she told me. "I've just found out there's an old acquaintance of mine working there. I think the police'd be interested to know it, too."

From the general tenor of this speech, it was easy to see that Felicity had not parted on good terms with her old acquaintance. I thanked her again and promised to pass the word along. In the same measure that Felicity is a wonderful friend, she is also a most dangerous enemy.

With the séance coming off the next day, I did not have a chance to pass Felicity's tip to the Inspector beforehand. Between you and me, Dear Reader, I was just as glad that it should be so. I had quite enough to do, rehearsing my players in their rôles.

The element of uncertainty made it difficult to rehearse beyond a certain point. I warned Miss Emily that she must be prepared for departures from the script. As the presiding Medium, I would endeavour to keep the performance running as smoothly as I could, but unexpected developments were entirely possible.

Of course every séance necessarily involves an element of the unexpected, Dear Reader. I cannot know the exact questions my clients may ask, how they will react to the answers, or what revelations may appear in the course of a sitting. But this séance, involving as it did a police inspector, a murderess, the murderess's husband, and a full-figure materialization of one of her would-be victims, bade fair to be an especially tricky business. I was glad to learn I would have Hilda to help me mediate.

She arrived mid-afternoon on the day of the séance, as calmly composed as if no murder had occurred since the last time we had seen her. "I could not come before," she apologized. "The police have been much occupied with this business of Miss Morton. I did not think it wise to leave Waterloo House while they were perhaps watching it."

I told her this was sensible behaviour. "You don't think they followed you here today, do you?"

"No," said Hilda. "But it would not matter if they did. For I am attending the séance here tonight. This I have told the police inspector, and he has given me permission."

I was surprised to hear it, but after thinking the matter over I decided to accept it at face value. Hilda was Miss Emily's long-time companion and a veteran of many séances. It was only natural that she would be interested in an attempt to contact her missing mistress via the Spiritograph. I thought Inspector Harper, as well as the Frosts, must accept it as such.

Miss Emily was delighted to see Hilda. Weeping, she fell into her arms and proceeded to tell her everything that had passed since she had last seen her. Of course there was much to tell. Hilda listened to it all with unimpaired calm and no exclamation more emotional than "Yes, yes."

The disclosure that Miss Emily was the mother, not aunt, of the late Arthur Wellesley Morton did not seem to shock her. Neither did the idea that Miss Emily's nieces had used this information to blackmail her. "I wondered," said Hilda. "But I did not like to say anything. It was not my place."

We also took her into our confidence about the séance that evening. She listened to it all calmly, and I could not tell if she approved or disapproved. "I wish it may answer," was all she said.

"So do I," said Miss Emily. "It will be a comfort to have you there, Hilda." Smiling a little, she added, "I have often wondered if I might be allowed to come back as a Spirit after my death. I never thought to be doing so while I am still alive! But dear Madame Fox has planned it out so cleverly. If it were not that I dreaded facing Catherine, I think I should be looking forward to it."

Hilda bent a searching look upon me, but said she would certainly be there, and that her mistress might rely on her for support.

I was glad to have Hilda's support, too. She had already proved herself a staunch ally on previous occasions. Taking her into the Spirit Parlour, I showed her the arrangements. We agreed she would be posted on Lady Frost's left flank—that is to say, on her left side, while Inspector Harper would be on her right. "Mind you keep hold of her hand, whatever happens," I warned Hilda. "There's no saying what she'll do when Miss Emily materializes. After all, she's a murderess twice over."

"On me you may rely," said Hilda. "I will see she has no opportunity to do any more harm than she has done already."

## CHAPTER 19

It felt strange to seat Inspector Harper at the séance table like any other client. "You will be here at my left," I told him. "Between me and Lady Frost."

Lady Frost's lip curled at these words. I half expected her to object to the idea of holding hands with a plebian policeman. She said nothing, however, Dear Reader. She had said little thus far in any case.

On entering the Spirit Parlour, she had looked around with amusement—unlike Hilda, she had never been there before, having previously attended only the Waterloo Night séances at her aunt's house. She was dressed in street attire rather than evening dress: a green dress made high to the neck, worn with a small straw hat trimmed in the same colour. Her husband was more formally clad in black and white evening clothes, having just come from a dinner at his club. I put Lord Frost at my right hand, with Hilda between him and his wife.

Because there were five of us, I had arranged the chairs so that Lady Frost was across the table from me and thus facing the curtained bay at the back of the room. Normally I sit with my back to the bay, but I had angled my chair slightly to the left, so that I, too, could see the bay. I wanted a view of it myself tonight, for it was here that Miss Emily was due to materialize in about an hour's time.

Once everyone was seated, I set about extinguishing the lamps. At the same time, I made a point of going to the Japanese screen and folding it back and forth a couple of times, under the pretence of adjusting it. I also pulled open the curtains in the bay before drawing them closed again, murmuring that a crack of light was showing from the streetlamp outside. In fact, both these actions were equivalent to a conjuror rolling back his sleeves. I wanted to show my audience I had nothing concealed anywhere in the room before we got down to business.

Inspector Harper's face wore a look of polite interest as I seated myself at the table. Lord Frost looked ill-at-ease and Lady Frost coolly amused. Hilda, of course, merely looked stolid. "Let us begin," I said. "Join hands, and remember that whatever happens, *do not break the circle.*"

The clients obeyed me, and we sat in a darkness only slightly alleviated by the candle in the hanging lantern. Its flickering light caught the brass fittings of the Spiritograph, making them gleam like gold. Lord Frost sat staring down at the machine, his anxiety almost palpable. I caught Lady Frost stealing a look at it now and then, too. I could have told them both they were wasting their time, for we were dispensing with the Spiritograph tonight in favour of more direct Spiritual Communication. But we still had some time to go before that was due to happen.

It was about half an hour, more or less. My audience bore the wait patiently, on the whole. At one point Lady Frost, in a long-suffering voice, did inquire how long we were going to have to wait. "Because I, for one, would welcome the certainty that *anything* is going to happen besides just sitting in the dark."

I told her sternly that it depended on the Spirit Energy, and that her attitude was a hindrance rather than a help. "You must concentrate," I told her. "Concentrate on summoning the Spirit of your aunt."

I shut my eyes, as though demonstrating the level of concentration she should strive for. In fact, my eyes were not wholly closed, for I was watching her from beneath my lashes.

Lady Frost sighed, but shut her eyes obediently. I saw her husband glance at her before returning his gaze to the Spiritograph. Hilda sat with stolid aspect and eyes downcast. Inspector Harper alone ignored my instructions to concentrate, letting his gaze flicker from one to the other of us. Although his hand in mine felt relaxed, I guessed he was alert enough.

This proved to be the case when the candle suddenly sputtered and went out.

As the room was plunged into darkness, there was a shocked exclamation from Lord Frost and a hiss of surprise from his wife. As for Inspector Harper, I heard him mutter something and seek to free his hand from mine. "Do not break the circle," I said sharply. "There is a Spirit among us. Concentrate—concentrate to give it form and power. Miss Emily," I said, raising my voice. "Miss Emily, is it you? Miss Emily, we seek to hear from you. Give us a sign that you are with us."

As I continued to murmur supplications, I could only hope Hilda was doing her part and keeping Lady Frost in her seat. That is the mischief of a dark séance, Dear Reader. Although one has freedom to trick one's audience, one cannot be sure the audience is not playing tricks of their own. At any rate, I was sure of Lord Frost, and Inspector Harper seemed to have settled down, too, though I could feel the effort it was costing him in his tightened grasp on my hand.

Presently, there was a little gasp from across the table. Lady Frost, from her privileged position, had seen it first: a glimpse of something luminous spilling out beneath the curtains of the bay. By turning my head, I could see it, too.

"By Jove," said Lord Frost, his voice expressing the most flattering tone of awe.

The luminous substance had spread until it was like a puddle on the floor. It behaved more like a vapour than a liquid, however, swirling and swaying, rising now above the floor, then settling back down to floor level.

"Miss Emily," I said, raising my voice. "Miss Emily, is it you?"

These words caused the vapour to swirl with a momentary agitation. Then it began to rise. Higher and higher it rose, higher than a human form, a faintly luminous column against the black curtains.

"Miss Emily," I said. "Can you show yourself?"

At these words, the column rose higher, swirled in agitation once more, then began to sink downward. In doing so, it gradually took shape as a veiled figure. The figure was indistinct in outline, yet suggestive of Miss Emily in its diminutive size. It stood silent and motionless against the curtains.

"Miss Emily?"

The veiled figure moved forward. "Yes," it said. The voice was soft, breathy, a trifle uncertain—but unmistakably Miss Emily's.

"Dear God," said Lord Frost.

He sounded reverent. I would have been glad to have gauged Inspector Harper's reaction—and even more Lady Frost's. But the room was too dark to see anything except the luminous figure.

"Do not break the circle," I said again, softly. "Whatever happens, do not break the circle."

"I don't believe this." said Lady Frost, in a conversational tone.

"You may believe it, Catherine. It is I." The voice from the veiled figure was grave and composed.

"Are you *dead*?" said Lord Frost. He spoke as though the words had been wrenched from him.

The phantom Miss Emily appeared to consider this. "No," she said at last. "I am living yet."

"Where are you? Where have you been this past week, ma'am?" This, of course, was Inspector Harper, sounding very much his ordinary policeman's self.

"Kind friends took me in, when I feared for my life." The phantom turned, as though addressing me. "But I heard you calling and knew I must come forward. It is time the truth was told."

"Yes, indeed," said Inspector Harper. He sounded relaxed now, Dear Reader: even cheery.

"What truth?" said Lord Frost sharply.

The phantom came another step forward, facing now toward Lady Frost. "Shall you tell it, Catherine, or shall I?"

There was a long silence. "I beg your pardon?" said Lady Frost. She was doing her best to sound amused, but not entirely succeeding. "I don't understand your meaning, Aunt—if you are my aunt. Which I don't believe." In a stronger voice, she continued, "I don't believe any of this. It's nonsense—some kind of trick." There was a noise from her end of the table, as though she had pushed back her chair. It was followed by an angry gasp. "How dare you? Let go of me, you abominable woman!"

There was a pause, and then Hilda's voice, calm and reproving: "You must not break the circle."

In the silence that followed, Miss Emily spoke again. "It is not trickery, Catherine," she said. "It is a judgment. You tried to poison me and ended by poisoning your own sister. How could you be so wicked?"

There was a noise like a sigh from Lord Frost. No one else said a word. At last, Lady Frost, still struggling to sound amused, said, "I, poison you, Aunt? But what nonsense! Did your fool of a companion say I did? I daresay she did it herself. Ouch!"

This last exclamation made me suspect Hilda had revenged herself in some manner. There was a little pause before Miss Emily spoke again. When she did, her voice sounded sad. "Catherine, I know you did it because I *saw* you. I saw you with the box of sweets in your hand, on the night of the Waterloo Dinner."

"Box of sweets?"

I had to admire Lady Frost's composure. She sounded genuinely puzzled, as though she had never heard of such a thing as a box of sweets. It was Inspector Harper who took it upon himself to answer her. "You will remember, my lady," he said. "We have spoken of this before—several times before, in fact. The police believe your sister was poisoned through eating a box of sweets that were in Miss Emily's bedroom."

"Yes, of course, my dear Inspector. And if *you* will remember, I told you that if they were poisoned, then I could only suppose my aunt had poisoned them herself."

The veiled figure shook its head. "No, Catherine," it said. "You know that is not so. I saw you with the box in your hand. It is only by the merest chance that I escaped being your victim. How must you have felt, when you learned you had murdered your own sister?"

"I haven't murdered anyone. This is all a farce." In a stronger voice, Lady Frost continued, "You haven't any proof."

"Isn't the arsenic still in your desk, Catherine? From when you murdered the first Lady Frost?"

Although Lady Frost did not answer, she must have acted. Another, louder scuffle erupted at her end of the table. "Let go of me!" she cried angrily.

"Sit down, my lady," came Inspector Harper's voice. "I must insist you sit down, until we have a chance to explore this accusation.

Explore *both* these accusations." In a voice that was slightly unsteady, he added, "Remember, you must not break the circle."

"As to that," I said, "I think it is time we shed a little more light on this business. Please remain in your seats, all of you, while I get up and relight the lantern."

I took a good few minutes to accomplish this task, Dear Reader. In the time it took me to pull a box of vestas from my pocket, strike one, and reach up to light the candle in the hanging lantern—not the burnt-out stump, but a fresh, new one I had placed alongside it beforehand—an acute observer might have seen the phantom figure rise suddenly in a cloud, settle to the floor in a luminous puddle, and slide rapidly across to the curtained bay. By the time the lantern was relit, however, there was nothing to be seen of it. There was only Miss Emily herself—dressed in black from head to toe, but unmistakably human, and standing in front of the séance table.

Three of the five people at the table stared at her open-mouthed. "You *are* here," said Lady Frost.

"Yes," she said.

"How did you come here?" demanded Inspector Harper.

She smiled faintly. "Indeed, I hardly know. But I am ready to speak."

Lord Frost shook his head. "I can hardly believe it. It is incredible."

"Transportation," I said, in my most professional manner. "There have been many such cases—living people transported through the barriers of time and space, in response to a Spiritual Summoning. But none as spectacular as this, I think."

It may be I let a little too much satisfaction show in my voice, Dear Reader. Inspector Harper looked at me sharply. "Indeed," he said. "Well, we are all witnesses—of something. Let's begin by sorting out what has happened in the *earthly* realm." Turning to Miss

Emily, he said, "You spoke of there being arsenic in your niece's desk?"

Miss Emily nodded. "Yes," she said. "It's a small writing desk. There is a false bottom. The arsenic is hidden beneath it."

Lady Frost stared at her. "But you cannot know that!" she said. "How did you—when did you—oh, it's impossible!"

Miss Emily gave her stare for stare. "I know more than you think, Catherine," she said. "I know it was you who broke my Sèvres vase years ago and blamed it on the cat."

I was interested to see that this lesser accusation, unlike the accusation of murder, rendered Lady Frost momentarily speechless. I exchanged looks with Hilda, who permitted herself a very slight smile.

When Lady Frost spoke again, there was menace in her voice. "Take care, Aunt," she said. "If we are talking secrets, I believe you are in no position to cast the first stone."

Miss Emily surveyed her calmly. "Blackmail," she said. "You won't silence me that way, Catherine. I *will* speak, though my own sins are black enough, to be sure. But I will not be still any longer." In a voice that held a distinct note of satisfaction, she added, "'Publish and be damned!'"

This really did seem to render Lady Frost speechless. In any case, Lord Frost chose that moment to intervene. "Enough," he said. "It is enough, Catherine." There was anguish in his expression as he surveyed his wife. "I was afraid of this. I could not help suspecting. I did not want to believe it, but I think I have known all along."

Lady Frost turned away, but not before I had seen a glitter of tears in her eyes. "Spare me your reproaches," she said. "Indeed, you might have known, Edwin. It served your own purposes quite as well as mine."

As arrests for murder go, Dear Reader, it was ridiculously genteel. Nothing so crude as handcuffs or a police wagon was involved. After asking me politely to send one of my servants for the constable on the beat, Inspector Harper took the Frosts into my Sitting Room and shut the door. They remained there together a considerable time. Presently the Inspector came out, asked to speak with Miss Emily, and took her into the Spirit Parlour.

By this time the constable had arrived—it was our old friend P.C. Shaw.[13] He stayed with the Frosts while the Inspector spoke with Miss Emily. Hilda had insisted on remaining with her mistress, and the Inspector made no objection. I was perfectly sure she had knitted the whole time, adding an extra gloss of gentility to the proceedings.

Eventually, the Inspector emerged, asked P.C. Shaw to summon a couple of four-wheel cabs, and the whole party went off to Scotland Yard as decorously as if they were going to the opera.

After all our work and worry, it seemed a trifle flat. But I opened a bottle of champagne anyway, and we had a bit of a celebration, during which Susan handsomely confessed that I had been right and she wrong.

"They were took in, every one of them. I never would have thought it."

"You deserve at least half the credit," I said magnanimously. "You made a nice job of managing the phosphorescent gauze."

Our phantom had been merely a length of very light, filmy silk gauze, impregnated with a phosphorous solution so it would glow after exposure to light. Once the candle had gone out—it was a stump of a candle that would go out by itself after burning a half-hour or

---

13  See *Ghost in the Machine.*

so—Susan had opened the door in the wainscoting and helped Miss Emily through, under cover of the Japanese screen. She had brought the gauze with her, along with a telescoping rod.

From the screen, the two women had quietly made their way behind the curtains and into the window bay. Once they were there, Susan had made the luminous gauze appear by poking it out from beneath the curtains with the rod and then stirring it about. On the proper cue, she had lifted the gauze on the end of the rod and begun telescoping it upward. Once it was high enough, all Miss Emily had to do was part the curtains and step beneath it. Susan then allowed the gauze to settle over her, and at this point, Miss Emily's form was fully materialized.

While Miss Emily was speaking, Susan had waited behind the curtains until it was time for the phantom to disappear. Miss Emily achieved this simply by lifting up the gauze and letting it fall behind her. Susan had then whisked it out of sight with the rod and taken everything back through the door in the wainscoting. Both women were wearing black, with black gloves and veiling over their heads, so in the dark room they were completely invisible.

"It was a wonderful thing to see," said Jenny, with a faraway look in her eye. "Just like a play." She had been watching through the ventilator from the next room, Dear Reader. With a murderess on the premises, I thought it well to have all my troops standing by.

"I hope Miss Emily didn't have too much trouble getting through the door in the wainscoting?" I asked

Susan laughed shortly. "No, she made nothing of it—whisked right through. And she eighty years old! I'd more trouble myself. I tell you again: I'm too old and stiff for this business of scrabbling around on my knees."

I told her it was merely a matter of training, and that I would be happy to show her some exercises. I traveled with a circus sideshow for a time, Dear Reader, though I do not advertise it as a rule—it is an experience I generally prefer to forget. But it enabled me to pick up a few useful things from my fellow performers, including some excellent limbering-up exercises. To the philosophic mind, all experiences are opportunities to learn.

Susan said she would think about it and changed the subject. "Do you think Lady Frost will tell about young Mr. Morton being Miss Emily's son?"

I said I thought not. "I believe Lord Frost means to hush the matter up as much as he can. We'll see. If it has to come out, I think she can stand it now."

"She did wonderful well," said Jenny reflectively. "Very brave of her to come forward like that."

"Yes, it was very brave," I agreed.

"I'd never have thought it—a fine lady like her, having a secret like that."

"Nor did I, but I shouldn't have been surprised," I said. "Lords, ladies, or ordinary folk like ourselves, it's the rare person who *doesn't* have a guilty secret of some sort."

Jenny nodded. She seemed to be thinking about something else. After a moment's pause, she said, "Miss Emily talked a lot about how afraid she's been. How all her life, she was always afraid the truth was going to come out. She said she'd have done things different if she could go back and do them again."

"I daresay," I said. "It's the rare person who doesn't have regrets of that sort, too."

Jenny took a deep breath. "But how do you know? How do you know whether telling the truth is the right thing—or if you'd be better off holding your tongue?"

I started to give her the benefit of my own cynical opinion, which was that no matter what decision you made, you would end up wishing you had done something else. Susan, however, elbowed me into silence. "You can't know, of course," she said in her calm way. "Every situation's different. You're thinking about Sam again?"

"Yes," said Jenny wistfully. "I wish I knew what he'd do if I told him the truth."

"Well," I said. "He has already shown he's loyal and trustworthy—even to the point of breaking the law. For he didn't betray us over *this* business, and at one time that looked a lot like being an accessory to murder."

"It did, didn't it?" said Jenny, looking struck.

"As someone whose business is predicting the future, I will tell you that the best way to do that is to look at the past. People do change, but not often—and not usually fundamentally."

Jenny thought a while longer. "I think I *will* tell him," she said. "Even if he doesn't like it—even if he doesn't want me after I tell him—I think I'd feel better knowing I'd at least given him a chance."

Susan and I expressed approval of these sentiments, though my own approval was somewhat qualified. To give counsel in matters of the heart is "a fearful responsibility," to quote the Iron Duke. I hoped Jenny would not regret her decision, but even if the worst happened and Sam rejected her, I did not believe her secret would weigh upon her so heavily after learning of Miss Emily's. The fictional Lady Deirdre had helped, too. There is nothing like witnessing the difficulties of others to put our own in perspective.

## CHAPTER 20

We went to bed that night without seeing anything more of Inspector Harper. It was the next day before he got around to talking to us. When I came down to the Sitting Room, in response to Susan's summons, I saw at once that he was in a genial mood. This was a great relief, Dear Reader. Miss Emily had sworn to conceal our part in the affair as far as she might, but I did not know how far that might be, under expert questioning from Scotland Yard. I trembled to think what Inspector Harper might say if he learned we had been concealing her all along.

"Tea, Inspector?" I asked, once we had exchanged greetings and taken our seats.

"Yes, thank you," he said, accepting a cup from my hands. I took this as another favourable sign. In general, accepting refreshments meant he was there in a friendly rather than adversarial rôle.

"How is the case progressing?" I asked.

"It's progressing very well," he said. "I'll need statements from you and your servants, but that's merely a formality. Our evidence is complete enough without them. The Chief was very pleased. Of course, I was obliged to do some rather creative editing in my report of last night's events," he added thoughtfully. "But I'm used to that when you're involved in a case."

As I was pondering what to say to this, he went on, still in a thoughtful voice. "Then, too, there's always some awkwardness when the peerage is involved."

I was glad to pursue this alternate subject. "Is Lord Frost making trouble?"

"Not trouble, exactly. Naturally he's not eager to wash a lot of dirty linen in public. But he isn't trying to argue against his wife's guilt, either. In fact, he gave us some very damaging evidence against her himself."

"What a gentleman," I said admiringly.

The Inspector shot me a look. "Yes, well, she's a murderess—most likely a murderess twice over. And a poisoner at that. A man might be forgiven for wanting his wife safely behind bars, under the circumstances."

"Do you think she will be convicted?"

The Inspector put the tips of his fingers together, considering. "We've evidence enough, I should think," he said. "But it's always a challenge getting a murder conviction against a woman. Especially a woman as handsome as she is. And the murder of her sister was an accident, more or less. A clever counsel will be able to make something of that, I've no doubt. And Lord Frost isn't sparing any expense in *that* department. Yes, the Crown will have a fight to prove its case, all right."

I remarked that at least Lord Frost was gentlemanly enough to see to his wife's legal defence. Inspector Harper agreed to it, albeit in an absent-minded manner. I judged it might be safe to ask the question that was chiefly concerning me. "Is Miss Emily back at Waterloo House?"

This earned me one of his sharp looks. "Yes, she and her companion went back last night," he said, "once we'd taken their statements. For what they were worth," he added cynically.

"Were they not worth much, then?"

"What do *you* think?" he said.

I pretended to consider. "I thought she gave a lot of valuable evidence in her testimony last night."

"Yes, so she did, and I'm grateful for it. But I don't understand why she couldn't have come forward a long time ago, in a proper manner, rather than—than—"

"Transporting," I said helpfully. "Arriving here via Spiritual means."

"Yes," said the Inspector. He eyed me with skepticism. "Does that happen often?"

I said truthfully that I had never witnessed it before. "But there have been some celebrated cases," I told him. "Mrs. Guppy, the famous Medium, was once transported from her house in Highbury to a séance several miles away. In a sense, that was an even more impressive feat, for you must know that Mrs. Guppy is enormously fat, while Miss Emily is just a little slip of a thing. So if you consider only the *weight* involved in the Transportation, what happened last night was, perhaps, a lesser achievement. But in another way, ours was *more* impressive. To summon a living witness, to answer in an investigation of murder, is a thing quite unprecedented. I expect the Society for Psychical Research would be very interested to hear of it."

"Yes," said the Inspector.

We looked at each other. "Damn it, she was here all along, wasn't she?" he said.

"In a *sense*," I said earnestly. "Given the nature of Spirit Energy, she would indeed have been here all along—*spiritually*. As we know, electricity pervades all nature and forms a reservoir of energy which may be—"

The Inspector broke in at this point to say some very rude things about Spirit Energy, Dear Reader. They seemed to relieve his feelings, for after that he became calmer and even complimentary.

"I'm glad I got to see it for myself," he said. "Between you and me, I had always supposed believers in Spiritualism were fools, plain and simple. I couldn't imagine how anybody who wasn't a fool could be deceived by it. But now I've seen it with my own eyes, I can understand completely. I tell you, I still can't reconcile what I saw with what I believe—and I'm not a fool at all. In the normal way, at least."

I inquired with interest what way he was a fool, and he said that would keep for another time. "But for now, I wanted to let you know that we finally turned up a piece of evidence that supports your theory," he said, passing me his teacup for refilling. "Rather late in the day, of course, but we got there in the end."

"My theory?" I repeated. I had presented him with so many theories, both real and spurious, that I had not the least idea now which one he was talking about.

"About Miss Morton drugging her aunt's tonic," he prompted. "To make her appear mentally incapable."

"Oh, yes, that," I said, as I refilled his cup. "You found the bottle of tonic?"

"No, but we found the datura." The Inspector smiled ruefully. "We hadn't far to look, either, as it happened. There's a flourishing specimen right there in the conservatory at Waterloo House."

"No!" I exclaimed.

"Yes, so it seems. I was as surprised as you were."

"I wonder how it came there?" I speculated, as I passed him back his cup.

"It seems Miss Emily had a nephew—elder brother to Miss Morton and Lady Frost. He was a soldier and stationed in India," said the Inspector, surveying me with a meditative eye. "He's dead now, but apparently he sent her the original seeds years ago, as a curiosity."

"My goodness," was all I could think to say.

"We didn't make the connection earlier because the gardener called the blasted thing a thornapple. Not meaning to deceive us, you understand—it appears that's another name for it, right enough. But of course it threw us off the track."

"Of course," I agreed. After a pause, I added, "I believe it's also known as jimsonweed, in the States."

The Inspector nodded and took a sip of tea. "At any rate, the plant is there, and it shows signs that someone's been clipping the leaves. And the gardener remembers seeing Miss Morton doing something in that corner of the conservatory, though he didn't think much about it at the time. Of course, it proves nothing at this point and wouldn't matter even if it did. But I thought you'd like to know, if only because it ties up a loose end."

"Thank you," I said. "I appreciate it."

"Thank *you*," he said, and we finished our tea in companionable silence.

Once the tea was gone and the cups back on the tray, he got out his notebook. "Only one loose end left, and that's taking your statement—yours and your servants'. They won't be any better than Miss Emily's," he said with a cynical smile. "But I'll add them to the collection."

In the event, he had to be content with taking my statement and Susan's, because it was Jenny's day off. But he said this did not matter, as he doubted she had seen much of the business anyway. I saw no reason to disabuse him of his error.

"That's it, then," he said. "That ought to wrap the business up, with any luck." He started to put his notebook away, then paused. "Oh, yes, and that reminds me. I've got a new line on your Captain Ingram."

I said he was not *my* captain, a little too emphatically. The Inspector shot me a quizzical look. "Nor anybody's captain, by the sound of it," he said. "Seems the fellow's been unmasked as an imposter. He had to leave London in a hurry, in the dead of night, and he left a lot of debts behind him. I doubt he'll be back."

This was satisfactory news, Dear Reader, though not necessarily news to me. I took care to thank the Inspector, however, and to say I appreciated his investigating.

"I am glad if I could help. I hope the fellow won't worry you anymore." He gave me another of those direct looks that always makes me wonder how much he sees that I would rather not.

To give his thoughts a different direction, I told him about Felicity's acquaintance at the pawnbroker's. He was very interested, taking down the information in his notebook and thanking me for it. "I suppose you can't tell me how you came by this information, any more than anything else," he said, as he put the notebook away and prepared to take his leave. "But there's one thing you *could* tell me, if you will." He paused, with an inquiring look.

"Yes?" I asked warily.

"You can tell me when you first became certain Lady Frost was a murderess. She swears you knew it all along."

I blinked. "Does she? But how odd. I don't know exactly when I became *certain*, but it hasn't been very long. I wonder why she would say that?"

"She said something about your telling her she had blood on her hands."

"Oh!" I clapped a hand to my mouth. "Yes, to be sure. The night of the Waterloo Dinner. I had forgotten." I was almost overcome to think of that incident and what an eerie coincidence it had been all around.

The Inspector was eyeing me with a curious expression. "Don't tell me it was a genuine Spiritual Communication?" he said, his voice only half joking.

I opened my mouth to deny it, then checked myself. "I would have said at the time it was merely coincidence," I said. "But really there have been too many coincidences altogether about this business. So let us say it was a very odd little incident and . . . leave it at that."

After he had gone, I went down to the kitchen to talk the matter over with Susan. I found her hovering over Jenny, who raised a tear-stained face as I entered the room. My heart gave an awful jolt, for I recalled then that she had been going to confide her secret to Sam and had doubtless used her day off for the purpose. For a moment, I feared the worst; then I saw she was smiling through her tears.

"It's all right, ma'am," she said. "It's all right." With a fresh gush of tears, she sobbed out, "He was so kind—so good. He didn't care about it on his own account at all, only on mine. I might have known it, indeed. I'll always feel bad I didn't tell him before."

"So now you have something *new* to regret," I began in a congratulatory tone. Susan scowled at me so fiercely, however, that I broke it off to express my best wishes instead. "I collect there is nothing to stop you and Sam from marrying now. I will be very sorry to lose you, Jenny, but of course I wish you both every happiness," I said, with strong fortitude.

"Oh, I don't know how to bear it, ma'am! It breaks my heart to leave you. I wish I didn't have to go. I've been so happy here." Jenny looked at me timidly. "Do you think—do you think it might work if I just came in days? Or nights, if you'd prefer? I've been talking it over with Sam, and he quite sees that I hate to leave you. And though his milk route is enough to keep us well enough, there's no denying that we'd do better with both working."

Susan looked at me pointedly. I sighed and shut my eyes. "Business has been good lately," I said. "I have been thinking for some time of setting up my carriage. I expect Sam could drive it. I'll see about renting a place in the mews behind to stable the horse, with a little flat above for both of you to live in."

It was almost worth it, Dear Reader: such a shower of tears and thanks and general rejoicing that ensued. I decided we might as well open another bottle of champagne. Jenny, of course, was full of wedding plans, and we had to listen to these at interminable length, but eventually she allowed me to introduce a few of the things Inspector Harper had said into the conversation.

Both she and Susan were struck by the coincidence of the blood-on-her-hands business. "Pretty strange, that," commented Susan. "But as you've said before, coincidences do happen. No need to look any further than that for an explanation."

"I suppose not," I said, slightly disappointed. Taking a sip of my champagne, I bethought myself of another piece of news. "Oh, yes! And it looks as if I needn't worry any more about Captain Ingram, so-called. The Inspector says he's left London and not likely to come back."

Susan shook her head dubiously. "I hope he won't. But a man like that—if he scents there's money to be made from you, I'm afraid he's not going to give up that easy."

By now, the champagne was having its usual exhilarating effect. I grandly defied John Colley or any other man to get the better of me. "What's he going to do—write anonymous letters to all my clients?" I scoffed. "As long as he isn't actually here in London, I'm not going to worry. Besides, I think he was impressed by my parting words!"

Having previously neglected to give Susan a full accounting of the "publish and be damned" episode, I did so now, relating with gusto my own and John's words. "I think he was impressed," I said again.

"As to that, ma'am," put in Jenny hesitantly, "you know I saw him out the door. And it seemed to me he was still pretty hot against you. He was breathing threats and so forth, and it was easy to see he meant to do you a mischief if he could."

"Yes?" I said, as she paused.

"So I just told him about you and the Inspector."

"Told him about me and the Inspector?" I repeated. "Told him *what?*"

Jenny looked angelic. "Why, how much the Inspector admires you, and how you've been a-helping him with his cases," she said. "And P.C. Shaw happening by on his beat just then, I called him over and asked if Inspector Harper didn't think a lot of you."

"And what did *he* say?"

"He said the Inspector thought you was the goods, all right."

"Go on," I said grimly. "What then?"

Jenny laughed in her throat. "Why, all the fight just went out of him," she said. "He said never a word, but looked queer as Dick's hatband,[14] and slunk off with his tail between his legs. I misdoubt you'll be troubled by him again, ma'am."

"Well," I said, "that is very . . . satisfactory." And it was, too. Although being thought a police informer is at least as damaging an allegation as being a man's mistress, on this occasion I could see it served my purpose very well. Indeed, it was such a simple idea that it had never occurred to me. While I was formulating elaborate strategies, Jenny had cut through the Gordian knot and found the means most likely to frighten John into remaining quiet. I had to chalk it up to another misjudgment on my part.

⁓

14  History has failed to record who Dick was and what was so curious about his hatband. But to quote dear Mr. Dickens, "the wisdom of our ancestors is in the simile, and my unhallowed hands shall not disturb it."—*Ed.*

Despite all my misjudgments, I could not help being pleased by the way matters had turned out. If John were no longer a threat to me, it stood to reason he was not a threat to Miss Waring, either. That being the case, I was delighted to receive a call from her mother the following day. I hurried down to the Sitting Room with a smile on my lips and the hope of a thousand-pound reward in my heart.

Mrs. Waring was smiling, too, as we exchanged greetings. "I had to come tell you the good news," she said. "My dear Madame Fox, the most providential thing! My daughter has broken her engagement to that dreadful Captain Ingram."

I began to say how pleased I was, with some idea of mentioning my own rôle in the business. Mrs. Waring barely allowed me to speak, however. "I can still hardly believe it," she said. "For it seems I was quite correct. The man was a thorough-going scoundrel and fortune hunter. Not only was he *not* a captain, but it seems he was never in the army at all. We never would have known it, but by the most fortunate chance we received a visit from a gentleman who actually *knew* Francis Ingram—the real Francis Ingram, that is."

"Colonel Sir Cyril St. Simon," I said with pride.

Mrs. Ingram threw me a look of awe. "Yes! So it was. And it seems he had been Captain Ingram's commanding officer—the *real* Captain Ingram, that is. The minute he laid eyes on the other, he denounced him as an imposter. The fellow tried to argue, but the colonel simply overbore him and ended by physically ejecting him from the house. Julia said it was most *masterfully* done."

"Yes, indeed," I agreed. "It happens that I—"

"Of course poor Julia was dreadfully upset at first," continued Mrs. Waring. "But the colonel has been so kind. He calls on her daily, and has taken her riding—and really, Madame Fox, I should not be surprised if they do not end by making a match of it."

With some curiosity, I asked if such a match would meet with her approval. Colonel St. Simon was, after all, nearly as old as the false Captain Ingram, and age had been one of Mrs. Waring's objections to their marrying.

It turned out, however, that Mrs. Waring had no objection to her daughter marrying a man twice her age when he possessed a pedigree as exalted as the colonel's. "His uncle is actually a *duke*, Madame Fox. And he himself is a *baronet*. And though I don't really care about such things, it is a comfort to think he comes from a family of such undoubted respectability. Of course, he *is* quite a bit older than Julia, but I don't know that it signifies. He is such a steady character—and such an undoubted *gentleman*. I declare I am half in love with him myself. The first moment I was able to speak to him alone, I told him I had vowed to pay a thousand pounds to anyone who could save Julia from marrying that villain. And I said *he* was entitled to the reward. But he said he couldn't think of taking money for such a thing. He said to serve me and my daughter was all he cared about."

I sat there with the smile frozen on my lips. "Yes?" I managed, after a while.

"Yes, indeed! Was that not pretty? I declare, it makes me laugh now, to think how despairing I was only a week ago." Mrs. Waring gave me a glowing smile. "Of course you predicted it would all come out right. I ought to know better than to doubt you, Madame Fox."

I managed a feeble smile in return. "You are . . . too kind, ma'am."

She waved this away. "No, I must say it. Such amazing powers! I keep thinking of how the Spiritograph spoke of Hidden Knowledge and said the Truth would emerge in time. Julia and I have agreed it was quite miraculous. I know there are those who sneer at Spiritualism, but I think this would convince even the most skeptical unbeliever. You are a true Seeress, Madame Fox. Only look at how you knew Colonel St. Simon's name—and I had not even told it to you yet!"

I let her babble on in this way for some time, as I didn't feel equal to talking. I had been counting on that thousand pounds, but it was evident I had miscalculated. Mrs. Waring saw Colonel St. Simon as her daughter's saviour, not me. I was rather the priestess in the temple, predicting events but not influencing them. Much as I might wish to, it was obvious to me that I could not send her an itemized bill for my fairy godmothering expenses without cheapening myself in her eyes. Better to preserve her belief in me and my abilities, with the hope of recouping my expenses in the long run, rather than risk ruining all for less than a hundred pounds.

After she had gone, I remained sitting where I was in discouraged silence. Susan came in after a while, took one look at me, and fetched me a glass of brandy without asking. "Bad news?" she ventured, after I had taken a few sips.

"Yes," I said.

"Don't tell me Miss Waring still means to marry the captain, after all that's happened?"

I gave a hollow laugh. "No, it's not that."

In as few words as possible, I told Susan what had happened. She tried to appear sympathetic, but I could see her biting her lip, trying not to laugh. "You think it's funny?" I demanded.

"In a way," she said apologetically. "All that work and worry and expense, and she gives the colonel the credit!"

"I know," I said. "Damn the woman. It would serve her right if I'd let her daughter marry whom she pleased and not bestirred myself in the matter."

Susan pointed out that I had had my own score to settle with the captain, and that it was worth something to have that old debt cancelled out. "Indeed, you said you'd pay a thousand pounds yourself just to put a spoke in his wheel."

I frowned. "Nonsense," I said. "I'm sure I never said any such thing. Not but what it was worth *something*." With satisfaction, I dwelt on the memory of John's forcible ejection from the Warings' house. "Yes, that was worth something, to be sure."

"Well, then!"

"But still, the expense I have been at over this business! That door in the wainscoting, and the train fare, and the cab fares, and the bribes to the landlady's maid, and Felicity's fee—"

"You'll make it up in no time," said Susan bracingly. "Mrs. Waring's a good client, and she pays generously."

"Yes," I said. This, too, was a satisfying thought. "And she has scheduled another sitting for this next week—and she always pays in advance."

"And don't forget, that door in the wainscoting came in handy with Miss Emily's business, too," Susan reminded me. "I daresay we might use it a fair bit, now we've got it."

"True," I agreed.

"If I was you, I'd just look on the whole business as some of that *pro bono publico* work you like to talk about."

It seemed the sensible thing to do, upon the whole. Susan is never less than sensible and often very wise indeed. Taking a sip of my brandy, I said I would try.

Susan, meanwhile, was mulling over a different matter. "Did you ever find out from Mrs. Waring whether her party came off, after the captain was sent about his business?" she inquired. "I must say I'd like to know."

"No, I forgot to ask," I said. "But if I had to guess, I would say it did. It sounds as if Miss Waring found consolation pretty quickly with the colonel. Mrs. Waring thinks they will end by making a match of it."

"You don't say," exclaimed Susan. "Well, that's one way to get over an unsatisfactory love affair. Just have your new sweetheart kick the old one down the stairs!"

"Yes," I agreed, raising my brandy glass in salute. "There is nothing like the expulsive power of a new affection."

## CHAPTER 21

Having put aside all hope of being rewarded by Mrs. Waring, I pinned my hopes on Miss Emily instead.

If this sounds mercenary to you, Dear Reader, please remember that I am obliged to work for my living. Remember also that I was now going to be supporting a staff of three, not to mention a horse (heaven knows where this will end).

Let it be remembered also that I had no mercenary motive in helping Miss Emily in the first place. I acted from simple principles of humanity—and, perhaps, a reluctance to let a good client pass to the Summerland before her time. But after everything that had happened, it seemed reasonable to hope Miss Emily might reward me in some way. She had, after all, expressed her gratitude to me many times. And when a client tells you she owes her life to you, and you know the claim is not without foundation, you naturally expect at least some small token of appreciation in return.

Alas, I had miscalculated again. Miss Emily's gratitude was so overflowing that no small token of appreciation would express it. She gave me the most precious thing she owned.

She gave me the Boot.

I tried very hard to appear grateful.

"But Miss Emily, I know how much it means to you," I protested, eyeing the thing with dismay. "I cannot accept such a—such a *munificent* gift."

"No, I want you to have it, Madame Fox," she said firmly. "It is fitting that you, who are in such close communion with His Spirit, should have it."

I met Hilda's eyes. She nodded. "It is fitting," she said.

In the next room, I could hear Susan laughing her head off. I forced a smile to my lips. "Well," I said, "this is certainly *unexpected*. And . . . and *delightful*. I shall . . . *cherish* it, Miss Emily."

She gave me a warm smile. "I know you will, my dear. I am glad I have some fitting way to express the gratitude I feel toward you. Of course, nothing can really repay such a debt. But I thought this very suitable and proper."

She looked so much in earnest that I was forced to reply in kind. "Thank you," I said. "I shall count it among my greatest treasures."

She had gifts for Susan and Jenny, too: simple monetary gifts, such as she would not insult *me* with. She went off to bestow them in person, leaving me alone with Hilda. "Is she well?" I asked in a low voice. "I know this business must have been a strain on her. I suppose she is dreading Lady Frost's trial?"

Hilda nodded. "Yes, but she is bearing up well, on the whole. Very well indeed, I should say. I think it has been a relief to her, to have that old business brought into the light."

"Has Lady Frost betrayed her secret, then?" I asked. Since Lady Frost had stopped short of telling the police about it on the night of her arrest, I had hoped she might continue to do so. Inspector Harper had seemed oblivious of it as recently as our last interview, when he had spoken of the late Arthur Wellesley Morton.

Hilda shook her head vigorously. "She has *not* betrayed it," she said. "I think Lord Frost has convinced her it would not serve her ends. To look well to a jury, she must not appear a blackmailer as well as a murderer."

"Murder, of course, being a more *respectable* crime," I said acidly.

Hilda shrugged. "It is at least more natural—although me, I do not think it either natural or respectable, in the case of Lady Frost. But then it is not for me to judge."

"For me, either, worse luck," I said, and told her what Inspector Harper had said about juries and their reluctance to convict attractive women. "But we shall see. In any case, I am glad Miss Emily need not face a public inquiry into her private affairs."

"Yes," agreed Hilda. "But as I say, it has been a relief to her to speak of it to those she can trust." She gave me one of her rare, slight smiles. "You have her trust, as you can see." She nodded toward the Boot.

"Yes," I said, repressing a sigh.

Being alone with Hilda, it occurred to me to ask her something else that had been puzzling me. "It would seem I have your trust, too, Hilda. And I wanted to thank you for it. That business on Waterloo Night," I explained, in response to her inquiring look. "You did not even question what I was doing, when you met me with Miss Emily in the hall that night."

Hilda shook her head. "I knew you were helping her," she said. "You and the Duke."

I was hard put not to roll my eyes. "You, too?" I exclaimed. "I know Miss Emily thinks he was there that night, but she was drugged at the time!"

Hilda frowned a little, as though seeking to recollect. "But yes," she said. "It was the shadows, you see."

"Shadows?"

"On the wall," she explained. "The lamp was lit, on the table in the hall—and I saw your shadows as you came toward me."

"Yes?" I said, as she paused.

"There were two of you," said Hilda. "But I saw *three* shadows." Lowering her voice, she said, "It was Him. I could not mistake it." She sketched the profile of a cocked hat and Roman nose.

I stared at her for a while. "I see," I said. "Well. That explains everything."

She smiled, nodded, and got out her knitting.

⁂

To this day, I am uncertain how much of her story to believe, Dear Reader. You may believe it or not, just as you choose. Belief is, after all, both a universal Human trait and a remarkably individual one. You have seen how Mrs. Waring, though a True Believer, nonetheless attempted to suborn the Spiritograph into endorsing her views over her daughter's. Miss Emily forms a yet more striking example: her faith in me and my Spiritualistic powers remains unshaken, despite her not only taking part in a fraudulent séance but herself playing the rôle of a Spiritual Apparition.

I am reminded of that verse in the Bible about not letting the left hand know what the right is doing. But perhaps an even better example is a child who clings to a belief in Father Christmas, even after becoming aware that the sugarplums come from Mother and Father. As humans, we are drawn to beauty and mystery, so much so that we will shut our eyes deliberately to the Truth rather than risk having our Belief destroyed. Given the nature of my business, I can only be glad it is so.

And I'm likewise glad that most of my clients pay me in something more substantial than used footwear.

Yet I am becoming reconciled to being the Keeper of the Sacred Boot (a title worthy of a secret society—and no less foolish than many such societies in this City—but I digress). As I say, I am becoming reconciled to Miss Emily's gift. Susan believes it might be quite valuable in time.

"Look on it as an investment," she counseled me. "The Duke only died some thirty years ago. Those kind of relics always appreciate with age. Give it another decade or two, and I'd be surprised if you couldn't sell it to some collector for a nice round sum."

This was a cheering thought. Also cheering was the news we received some weeks later that Lady Frost had been found guilty at her trial, though she escaped a capital charge. You, like me, may not think the fact that the poisoned sweets had been meant for her aunt rather than her sister would be much of a mitigating factor, but her counsel made great play of the fact that Miss Emily would have eaten the sweets one at a time rather than all at once, as Miss Morton had done. Really, he made it sound as if Lady Frost, by putting arsenic in her aunt's sweets, was guilty of no more than a girlish prank— "poison in jest," in Hamlet's phrase, and no offense intended.

The jury didn't quite swallow that, but they allowed her to get off with a life sentence rather than hanging her. Since she is as effectually removed from society by the one means as the other, I suppose we must be satisfied. And indeed, I think Miss Emily is glad that it is so. It was hard enough for her to testify against her niece, and she has not the proper vindictive spirit that would rejoice in the downfall of an enemy, however vicious.

And what, you may ask, of Lady Frost's other crime? Inspector Harper told me in confidence that even with the lady's maid's testimony, the Crown did not feel it had enough evidence to prosecute. That may be, Dear Reader, but my knowledge of Human Nature makes me suspect Lord Frost used his influence to have the matter hushed up. It would have reflected badly on him as well as his wife, although—to do him justice—I believe it to have been more for her sake. He has stood by her thus far, though there is nothing to prevent him from divorcing her at any time and making a third essay at matrimony. Should he do so, I would wish him better luck than he has enjoyed on his first two attempts.

I owe something to Lord Frost, Dear Reader, for he alone tendered me the only cash payment I received in this business. It was a very generous payment indeed, so much so that I suspect it may be meant as hush money. Whatever its motivation, I had no hesitation about accepting it. Lord Frost's secrets are safe enough with me, and certain it is that he owed me for a sitting, though I had given up any hope of his paying me for it. I would have felt delicate about dunning him, seeing that I helped convict his wife of murder. It was, as I told Susan, enough to restore one's faith in the English aristocracy.

In the meantime, I make strides toward becoming myself a lady. I refer, of course, to setting up my carriage. I have acquired a nice little second-hand brougham and am trying to settle on a livery. Susan thinks unrelieved black would make Sam look like an over-sized undertaker's mute, and perhaps she is right. At the moment, I am favouring black with purple facings.

There is the matter of a coat of arms, too. I fancy a lozenge charged with a fox rampant and an all-seeing eye. Susan suggests it be done in phosphorescent paint, but tempting as that idea is, I think it would be cheapening what is, after all, one of the tricks of my trade. Better to keep it in reserve, should another occasion arise where it might be useful.

Susan also suggests—in jest, I do trust—that Miss Waring's marriage might form such an occasion. The announcement of her engagement to Colonel Sir Cyril St. Simon appeared just the other day in the *Morning Post*. "Maybe they could be married here at the Temple," said Susan. "And you could summon up the Spirit of Howard Waring to give his daughter away."

In Felicity's round phrase, I told her I couldn't hold with *that* sort of thing. In fact, I do not plan to attend the wedding at all. Although I made the match myself, I cannot help feeling there might be some awkwardness in taking credit for it. The bridegroom, after all, believes me to be the bride's godmother. So I will content myself with sending her a wedding gift, in the form of her letters to John—anonymously, of course—and wishing her and the Colonel happy in their married life together.

There is little more to tell, Dear Reader, except the most surprising news of all. With the stress of her niece's trial behind her, and her health restored to its usual blooming state, Miss Emily made up her mind to achieve her life's dream of visiting the Waterloo Battlefield.

And she invited me to accompany her!

I have traveled a great deal in my life, Dear Reader, but it has always been in the way of business. I never had the opportunity to take a traveling holiday before. At any other time of year, I might have hesitated, but much of my clientele is out of Town anyway in the latter part of the summer. On the whole, it seemed too good a chance to pass up. Taking Susan with me, and leaving Jenny and Sam (newly married) to honeymoon in their new flat, I embarked with Miss Emily and Hilda for Belgium.

Miss Emily paid for everything in the most handsome style. I enjoyed myself immensely. I found Belgium a beautiful country and the Belgians very hospitable. Their food is not exactly the same as in France (where I spent several pleasant years before the Sûreté began to take an uncomfortable interest in my affairs), but I thought it very reminiscent of French cuisine and every bit as good. I had several opportunities to wear my taffeta dinner dress and made quite a conquest of a young Belgian senator during our stay in Brussels—but that has nothing to do with the present story.

The Field of Waterloo was, of course, our chief object. That field is not quite as it was in 1815: the mound and monument erected to commemorate the battle has changed the topography of the place a good deal. The Duke himself, on first seeing it, exclaimed, "They have spoiled my battlefield!"

Still, I had no difficulty discerning the chief landmarks. The same could not be said of our tour guide. When he misnamed Hougoumont for La Haye Sainte, I swept him aside and began giving my own account of the battle, drawing eventually all the English-speaking tourists in the place. When a few French-speaking ones wandered up, I generously translated my remarks for them, too. My French is voluble enough, if not strictly grammatical, and they seemed to understand me pretty well. Of course they cheered in the wrong places, but given that Bonaparte was *their* hero, that is only to be expected.

In the end they applauded me, French and English alike. Hilda smiled; Miss Emily shed happy tears; and even Susan admitted it had been an impressive performance.

"It would have been even more impressive," she told me, "if when you were describing the battle, you had not kept referring to '*my* men' and '*my* army.'"

"Don't be a damned fool," I said.

The End

# ABOUT THE AUTHOR

Joy Reed is the author of 16 romance novels, an award-winning master's thesis, and the Seraphina Fox mystery series. Her works have been published around the world and translated into four languages. She has dabbled in teaching, is a dilettante scientist as well as a fairly serious historian, and in her giddy youth passed the certifications tests for ASE Master Technician, not to mention Heavy Truck Diesels. Perhaps her proudest moment was to perform *pas seul* in the internationally acclaimed "Dance of the Seven Deadly Weapons." Ms. Reed lives with her long-suffering husband and an undisclosed number of cats and tarantulas in the Greater Little Rock area.

You can read her musings about life and literature on her blog BookJoy: http://bookjoy.livejournal.com/